THE TESLA LEGACY

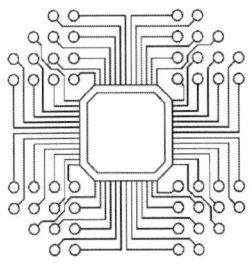

REBECCA CANTRELL

ALSO BY REBECCA CANTRELL

Mystery/thrillers in the award-winning Hannah Vogel mystery series set in 1930s Berlin:

A Trace of Smoke
A Night of Long Knives
A Game of Lies
A City of Broken Glass
On the Train (short story)
The Main in the Attic (short story)

Gothic thrillers in the Order of the Sanguines series (written with James Rollins) set in ancient and modern day times and following the adventures of an order of vampire priests.

The Blood Gospel
Innocent Blood
City of Screams
Blood Brothers
Blood Infernal

Young adult novels in the iMonster series (written as Bekka Black).

iDrakula
iFrankenstein

Happy reading!

THE TESLA LEGACY

REBECCA CANTRELL

Copyright Information

This book is a work of fiction. All of the characters, organizations, and events portrayed in this novel are either products of the author's imagination or used fictitiously. Any similarity to any real person, alive or dead, is completely coincidental.

THE TESLA LEGACY

Copyright © 2015 by Rebecca Cantrell

Cover Design by Kit Foster www.kitfosterdesign.com

All rights reserved.

Dedication

For my husband, my son, and all the other Nikola Tesla fans, and most especially Karen, the snotty actress.

PROLOGUE

Winter, 1896
46 E. Houston Street
New York, New York

Most men would not care about a simple pigeon, but Nikola Tesla was not most men. And so, when the pigeon found him in the vastness of the city, he recognized her as his own. Each dawn, her white wings cut through the cold air of New York and carried her over the bustle of horses and men to his windowsill. In the many months he had known her, she had come to trust him enough to feed from his palm, her cold beak tapping against his skin.

On this winter morning, he stood with his window thrown open longer than usual, waiting for her. He checked his gold pocket watch again and again.

Finally, a white dot appeared against the gray light of dawn. The dot stuttered and dropped in changing air currents. Worry fluttered in his heart as he watched her erratic flight.

She landed on the snowy windowsill, scattering clots of snow onto his rug and down toward the street below. With extreme care, he cupped her body. Her feathers were scarcely colder than the flesh beneath. Her silver eyes looked dull, but showed no alarm—she trusted him.

He brought her inside to the perch in an empty cage next to his bed. His other pigeons cooed in their cages, but she took no notice of them. Her head drooped down to her white breast. She had spent her energy reaching him.

When she warmed, he would feed her. His pigeon keeper, Mr. Smith, would arrive later that morning, and Nikola would ask him what else they could do for her. Mr. Smith had a deep knowledge of pigeons and their maladies. Surely he could make her well.

Nikola washed his hands and watched her from his stiff chair. With each blink, her familiar silver eyes disappeared for longer and longer, until they failed to open at all. Her chest no longer vibrated with breath.

With a sigh, he lifted the limp body from her perch. She had come to him, not to be healed, but to die in warmth and peace. At least he had been able to grant her that.

He cradled the soft body between his palms before placing her inside a plain wooden box lined with a monogrammed handkerchief. He wrapped the warm silk around her like a shroud. Later, he would bury her in the park, but he must first do his day's work.

He set the box on the table next to his bed, washed his hands again, and went to breakfast. He met with Mr. Smith to tell him only that the white pigeon had passed away, and that he would bury her himself. Mr. Smith said that nothing more could have been done for her, and she was fortunate to have a safe, loving place to take her last breaths. Nikola only nodded, and Mr. Smith did not press him further.

Mr. Smith was the only person who understood about Nikola and the pigeon. Other men would have considered him mad, but Nikola had loved the hen for a long time. The sight of her coming for her morning corn had moved him more than the arrival of his most distinguished visitors. Today was to have been a day of triumph, but melancholy had marred it. She, the most loving constant in his life, had left him.

Her image followed him down to his basement. With one hand in the pocket of his overcoat, he walked through the empty room. Today's experiment must be conducted here, and not in his upstairs laboratory—not in front of his assistants. He wanted no announcements in the press before he was ready, as had happened so often before.

Tall wood-framed cages held the tenants' belongings—ordinary items like bedding and furniture and brass candlesticks. Between the cages ran a line of steel columns. Those steel bars faithfully bore the weight of the building above. Taken for granted, they performed their essential task year after year, unyielding and eternal.

He stopped next to the column in the center of the room. Its base rooted deep into the earth beneath his feet, and its crown rose far above his head. This humble steel would serve as the perfect material on which to test his newest device.

When he drew a metal object about twice the size of a deck of cards from the pocket of his jacket, a feeling of satisfaction dulled his grief. He held the device in his palm just as he had recently held the pigeon, with reverence. An uninformed observer would see only the object's square base with its dial and a curiously turned steel cylinder rising a few inches from the top. This rounded casing could withstand temperatures of more than two hundred degrees and pressure of more than four hundred pounds per square inch.

Nikola visualized the highly efficient pistons he had built inside, supreme examples of the art and skill that marked his peculiar genius.

His long fingers stroked the casing. Ordinary looking, but holding immense power. He had built it to test a principle that appeared innocuous, but could destroy Earth itself—a bountiful earth that contained him, his family, and, until recently, a precious white pigeon.

No one else had recognized this resonance, nor thought to harness it, because no one else heard the vibrations of objects as he did. No one else but he felt the telltale tremble of everyday things with their fingertips.

Using simple wooden clamps, he affixed the device to the steel column, tugging on the cylinder to make certain that it couldn't be dislodged easily. He touched two fingers to the thick column so that his fingertips barely grazed the metal. With the other hand, he turned the dial.

He pictured pistons inside moving in silent precision as they slowly accelerated to the requested speed, like a pigeon pumping its wings to fly. For a long moment he stood next to the column with his head cocked, listening with his ears as well as his fingers. He adjusted the device's oscillation rate. Again, he waited and listened. He repeated this action countless times, seeking to tune his Oscillator to the natural vibration of the steel.

Eventually, the metal under his fingertips trembled to a faint life. His device had matched the frequency of the steel's resonant frequency. Time would do the rest.

He left the Oscillator to its work while he unlocked a wooden storage unit containing spools of wire, a stained metal table holding egg-shaped globes of blown glass, and a ladder-back chair. He grasped the chair by its top rung and placed it next to the column, then dusted the seat with his handkerchief, sat, and crossed one long leg over the other. Again, he placed two fingers against the steel, like a doctor feeling for a pulse.

The metal's deep song thrummed through his fingers and up his arm. The music vibrated in the synovial fluid in his shoulder, trilled through his stomach, and pressed against his ears. He closed his gray eyes to concentrate on the metal's song, and a small smile crossed his pale face.

He was in tune with the steel.

Mesmerized, he listened too long. The steel trembled too quickly. An ordinary man might not have seen the change, but he did. Tiny oscillations, no bigger than a pigeon's heartbeat, shivered the length of the column.

The column cracked, like lake ice breaking free after winter.

Sounds intruded on his consciousness—a siren, the tinkle of breaking glass, the creak of other steel columns flexing. His device had succeeded, but perhaps too well.

With one decisive movement, he stood and reached to turn it off. Hot steel seared his fingertips. He gritted his teeth and tried again, but the dial had frozen in position, and the clamps, too, would not budge.

His device pounded remorselessly on.

His usually calm heartbeat sputtered in his chest. If he didn't stop the motion soon, the column itself might shatter. Even the surrounding columns might break apart. If so, this beautiful building would collapse and bury its occupants, including him and his pigeons upstairs. He would not let this building become their tomb.

He wheeled on the heel of one patent leather shoe and ran for the cage. Thinking it a useless precaution the night before, he had nonetheless given in to a niggling doubt. He had taken a sledgehammer from its usual location in the corner and rested its handle against the table's edge.

Now he was grateful he had. In two long steps he reached the hammer. He wrapped his long white fingers around the handle and returned to his device. He lifted the hammer high and brought its head down on the deceptively small cylinder. The metal case cracked, but gears within continued to turn. He had engineered his device to withstand shock and force. Again, he brought down the hammer, and yet a third time.

The gears shrieked like a baby bird as metal ground against metal. He flinched, then hardened his heart against his creation. He smote it blow after blow until the misshapen steel fell to the floor and was still. He had stopped its mechanical heart.

Heavy fists pounded on the front door to the building, and angry voices outside shouted for admittance. He had only minutes before one of his neighbors let them inside. He must not be found down here with the device. It was still too hot to touch, so he kicked it into a corner with the toe of his shoe. He polished that toe against the back of his immaculate trousers, smoothed his hair, and settled his jacket into place.

His long legs skipped every other stair as he flew to his laboratory. He entered and closed the door quietly behind him. His assistants looked at him with surprise. He smiled to allay their suspicions and glanced around the laboratory.

Glass had broken in this room, too. The windows had given way, and one assistant sported a thin cut across his cheek. An oval bulb lay shattered on the floor.

His device's power was writ large in the destruction that surrounded him.

Curious and exhilarating to think that something so small could produce such dramatic changes in the world. Yet he himself, like every man on Earth, had grown from something as small as an egg.

Angry voices grew louder. He couldn't yet make out their words, but he understood the tone and recognized an Irish accent. The local constabulary, then.

Knuckles rapped against the door to his laboratory. Nikola glanced around once before calling out, "Enter!"

The door slammed open, and two men strode inside. They looked like life-size windup dolls in matching blue uniforms with silver buttons and with handlebar mustaches and worried eyes. They glared at him, although they could not know that he was at fault.

"There was an earthquake!" shouted the one in front, the leader. He was the fatter of the two, and he had the larger mustache—blond shrubbery against a face as freckled as a plover's egg.

"A horse fell down and was almost run over by the cab." The other policeman clenched his meaty fists.

"I don't suppose you know about that?" asked the leader.

Both men hovered in the wooden doorway as if afraid to venture inside.

Nikola would not have let the building bury his hen, or himself. "The danger is past."

"What danger do you mean? Why is it past?" The man's freckles squirmed when he spoke.

"Why, the earthquake. I felt it here in the laboratory." Nikola gestured to the broken glass on the floor so that they would see he hadn't been spared. "It knocked my bulbs off the table and broke my windows, but it is over now, yes?"

Such a machine! It intrigued him; it did not frighten him. His heart soared at the thought of what such a device could do—send messages perhaps, or destroy rock for mining. Glorious possibilities flashed through his mind. If only mankind had the wisdom to harness such power for good use.

The freckled policeman looked at him with his mouth still partially open. Native intelligence and suspicion shone from his snapping blue eyes. "Just a simple earthquake then?"

"What else could it be, my good man?" Their imaginations could conceive of nothing but this natural explanation.

The man fingered the long black stick he carried in his belt. He looked as if he wanted to take it and strike Nikola.

Nikola drew himself up to his full height and stared him down. "That will be all."

Anger flashed across the man's face, but he turned away, dismissed. He had not found what he sought, and so he retreated.

Nikola thought again of the wisdom and courage his beloved bird had displayed by knowing how to find him and coming across snow and cold to say farewell. He had never met a person like her. And he never would.

He had already filed a patent for his device, which he had named the Oscillator, but he must revise the patent's specification so that the device could not be built properly from those plans. Mankind was not ready for a weapon of such power.

He would rebuild the device, refine, and test it again, until he knew that he could control it, because he could not leave it uncompleted. After that, he would hide it away. The true device could be used only by one of uncommon courage and wisdom. He doubted that he would ever come to know such a person.

And so the device must remain hidden.

June 28, 1983
Mianus River Bridge
Greenwich, Connecticut

George Tesla was drunk. This wasn't new for him, but the reason was. He was going to be a father. Fifty years old, and he'd knocked up a thirty-year-old carnie. Someone careful enough to live through a trapeze act ought to be careful enough to not get pregnant. But she hadn't been.

Tatiana flat-out refused to talk about abortion or adoption or any sensible solution to the problem. She was perfectly willing to talk about leaving him to raise the baby alone, but nothing else. Her mind was set.

He leaned against the cold side of the bridge and took a long sip of Jack Daniel's from his silver hip flask. He'd bought the flask when he was first made professor of mathematics at New York University. Another thing that would have to change, since Tatiana had told him she had no intention of giving up performing to move to New York and be a faculty wife. He couldn't imagine the fiery Romanian trading her sequined leotards for wool skirts and pearls.

He dropped the flask in the pocket of his tweed jacket, where it clinked against the other metal object he carried. Before he met Tatiana, he'd gone on a quest to find this little thing. It had been hidden before his birth, but he'd found it anyway. He'd carried it around for years—its weight a constant reminder that he was squandering a great legacy. Many things were possible for those smart enough and daring enough. He suspected that he was neither.

A car roared down the road, its headlights blinding him. For good measure, the driver honked at him—another good citizen chastising him for being up here on a public road, drunk, at one in the morning. But he had nowhere else to be.

Seventy feet below, the black river rolled along like tar. If he jumped, that would solve his problem. He filed this away for later consideration.

He fumbled the metal object out of his pocket and set it on the railing next to him. It didn't look like much—a square metal base with a cylinder sticking out the top—but Nikola Tesla had told his father that it could do great things. Nikola Tesla had patented it, but it had never worked. George wondered if he had patented a flawed device on purpose, to discredit his own theory. If so, maybe the object next to him could do great things.

He tapped his flask against the side of the device in a fake toast. "To great things. For one of us."

The device didn't answer, so he wasn't that drunk. Maybe it knew it wouldn't work.

But if it didn't work, why had its creator entrusted the secret of its existence to only one man? George's father said that he was the only one who knew about it, and he must have been, because once George had figured out its location, he'd found the device waiting for him. If anyone else had known where to find it, they would have taken it.

He dumped the flask and the device into his pocket and swung one leg over the railing. He wasn't going to jump. He was a scientist, and he was going to do an experiment.

He rested his feet against the outside lip of the bridge. The river rushed below, dark and deep and cold, and he held on to the cold metal railing with both hands. At least now nobody above could see him and beep at him.

Eventually, he persuaded himself to unclench one hand from the railing. It took him a few tries, because he was working one-handed, and he nearly dropped the device twice, but eventually he managed to clamp it to the side of the bridge. The device stuck out like an accusing finger. Like Tatiana's accusing finger.

He cocked his head and listened. No cars close by. The bridge was empty. Timing wouldn't get any better than this. Time to start his experiment.

He turned the tiny dial on the top of the device. It immediately started thumping away. He gaped at it. He'd replaced the power source with batteries, but he hadn't expected the old mechanism to work. He played with the dial, trying to match the natural resonance of the steel. Eventually, he seemed to get it dialed in, because the bridge started to vibrate against his stomach.

It didn't feel like much, maybe like a truck driving by. Not even a truck. A car. A little convertible. Not a threat.

Headlights appeared in the distance, and he swore. From the sound of the engine, a semi-trailer truck was approaching. Probably nothing to worry about, but he ought to shut the thumper down just in case. He reached for the device, missed it on his first drunken swipe. Was it his imagination, or was the bridge shaking?

Heat blistered his fingertips when he touched the dial, and it didn't budge. He couldn't turn the damn thing off. He could let go and fall in the water, let all this be someone else's problem, but his hand refused to release the railing. Maybe fear, or maybe a sense of responsibility.

Either way, he had to do something. He pulled the flask out of his pocket and used it to pound on the device. It moved a hair, then another. The truck thundered closer, its driver completely oblivious. Another truck was tucked behind it. A convoy, trucking through the night.

When the truck hit the span George was holding on to, the bridge let out a tremendous crack. The device fell, and he instinctively caught it, his hand slipping off the bridge.

He tumbled toward the river. His feet hit the water first. It felt like he'd landed on concrete, and the force drove him deep underwater. He fought for the surface. He didn't want to die. He wanted to stand by Tatiana. He wanted to see his child.

By the time his head broke the surface, he'd traveled a hundred yards downstream, still clutching the device. The span he'd been standing on had collapsed. He watched as a semi barreled right over the broken edge of the bridge and landed nose-down on the stony bank where another truck had already fallen. The drivers were likely dead.

Another car piled on, then a screech of brakes.

His head went under. He still held the device. It had burned his palm, but he didn't let go. He couldn't let it out of his possession.

He'd killed the men in those trucks, the people in that car. One drunken mistake, and now those people weren't going home to their families, to their daughters and sons. He could never make that right.

The current dragged him relentlessly onward.

1

Present day

Subway tunnels trap New York's heat. Heat soaks into sticky pavements and tired sidewalks. Hot, humid air blows into the tunnels' open mouths and lingers in the dark places until fall.

Joe Tesla tried to pretend he enjoyed the heat in the upper tunnels, but it reminded him of the second ring of hell. Summer was meant to be spent outside, basking in the sun, his father had always said. Good times, not the second ring of hell.

Joe walked between steel rails that brought trains from the rest of New York into Grand Central Terminal. His service dog, a golden retriever/yellow Labrador mix named Edison, panted at his side. They were performing what was becoming a daily ritual in which Joe went to the limits of the darkness, just to see if today he could break out into the light. Aversion therapy, psychiatrists called it.

It wasn't working, but he would not give up. Today, more than ever, he wanted to break free of his self-imposed darkness and go outside into the light and fresh air. He wanted to go outside to say good-bye.

Ahead, a square of daylight beckoned. Gray light filtered in at the end of the rectangular tunnel. He drank in the sight of shining silver tracks, a bird's shadow on the ground, a tree in the distance. A real, green, living tree. Outside.

He'd long ago memorized the train schedules, and he and Edison had enough time to make it to the light before the next one arrived. Following his training, Edison stayed closed by Joe's leg and far from the third rail. They were safe, from trains at least.

Joe knelt to cover Edison's sensitive ears as a scheduled train approached on a nearby track. It posed no threat to him, but he worried that the noise couldn't be good for the dog. The animal's brown eyes met his, calm as always. Nothing seemed to faze the yellow dog. If Joe could be like one creature on Earth, he'd pick Edison. Not that he got to pick.

The train passed, and Joe let go of the dog and started forward again. He was still in the shadows where the gray light didn't reach. Hot outside air stroked his cheeks. It smelled of cinder and smog, but also a little of the sea and green grass, or so he liked to think.

He walked toward the light, and his breathing sped up. He forced himself to slow his breaths, hoping that would calm him down, but knowing it wouldn't. He fought this knowledge with each shuddering breath. He wiped his wet forehead on his sleeve and kept breathing.

Then full adrenaline kicked in. His heart got into the action, beating at twice its normal rate. It felt as if he'd just sprinted across a football field.

If his heart didn't stop racing, he was going to die. Panic coursed through his veins. He had to run back into the tunnels. He'd be safe there.

He used every scrap of willpower to keep his trembling legs from bolting down the tunnel of their own accord. He wasn't going to die. Nobody ever died of a panic attack. He repeated that twice, as if his body might believe the words. It didn't. But today he had to try harder. For his mother's sake. And his father's.

First, he must get his heart under control. He closed his eyes and imagined he was somewhere safe. He was standing in front of his underground house. The house was a yellow Victorian, with red and white trim, bright and sturdy, protected in its cocoon of rock. Its paint gleamed in the orange light shed by round, hand-blown light bulbs strung overhead.

He pictured each detail—the three steps up to the front porch, the white door he dusted until it gleamed, the wrought-iron wall lantern that he always left on, the windows upstairs and down decorated with stained-glass flowers and leaves. Inside that house, he was safe. He took a deep breath. Safe.

Keeping the picture of his house in his head, he took a step forward. He didn't dare open his eyes. Edison pressed against his leg, and the contact comforted Joe. He wasn't alone. Edison was always there. He took another step.

Hot air brushed his face, a breeze from outside. He opened his eyes the tiniest crack. A thread of light leaked in. His heart slammed against his ribs so hard it felt as if it might break out of his chest and roll into the tunnels behind him.

His breath came fast and ragged. He tried to control his breaths, slow them down, but his body had taken over. His tense muscles begged to flee. He was so close to the outside. And he couldn't take another step.

Retching, he leaned forward. Edison fastened his teeth on Joe's pant leg and pulled. He tottered, terrified he might fall into the light. He caught his balance and let the dog pull him backward, step by step, into the familiar darkness.

His stomach roiled. The first time he'd tried this had been after breakfast, and he'd thrown up on the tracks. He knew better now, and came here only on an empty stomach.

Edison nudged his nose under Joe's hand and tilted his head back. He urged Joe to pet him, to relax. Joe ran his hand along the dog's warm back. His legs still shook, but he didn't feel as if he were about to die anymore. He petted the dog, controlled his breathing, and slowly calmed down. He wasn't going to die, but he wasn't going to go outside either. Not today.

He'd turned his back on the light as he fled, but he faced it again now. The entrance was an empty mouth that mocked him. The light and wind and trees might be forever out of his reach. But he had gone nearly a yard farther than yesterday. Not enough, but progress.

A train came through, again on a different track, and he covered the dog's ears. The simple act of protecting Edison brought him all the way back to himself. After the train passed, he pulled a dog treat out of his pocket and gave it to Edison. "You earned this, buddy."

The dog swallowed it in a single gulp.

Joe headed toward the tunnels that led to Grand Central Terminal. Today, his brain had betrayed him—something he'd grown to expect. Once, he'd prized his brain. It understood things that other brains didn't. His brain had led him out of a difficult childhood into early entrance to Massachusetts Institute of Technology—on a full scholarship—while other boys his age were freshmen in high school. His brain had let him coast through his classes, earn his degrees, found his own company, and retire a multimillionaire before most people bought their first house. It had been a good brain, but now it wouldn't even let him sit in the sunlight.

But he had to cut his brain some slack—it wasn't at fault. Someone had poisoned it, and he had blood tests to prove that poison had caused his crippling agoraphobia. Since he'd found that out, he'd spent a great deal of time and money trying to discover who had poisoned him and why. He'd investigated everyone who had access to his food and drink on his last days outside, but all his inquiries had led nowhere.

A large key ring at his belt jangled when he stumbled over a train tie. The keys came with the house—they provided access to all the doors in the tunnel system. With these keys, he, and he alone, could open each door in his subterranean world and see what lay behind it. Too bad his brain wasn't so straightforward.

Edison bumped Joe's knee with his nose, as if to remind him he was OK. That his life still had good things. That he was safe.

If only it were that easy.

2

Vivian Torres hung on to the rock wall with every bit of strength in her chalk-dusted fingertips. She'd been mixing and matching holds all the way up, always trying to find something more difficult, and now she'd climbed herself into a spot she wouldn't be able to get out of without falling off the wall. Her fingertips were screaming, but she wasn't going to give up.

She ought to be safe. Her teenage sister, Lucy, stood below, belaying her. Lucy didn't like to climb, but had taken and passed a belaying class because Vivian paid her twenty dollars for each visit to Brooklyn Boulders—an indoor climbing gym where she'd had to sign more waivers to touch the walls than she had to enter the military.

Easy money, but Lucy wasn't earning it. Instead, she fiddled with her phone one-handed. If Vivian fell off the wall, Lucy would let her hit the mat like Humpty Dumpty. So, dropping wasn't an option.

Vivian had to get out of this on her own. She hadn't survived two tours in Afghanistan to kill herself falling off a fake climbing wall in New York City. No dignity there.

She blew a strand of black hair off her face and reached for a yellow handhold. She had to let one foot leave the wall, and her shoulders told her they were tired of her shenanigans. Her left hand slipped off the handhold, and the momentum knocked her off the one good foothold she'd been using. Pain shot down her right arm as it took her full weight.

Dangling by one arm, she had a good view of Lucy. The rope was slack in her brown hands, and Lucy studied the graffiti-covered front windows as if trying to read them from the inside.

"Yo!" Vivian shouted.

Lucy didn't even flinch. White wires trailed out of her ears and down to the phone in her hand. She was wearing earbuds! Vivian had forbidden her to listen to music while belaying her. Back in the service, she had trusted her fellow soldiers with her life. Civilian life wasn't like that.

She looked down at the wall below her, but she was just over a curve, and she couldn't see far enough to find a safe place to put her legs or her arm. She blocked out the panic in her stomach and the pain in her hand. That was just her body. She could rise above that. She had scars on her back and a medal in her closet that would testify to it.

If she couldn't use her eyes, she'd have to use her memory. She closed her eyes and visualized the wall below, replaying each potential handhold and foothold in her memory.

A red foothold scrolled by. She stopped the picture and studied it. If she swung toward it, her foot might reach. If she misjudged the hold's position, she'd fall. But she'd fall in a couple seconds anyway, when her right hand lost its last bit of desperate strength.

She swung toward a foothold she couldn't see, caught it with her toe, and pulled herself onto the wall. Her left hand found a new grip. She let go with her right hand and clenched and unclenched it, sending blood to her angry muscles. She hauled in a few deep breaths.

That wasn't a mistake she could make on a real wall. That'd kill her. Next weekend she was going out to The Gunks with Dirk and a couple of friends, and she'd better get her head in the game by then. Outdoor walls were unforgiving.

But careful climbing wasn't what the indoor wall was about. On the indoor wall, she didn't allow herself to plan in advance. She went from one handhold to the hardest one she could see, training herself to react to the unexpected, getting stuck on purpose. Something that was a lot easier when she thought she had Lucy to back her up.

She reached for another handhold and pushed herself up with her legs. She wasn't going to climb down before she reached the roof. Below her, Lucy started tapping her foot to the music.

Damn little sister. Vivian was taking back those twenty dollars as soon as her feet were on the ground.

Lucy looked up. "Your phone just beeped! It says you have a funeral to go to."

Vivian touched the roof. "You're damn lucky that it isn't mine."

3

Ash gazed out the window of his eighty-fifth floor office. The surrounding skyscrapers faded into pollution-browned clouds. From his perch high in the Empire State Building, he was constantly reminded how humans had sullied even the clouds. Mankind was fast turning this beautiful blue and green ball into a waste dump. A few more generations and the planet would collapse. He could cope with the idea of losing a few billion people here or there, but the mass extinction of the innocent plants and animals troubled him deeply.

He cracked a window, and warm air flowed into the room. Another reason he loved the building—the windows actually opened. He'd spent so much time sealed off from nature at their last location that he'd vowed never to move into another building that didn't have windows that could open into the world.

A few quick breaths of the outside air—he could taste the metallic tang of pollution in it—and he went back to work. On his sleek bamboo desk sat the current quarterly report for his company, Wright, which played at the boundaries of ecology and commerce—snapping up money right and left by making a cleaner world profitable. On top of the report rested a *Forbes* article that described Alan Wright as "the man who has singlehandedly done more for the planet than anyone before him."

Most men would have been content with that, but not Ash. Repairing the planet one tiny piece at a time was pitiful. People had to learn to consume less and reproduce less, and it drove him crazy to see how sleepy and stupid they were, even when their self-interest was concerned. It didn't matter how often or how clearly the message went out—most people weren't listening.

So he had created the hacktivist network Spooky. Spooky's name came from Einstein's quote about quantum entanglement as "spooky action at a distance." The world was entangled whether policymakers recognized it or not, and each tiny human was a force with a spooky amount of power that could stretch around the world.

In the beginning, he had secretly played all the parts—creating bots and identities that interacted with each other and pulled off brilliant hacks. Once, Spooky sent pictures of oil-soaked pelicans, open-mouthed dead fish, and fires burning on the surface of the ocean to every employee of the oil company responsible for a giant spill. A few examined their consciences and talked to the media.

Then, he hacked the senior executives' emails and posted their ass-covering, contemptuous correspondence about the spill on the Internet. In the media firestorm that followed, he'd lunched with some of those very same executives as a peer, commiserating over the violations to their privacy, as if their privacy were more sacred than the ecosystems they destroyed for profit.

That action launched Spooky. He'd built it, and they finally came—young, eager hackers willing to risk everything to change the world. Powerless kids who suddenly felt as if they might have a chance to expose the powerful, to use their brains to even the odds of survival for the planet had poured into Spooky's secret chat rooms to plan and execute their own actions.

He'd intended to turn over control of Spooky and let the young ones bear it forward. But he loved the freedom his online anonymity gave him and, in the end, he couldn't give it up. In real life, Alan Wright was always deferred to for his billions, his brilliance, and his meteoric success.

In Spooky's world, he was merely Ash—either the wood used to stake a vampire or what remained after a fire. Both meanings were about transformation.

Ash tapped a button to open a secure window on his monitor. He'd finally hacked one of his favorite hacktivists—Geezer. Geezer was the oldest of the fluid consortium of troublemakers that swirled around Spooky. Geezer had helped build the Internet infrastructure they hacked, and he knew secrets that went deeper than the youngsters, but he sometimes missed obvious intrusions into his own space. Ash had finally nailed down his real IP address and accessed Geezer's camera. He liked to put a face to the name.

A man in front of a computer in an untidy room showed on Ash's screen. He hadn't expected Geezer to be bald as an egg. He had expected the long, unkempt beard and the tie-dyed shirt. The man's bloodshot eyes bulged, like Marty Feldman's, and he looked too thin to be healthy.

Geezer's long fingers were typing away, logging into a dark chat room often frequented by members of Spooky. Ash took a long sip of coffee and eavesdropped. This was better than television.

quantum: u don't have the courage of ur convictions, old man. spooky would be better off without u
geezer: I don't answer to you

> quantum: i don't ask u questions, because u don't know anything. maybe u used to, before ur Alzheimer days
> geezer: Wisdom is earned
> quantum: courage is born, and u didn't get any. u'll never do anything great, old man.

Quantum could be cruel, but his tactics ensured that only the strongest and most committed members stayed with Spooky.

> geezer: I have access to something great
> quantum: viagra? old news, old dude

Quantum was trouble. Ash had researched him when his importance within Spooky grew. He knew his real name, Michael Pham; his current location, also New York City; and that Quantum had been in and out of prison for hacking, stalking, and assault. He was brilliant, but unpredictable, violent, and more radical than the others. At some point, Spooky might have to cut ties with him and disavow that he had ever been part of their group. But not yet. He might still be useful.

So far as Ash could tell, Quantum and Geezer didn't know each other off-line, or even know they both lived in New York. Good. Ash liked having an overview that others didn't. Information was power.

> geezer: Any Nikola Tesla fans out there?
> quantum: who isn't?

Ash sat up straighter. He had been obsessed with Nikola Tesla since he was a boy.

> geezer: I know a guy with a box of Tesla's original designs.
> quantum: sure u do
> geezer: Including the Oscillator.

Ash leaned forward. Plans for the fabled Earthquake Machine? Nikola Tesla had said he had once used the

Oscillator to create an earthquake in Manhattan, frightening local police. But those words came from an elderly Tesla, one whose lucidity was often disputed. Tesla had said a lot of kooky things, but he'd also said enough brilliant ones that you never knew what to take seriously. The Oscillator was one of his more intriguing claims.

quantum: the one he said could 'knock down the empire state building with 5 lbs of pressure?'
geezer: That one.

Ash looked around at the steel and glass that encased him. He'd headquartered his company here because of everything the building represented, including reaching for the sky using green technology.

He certainly hadn't come here for the neighborhood. He shared a floor with the third-largest privately owned corporation in the United States. The Bakers, although he called them the Breakers because all they did was break things, were a brother-and-sister team. Their oil-drilling empire perpetuated legendary environmental destruction, and they were well-known for spending huge sums to finance the right-wing agenda. They were destroying the world faster than Ash could save it, and he had to be reminded of them every time he got out of the elevator.

They had moved into fracking, and were drilling deeper than had ever been possible. Their actions were causing earthquakes and widespread water contamination. They were set to expand their fracking activities into national parks in six months. No place on Earth would be safe from their depredations. Ash had his lobbyists working against theirs, of course, but he'd run out of time.

In weak moments, he thought of moving to another floor entirely, but he didn't want to give them the satisfaction. He'd tried to buy up the floor, but the Bakers had deeper pockets, and a deeper attachment to their office space because they had spent so much to set it up. They lived in paranoid fear of being hacked, so they had spent a fortune to install a top-notch security system. Their walls were shielded against electromagnetic emanations to keep out any kind of detection, including devices designed to recognize and reconstruct keystrokes. They didn't even send their data to be backed up off-site. Every single bit of intelligence about their company was in this building.

Could this building be brought low by a device so small it would fit in a pocket? It was a ludicrous thought, but Nikola Tesla had claimed that it could. He'd said more incredible things in his time—and gone on to prove that they were true.

> *quantum: saw a mythbusters episode on that. device didn't work. myth busted*
> *geezer: I saw it too. It didn't knock down the bridge, but it caused vibrations hundreds of feet away. It could cause a lot of panic without being destructive.*
> *quantum: unless nikola=right and mythbusters=wrong. then it could wreak havoc*

Quantum liked havoc a little too much. He'd come up from poor beginnings, and he didn't believe in the system. The first computers he hacked were in the library. Even now, the machines he worked on were probably stolen. He was no white hat hacker, and his connection to financial hacking schemes for profit could bite Spooky in the ass. Still, Ash was attracted to the edgier members of Spooky, becoming bored by those who simply wanted to do right and do good. They weren't as effective as someone like Quantum, who was willing to take big risks.

> *quantum: doesn't matter. oscillator doesn't exist*

Geezer sat back in his chair, bushy brows drawn down in what looked like frustration. He bent down to get something out from under his desk, and his face disappeared from the screen. Behind him, bright sun fell through his window onto what looked like a scale model of the Mars rover. He returned with a sheet of yellowed paper in his hand and a thoughtful expression on his face. For a few seconds, he studied the paper, as if trying to decide whether to reveal it to the group.

Ash's heart started to race. He had a hunch they needed to see that piece of paper, and he always followed his hunches. He entered the chat room.

ash: care to put ur $ where ur mouth is? show us proof
quantum: hi, ash!
ash: hello, fellow troublemakers
quantum: no proof. just words
geezer: Here's your proof.

He tapped a few keys, and a file link appeared in the chat room. Ash opened the image file. A yellowed piece of paper with writing appeared on his monitor. He quickly zoomed the image to a readable size.

The writing was unmistakably Nikola Tesla's. Ash recognized the classic Old World lettering and the forward-slanting N. Dots of darker ink showed in the corners of some letters where Tesla's fountain pen had paused at the end of a stroke. The document was an original, or a damn fine copy. But it looked like a shopping list.

ash: that's not for oscillator
geezer: It's from a larger collection. Plans for Oscillator in that collection
quantum: u can get it, old guy?

geezer: It belonged to another old guy, and was written by yet another old guy—Nikola Tesla himself.

Ash had been through every known collection of Tesla memorabilia, but he never read the document currently on his screen. Geezer must have access to previously unseen material.

ash: what collection?
geezer: A friend of the family. I know them. I can get the plans quantum: if they let u out of the home to look for it

Ash stared at Geezer's lined face and wondered what secrets it was hiding.

Ash would have to keep an eye on him. If the Oscillator was out there, he wanted it for himself. Spooky's job was to shake things up, maybe knock things down. The Oscillator might be a devastating tool—something that could save the world, or destroy it. The possibilities were limitless.

And the Breakers didn't have one.

He laid his palm against the cool glass shell that separated him from the hot and polluted world outside. With the Oscillator in hand, this building would be fragile. He could wound the Breakers with an act of great physical and metaphorical power, and save countless acres of the most pristine country left in the United States. He could buy himself the time he needed to fight back against their lobbying machine.

What a glorious symbol the Empire State Building laid low would be! American hubris brought to the ground for the world to see by destroying the most iconic building in the city, perhaps the country. The repercussions would be more than financial—the entire modern world would again feel at risk.

What could he grow from the ashes of that destruction.

4

Together Joe and Edison climbed the *Employees Only* stairs onto Grand Central Terminal's Track 42. The numbers triggered Joe's synesthesia (green for four and blue for two). He'd been five (brown) before he discovered everyone else didn't see colors in their heads when numbers were mentioned, eight (purple) when he realized it let him understand mathematics at a completely different level than others, and sixteen (cyan, orange) when he'd used it to get into MIT and take control of his own life.

Joe glanced at the simple white-faced clock hanging from the ceiling—just after noon (cyan, blue). Lunchtime. He wasn't hungry, but he thought it best to stick to his routine today.

He picked up the pace and strode across the empty platform and out into the terminal itself. The air felt cooler here, but still uncomfortable. Summer had come even to the vast concourse. The weather brought heat and humidity, but also a lot of women in shorts and miniskirts. An acceptable tradeoff.

He snapped a leash onto Edison and adjusted the dog's blue psychiatric service vest. Joe didn't expect to be hassled, but it was easier to put on the vest than have a conversation with some cop.

The dog tugged on the leash, pulling them toward the food court, but when Joe headed over to the Apple balcony, Edison obediently followed. The glowing white apple meant different things to different people, but in Grand Central, it meant free Wi-Fi.

He touched the pocket where he kept his phone in a pouch. He'd designed the pouch to block cellular signals from reaching his phone. It was his mini-Faraday cage. Somebody was marketing them now, but he'd made his years ago. He used the cage so his phone wouldn't always be communicating with Apple, telling them his location so that they could track his movements. They didn't need to know what he was doing.

He took out the phone, connected to the free Wi-Fi, and discovered that in less than an hour's walk, he'd accumulated a long list of work-related emails. California and Pellucid, the company he'd founded, were waking up. He still consulted there. He was helping to catch bad guys, or at least that's what he used to tell himself. Now he wasn't so sure.

He scrolled through the list of emails and opened the one he'd most been dreading. It was an automated email sent by a tracker he'd installed in his company's facial recognition software. The tracker checked to see how many facial recognition requests were made and how quickly they were matched. The volume of faces being fed into the system had skyrocketed to hundreds of times more than expected. Either something new had come online recently, or he had a bug to track down.

By force of habit, he logged into the darknet and scanned through emails sent by those who'd had the opportunity to administer the poison that had caused his agoraphobia. Still nothing interesting, but they would slip up eventually and, right now, all he had was time. He would wait them out.

With a few quick movements, he disconnected and returned to his own email. The last message in his inbox caught his eye again. It had been sitting there for days, and he couldn't bring himself to delete it.

From: George Tesla
To: Joe Tesla
Subject: Be careful

Son,
I've said things I shouldn't, to people I shouldn't. I've set them on paths. I don't know where they might lead. Watch your step.
Dad

He sighed. He'd read it many times. It was part of the one-way conversation that his father had started up with him when Joe moved to New York. His father had once been a brilliant statistician and, despite his failings as a father, he'd at least bequeathed Joe the Tesla brains. That should count for something. So, Joe read his daily emails, but he never answered them. He'd never forgiven his father for his many sins of omission and commission during Joe's childhood.

Today, too late, he wished that he had.

Edison nuzzled his hand. His brown eyes looked worried.

"I'm OK." Joe scratched the dog behind the ears and dropped the phone into his pouch, cutting himself off from the grid again. "Lunch?"

Edison's tail wagged at the familiar word, but his eyes said he knew Joe wasn't OK.

Joe headed over to Grand Central's underground food court. At the Tri-Tip Grill, he ordered steak sandwiches for himself and for Edison. Joe also got fries and a Coke, but Edison would have to make do with water once they got back to the house.

The dog's eyes fastened on the brown paper bag, and he licked his lips.

"Soon enough," Joe said. "Greedy Gus."

Edison gave him an injured look and stood, ready to go.

By way of apology, Joe fished a piece of meat out of Edison's sandwich and fed it to him, resting his hand on the dog's shoulder before they hurried up the long ramp to the concourse.

He usually stopped to admire his surrogate heaven—the green-blue ceiling painted with Zodiac constellations was the only sky he saw these days—but today he gave it only a quick glance because he caught movement out of the corner of his eye. A gray and white pigeon flew diagonally across the space, landing behind a carved ship's wheel far from the floor.

A pair nested at the edge of the green-blue ceiling—the only wild animals in this man-made room. He wished that he had some dry corn to feed them. He and his father had fed the pigeons in Central Park during Joe's rare visits. His father had practically tamed the pigeons, and they had perched on his wrist and had taken the corn from his palm. Joe would have liked to have tried to tame these two, but suspected that feeding them would draw unwanted attention and maybe get the birds in trouble, so he left them alone and admired them from afar.

He wove between travelers to get to the iconic clock mounted on the round information booth at the very center of the concourse—a familiar meeting place to any New Yorker. The clock read almost 12:30 (cyan, blue: red, black). He tapped on the brass door, and waved to Miss Evaline, the woman who presided over the booth with good-natured authority.

The information booth was built around a large, hollow column. Inside the column, a spiral staircase led to the creaky elevator that would carry Joe and Edison to their underground home.

"Did you have a nice walk?" Miss Evaline opened the door to the concourse and let them in. Curious tourists stopped to look. Civilians didn't go through that door.

"We did, thank you." Joe stepped inside and fitted his key into the second door. He needed to go downstairs, and he dreaded it. "How was your morning?"

"Busy. Can't complain." She straightened the black cap on her head before stooping to pet Edison. He was on duty, so he kept his serious face, but the tiny wag of his tail betrayed him. He liked her. "But I'm sorry to say you can't go down right now."

The bottom fell out of Joe's stomach. "Why not?"

"Elevator inspection," she said. "Should only be a few hours."

Edison licked his hand, but it didn't calm Joe down.

He thanked Evaline, but the words stuck in his throat. He needed to go home, but he didn't have time to wind through the tunnels again. He had to be somewhere with Wi-

Fi by one (cyan). Quickly, he ran over his Wi-Fi options: the Apple Store—too public; Track 36 (red, orange) by the Station Master's office—even more public, he might not even get a chance to sit down; and the Hyatt—which would have to do. He could check into a hotel room for a few hours and get the Wi-Fi password from the concierge. Not long ago he would have balked at the expense, but it didn't matter anymore. After Pellucid went public, he'd never had to worry about money again.

He jogged across the terminal, slid through the hallway separating the Hyatt from Grand Central without looking toward the glass doors leading outside, checked in, and took the elevator up to his temporary room. Even though he'd lived in the Hyatt for months before moving down below, he didn't feel comfortable in the room. Its anonymity felt wrong, today of all days. This wasn't where he should be for this call. But he didn't have a choice.

He dumped Edison's sandwich onto a towel in the bathroom and filled the ice bucket with water so the dog could have a drink. Edison bolted his sandwich in three bites and lapped noisily at the water.

Joe glanced at the window that ran along one side of the room. The window looked onto the outside edge of Grand Central Terminal. He never saw the building from the outside.

Sunlight poured through the window onto the carpet. He couldn't go near the light. The curtain was so close, but he'd have to cross the light to get to it. That wasn't possible, so he'd have to sit on the floor on the other side of the bed with his laptop in his lap. Not ideal.

Edison trotted across the room, took the curtain gently in his mouth, and pulled it closed. The room was safe again.

The dog's ability to read Joe's moods and respond was uncanny, and Joe loved him for it. He took another treat out of his pocket and gave it to him.

Joe clicked on the desk lamp and took his phone out of his pocket. He settled down to wait. He had made it with a few minutes to spare. He chewed his sandwich, not tasting it, and washed it down with a swig of cold Coke. He was too upset to stomach the fries.

The clock at the corner of his computer screen read one (cyan). He tapped his fingers against the desktop. He wanted the call to come in, and he didn't want it to.

His phone rang. Vivian Torres was calling him on FaceTime. Characteristically prompt.

Sweat sprang up on Joe's palms, and he wiped his hands on his pants before accepting the call.

Vivian looked tanner than usual. She'd been soaking up the summer sun, like nature intended. His father would have been proud of her. She'd also cut her black hair shorter, into a bob. It suited her, but just about everything suited her. Even though she didn't seem to know it, she was a beautiful woman.

"Torres here. I'm at the entrance to the cemetery," she said.

Hydraulic brakes sighed behind her, probably from the bus she'd arrived on. She tilted her phone to show a wrought-iron gate with *New York Marble Cemetery* written across the top.

Joe's mouth went dry, and he croaked, "Thanks."

The funeral was about to begin, and he wasn't there. He was in some hotel room, alone with his dog.

"I can't see anyone from out here," she said. "I'm going to walk into the cemetery and see what's going on."

Joe nodded, then remembered she wasn't looking at him. "OK."

He took a long sip of Coke and cleared his throat.

She panned her phone from side to side to show brick walls and a faraway strip of bright green grass. "I don't know how they'll feel about me filming once I get in the cemetery, so I'm going to put you in my front pocket to be discreet."

The view dropped a foot, dipped behind white fabric, then settled.

"I feel short," Joe said.

"If you think I'm taping this thing to the side of my head, you've got another think coming."

Joe smiled, grateful he could. "I'll go on mute now."

He didn't want any hotel noises beaming out into the cemetery during the service.

"Gotcha, boss." The phone wiggled as if she had nodded. She started forward, and the green grass neared. That must be the cemetery itself.

A guy wearing a black suit and a professional mourner's face hurried up to her. "Are you here for the Smith funeral?"

Smith funeral? His father's last name was Tesla.

"I'm here for Mr. George Tesla. Am I in the right place?" Vivian asked.

"Of course. Mr. Tesla is descended from the Smiths, so he will be buried in their crypt. It dates back to 1836." He gestured to a white plaque resting on grass in front of a stone block wall. "So few families have kept up the tradition. It's an honor to be able to lay someone to rest here today."

As Vivian moved closer, Joe saw the name SMITH engraved on the marble plaque. But his father wasn't a SMITH. He was descended from Nikola Tesla. The Teslas had lived in Croatia, not New York. Nikola Tesla himself hadn't immigrated to the United States until 1884 (cyan, purple, purple, green). This couldn't be the right place. Maybe his father was a Smith on his mother's side, although Joe was pretty sure his grandmother's maiden name was Morris.

He wanted to ask Vivian to double check, but he didn't want to make his presence known and maybe get her kicked out. She turned in a slow, unobtrusive circle, clearly trying to show him the full scene. Two older men in black suits stood near the plaque. They must be his father's chess club—professors who had visited his father in the home. One had removed his suit coat and hung it over his arm, but the other seemed more concerned with propriety than comfort, even on such a hot day.

From his father's emails, Joe knew more than he wanted to about both men. One was a brilliant mathematician who had never achieved the recognition Joe's father thought he deserved. The other one might have had an affair with Joe's mother, or at least his father had hinted at it. In a movie, one of them would have murdered his father, but they hadn't.

Ever wary, Joe had asked his lawyer, Mr. Rossi, to hire a medical examiner to review the autopsy performed on his father's body. The second doctor concurred that his father had died of a heart attack. He was eighty-two years old and had suffered two previous heart attacks. The medical examiner had tested his father's tissues for poisons, and every test that had come back so far was negative. He was an old man who had died of natural causes, like the original report said. Joe was still glad he'd double checked.

The camera moved past the professors to settle on a woman who had just arrived. She held a simple black box and wore a black dress, a wide-brimmed black hat, and a dotted veil that looked like something Marlene Dietrich would have worn. Even though his mother hadn't performed for decades, she walked with the graceful step of a young dancer, each movement elegant and choreographed. She looked the part of the grieving widow, even though she had divorced Joe's father twenty years before.

Vivian must have recognized her, because she kept the camera pointed there. His mother looked from side to side, as if searching for someone in the small group of mourners. Her veil fluttered in the breeze.

Guilt rose up in Joe. She was looking for him, her only child. She expected him to be at his father's funeral, and he wasn't. The man she had raised wouldn't have shamed her by missing such an important event. He would have paid his respects. But he hadn't.

She pulled the simple black box closer to her chest. The box's ebony surface gleamed in the sun. That box contained his father's ashes. Joe swallowed the lump in his throat. After he'd received the phone call from his mother telling him that his father was dead, he'd arranged the funeral and picked out the box to hold his father's ashes, but he hadn't really accepted that the man was dead until he saw the box in his mother's arms.

Edison dropped his warm head in Joe's lap. He stroked the dog's ears, and Edison wagged his tail—one solid thump (cyan). Joe took a careful breath, held it, and let it out. His father was gone. There would be no reconciliation for them now. Joe had had very good reasons to cut his father out of his life, but looking at the black box made it all so very final.

A man took his mother's arm. He looked about fifty, ten or so years younger than she, and handsome in a craggy thirties movie star way. Vivian caught the man's solicitous face in profile, and Joe was struck by how much the man looked like a younger version of his father.

Joe had no doubt this man and his mother were romantically involved. Men had always flocked to his mother.

The camera stayed on her as she stepped across the grass. The chess players watched her advance, both smiling a greeting as if they knew her. Had his mother and father stayed in touch till the end, so much so that she knew his friends?

They'd separated when Joe was ten, and he and his mother had moved around with the circus while his father returned to New York, teaching statistics at New York University, and forgetting Christmases and Joe's birthdays.

Vivian moved the camera to show a priest walking behind his mother. The man looked fresh out of missionary school. His fresh-scrubbed face was pink, and his priest's collar looked too tight. He clutched a Bible and marched with the determined steps of an African explorer about to set off into the jungle. Joe bet it was his first funeral.

The priest nodded to his mother, then to Vivian, as did the chess club, even though they didn't know who Vivian was. Joe's mother, however, gave her such a knowing glance that he inched back in his flimsy hotel chair. His mother pressed two (blue) fingers to her lips and dropped them to her side. That was the secret "I love you" sign she and Joe had invented when he was a kid. He hadn't seen it in years, but he instinctively made it back, even though she couldn't see him.

The priest lined his mother, her paramour, and the retired professors in front of the wall. Vivian fell in last. A giant arrangement of flowers Joe had selected online stood on an easel next to his mother like a proxy for her son. It wasn't enough, of course—she needed a flesh-and-blood son to hold her hand—but it was the best he could do right now.

Words were intoned, but Vivian's microphone picked up mostly wind and the faint drone of traffic. It didn't matter anyway. The priest hadn't known his father, so what could he say that Joe needed to hear?

He closed his eyes and prayed for his father. He prayed death had brought his father peace from the demons that had haunted him. He hadn't been an easy man, and there must have been reasons.

But even now Joe couldn't forgive him everything. The demons that his father had set upon Joe would be with him always. As they say, we carry the dead with us.

When he opened his eyes again, the priest had finished. His mother lifted the urn to hip height and slid it into an empty niche in the stone wall. Her lips moved as if she whispered something, but he couldn't make out the words. He turned the volume up to full, but heard only the murmur of traffic and the slamming of a faraway door.

5

Vivian hated funerals. She'd attended plenty back in the service, and they'd never offered her comfort or closure. They made her angry that everyone was boxed up in the same generic ritual, just like their bodies were boxed up in wooden caskets. When she died, she wanted to have her ashes scattered out the back of an airplane. Then the mourners could parachute after and go have a beer when they landed—adrenaline and alcohol would be a good send-off.

If her mother outlived her, though, Vivian knew she'd insist on this kind of awkward service, where everyone felt compelled to make up something nice, maybe toss in a joke, and cry. At Vivian's funeral, Lucy would feel guilty because she let her big sister fall off some indoor climbing wall and die and sad because she'd inherited Vivian's shoes. Vivian's shoes were too boring for Lucy. She suppressed a smile.

A couple of guys from the funeral home lifted the stone block into place, and that was it. Nobody but the priest gave a eulogy, which was weird. It looked like it was over.

One more thing she had to do, although Tesla hadn't told her to, and probably didn't want her to. Whatever. It was the right thing to do.

She walked over to Mrs. Tesla and held out her hand. "My name is Vivian Torres. I'm here on behalf of your son."

The woman shook her hand. She wore silk gloves, like a movie star, but her tiny hand was surprisingly strong.

"Thank you for coming." Mrs. Tesla waved her hand at the phone in her pocket. "And thank you, too, Joe."

"Would you like to speak to him, ma'am?" Vivian fished the phone out of her pocket. Tesla would probably be furious he was being ambushed like this, but the least he could do was talk to his mother. She needed him, and he probably needed her, too.

Mrs. Tesla took the phone and turned away. Speaking in a low voice, she walked a few steps to the wall. Her finger traced the S in SMITH on the plaque.

Her good-looking older escort made a move to follow her, but Vivian intervened. "Had you known George Tesla long, Mr.…?"

"Hugh Hollingberry." He shook his head. "I never met the man, but my fiancée was married to him once, many years ago."

Fiancée? Knowing how rich Joe Tesla was, an alarm bell went off in her head. Mrs. Tesla seemed as if she could take care of herself, but even the toughest of women might have a blind spot about men. "I didn't realize you were engaged to Mrs. Tesla."

"Two years ago," he said, which took him out of suspicion. Joe Tesla had been crazy rich for less than a year. "She humors me. How did you know the deceased?"

"I'm a…friend of his son's." That made it sound like she was sleeping with him, but she couldn't say she'd been hired to cover the funeral, even if his mom would probably tell the man anyway.

"The mysterious software genius." Hollingberry glanced over at Mrs. Tesla. "I've yet to meet him. What's he like?"

"Mysterious." She softened her non-answer with a smile. "How'd you meet Mrs. Tesla?"

He pointed to a looped ribbon that looked like the pink ones she'd seen for breast cancer, but this one was denim blue. "I met her at a charity event I sponsored to raise funds and awareness for rare genetic diseases."

Vivian hadn't expected that answer. She'd Google him later, but she doubted this guy was after Mrs. Tesla's money. He sounded as if he had money of his own. "A pretty good cause."

"I think so." His blue eyes lit up, and he spoke with a passion that reminded her of Tesla. "My sister died from a rare genetic disease, and I realized how few resources are devoted to them. But these diseases can have profound effects not just on those who suffer from them, but also on our understanding of genetics as a whole. I believe these conditions hold the secrets to understanding many of the body's processes, like aging, metabolism, mental illness, how—"

Mrs. Tesla had returned. "There now, Holly, no need to bore the young woman."

"It sounds fascinating," Vivian countered.

Hollingberry took Mrs. Tesla's arm. "Are we ready to go home, my dear?"

Mrs. Tesla handed Vivian her phone and thanked her, then the two walked across the grass, through the passageway, and turned left at the street. Vivian decided she liked them both.

She looked at the phone in her hand. She was still connected to Tesla. She popped the phone into her pocket and turned so he could see the wall where his father was entombed and the two old guys who seemed to be the only other mourners. The priest and the two men from the funeral home waited as if they had all the time in the world, although they, more than most, had to know that wasn't true.

Deciding Tesla might want to learn more about those mourners, she headed toward them. The cemetery was a beautiful place—an island of green and peace in the middle of Manhattan. She hoped that came through on the phone and gave Tesla some comfort.

"Hello." The taller of the two was Indian, with thick black hair, a good-looking face, and large brown eyes. "I'm Professor Patel, and this is Professor Egger."

Vivian felt like she was back in school. "Vivian Torres."

The bald man with the crazy beard held out his hand for a shake. He, too, wore a black suit, but had paired it with an egg-yolk-yellow bow tie that looked jarring at a funeral. He'd taken off his jacket earlier, but he'd put it back on for the service. "I'm Professor Egger, but you can call me Eggy. Everyone else does."

Well, that explained the tie. An inside joke.

"Please tell us you are a mysterious beauty who helped to ease George's last hours." Patel smiled. "Give some old men hope."

"I'm a colleague of his son's," she said. "I never met Professor Tesla, Senior."

Egger looked as if he held back a smile. "Ah, Professor Tesla."

He stressed the last name in a way that piqued her interest. "He didn't like being a Tesla?"

"To the contrary, he loved being a Tesla very much." Egger straightened his bow tie.

"He wasn't, of course." Patel had a slight Indian accent.

"Wasn't what?" Vivian wished she'd turned the phone off. She had a feeling Joe wouldn't want to hear whatever was coming.

"In America, you can change your name to whatever you want." Egger fussed with his yellow tie again. "I could be George Washington if I wanted to."

6

People swirled around Joe, heading for the doors, the tracks, the shops. Everyone was in transit to somewhere else. He was as stuck here as the clock or the light fixtures.

He sighed. He'd get back outside again someday. For now, he was waiting to meet his mother for dinner. They'd set the time and place when he talked to her at the funeral, but he'd kept his phone out of its Faraday cage since in case she changed the plans.

His phone rang, and he glanced at the screen, expecting to see a picture of his mother, but it was Celeste. A picture of her from the days when they dated in college flashed across the screen. Her smile still gave him butterflies.

He couldn't talk to her here. Her voice was hard to hear under the best conditions.

With Edison at his heels, he scooted across the concourse to the Biltmore Room, also known as the Kissing Room. Originally, passengers met in this room to travel to the luxurious Biltmore Hotel. Later, it became a meeting place for families waiting for incoming troops—a place to kiss them hello. These days the room was usually deserted, but the station had plans to restore it into a new hub. For now, it was the only quiet place in the concourse.

He sat down next to an abandoned shoeshine stand. He liked the Biltmore Room, not just because he cherished the quiet, but also because it was a time capsule—from its old-fashioned signs to the slate board with the arrival and departure times of long-forgotten trains printed in dusty chalk.

He called Celeste back and listened to the faraway ringing. Edison sat next to him, attentive and on duty.

"Hello!" said Celeste in her now-breathy voice. She had good days and bad days since she'd been diagnosed with ALS, but even the good days weren't that good anymore. Still, she sounded stronger than yesterday.

"Greetings," he answered.

"Are you home?" she asked. "Haunting the old boards?"

"I can't go down right now. They're inspecting the elevator, so I can plummet to my death with the proper inspection certificate in front of me."

"That elevator is perfectly safe! It hasn't killed anyone in over a hundred years."

"Makes it due. Those ancient cables will snap. Game over."

"I think that's only happened one time. The Empire State Building, in 1945 when a B-25 bomber crashed into it and damaged the cables. How likely is that to happen *underground?*" A quick wheeze told him she'd spoken too long.

"Have to be prepared for every eventuality." His sentences always got shorter when she was out of breath, as if he could make hers shorter, too.

"Including the final one. How was the funeral?"

"Lightly attended. And I found out my father, and by extension me, isn't descended from the great Tesla at all."

"All those years of 'do better, you're a Tesla' have come to naught?" She didn't sound as shocked as he felt.

"My father's last name was Smith. I looked it up online, and I think I might be descended from Tesla's pigeon keeper."

Tinkles of laughter came down the phone line, followed by coughs.

Joe glanced over at a sign that read *eppie's shoeshine & repair*. The little man on the sign was poised to drive a nail into a giant shoe to fix it. If only it would be so easy to fix Celeste.

"What the hell did you say to her?" That wasn't Celeste. It was her brother, Leandro. Joe and Leandro had been friends for years, but he'd become distant since Joe moved into the family house underneath Grand Central, taking possession of the place Leandro used for annual parties.

"Is Celeste all right?" Joe asked. She gasped out something in the background. He felt guilty for making Celeste waste her breath on him. She had so little to spare. Doctors still had no idea if her ALS would kill her in a matter of months, or if she might linger for years, like Stephen Hawking. They did know that she would never get better.

"It'll take her a minute to catch her breath," Leandro said. "You shouldn't make her laugh like that. It's not good for her."

Laughter, not the best medicine. "It wasn't a laugh line."

"Two laugh lines: not a Tesla and pigeon keeper," Leandro chuckled. "Just when you think the mighty can't fall any further."

Joe wasn't sure how to take that, but any way he looked at it, it counted as an insult.

Celeste came back on. "Sorry, darling, that was too funny."

"Don't go letting the tragedy of my life's circumstances cause you to work yourself into a state."

"Now you're angry." She cleared her throat. "But your ancestry is irrelevant. No less an august paper than *The New York Times* called you 'the reclusive genius who revolutionized law enforcement.' You are who you are and whether your great-great-whatever-uncle was a famous inventor or not, you've left your legacy."

"That makes it sound like I'm already dead."

"Aren't we all?" She coughed again.

"I have a surprise for you," Joe said.

"Tell me."

"Can you look out your window?" He'd already written the code to hack the smart lighting fixtures installed in the office building across from her apartment. The security on them was practically nonexistent.

Leandro came on the line. "I'm moving her. It's not easy, so this better be damn good."

"I'm at the window," Celeste said.

Joe pressed a button on his phone. It should run the code he'd set up a week ago.

"Oh." Celeste sounded surprised. "A heart."

He'd turned off every light on her side of the building, then turned on only the ones that would form a heart. He'd been saving it for some night, but Celeste often went to bed before the sun went down these days.

"That's lovely." He heard the smile in her voice. "A little sappy."

"I thought you'd say that." He pressed another button to change to a different set of lights.

Celeste laughed again and then went into another coughing fit.

Was it too much? He didn't want her to hurt herself.

Leandro's voice again, and he was laughing, too. "Damn fine work, Joe. You showed my sister a heart, then flipped her off."

It had worked. Joe tapped another key to restore the building to its original lighting. "She knows what I mean."

"Thanks, dude." For the first time in a long time, it sounded like Leandro meant it, but before Joe could say anything else, he hung up.

Edison leaned against his leg and thumped his tail once (cyan). The dog knew he was upset, but how could he not be when he thought about Celeste? She was an incredible, vibrant woman—tough, reckless, and phenomenally talented. Although she'd never needed to work a day in her life, she'd struggled to become an admired artist. Painting was one of the first things the disease had taken from her.

Just as his condition took her from him. They'd dated years before, but he had not been exciting enough for her, and she'd moved on. Now that they both were crippled, they'd become closer than ever, at least emotionally. But physically they would never meet again—she couldn't leave her penthouse apartment, and he couldn't get to it. He'd checked all the city plans, and her building was too modern to have steam-tunnel or subway access.

Edison nudged him, and he stood. No point in dwelling on all that he couldn't have. He should be grateful for what he did. Celeste on the phone was better than no Celeste at all.

"Good dog." He palmed a treat for Edison.

They walked out through the concourse and down to the Oyster Bar. Joe admired the vaulted ceilings in the restaurant, so different from the rest of Grand Central's architecture. They'd been state of the art when built, but they looked medieval. He liked that.

Giovanni hurried over. His wavy black hair was artfully disheveled, and his face was flushed. "Mr. Tesla! We have your corner table prepared. I will take you there!"

Joe followed him. He liked to sit in the corner so Edison could lie down next to the wall and be out of everyone's way. He didn't want anyone stepping on his dog.

Giovanni tapped a white dog dish on the floor, full of water. "It's such a hot day! Maybe Edison would like a drink, too? Nice and cold for him."

Joe thanked him, and Edison gave him a tail wag before ducking his head over the bowl.

Joe listened to the lapping sound of Edison drinking and the clinking of glass and silverware on plates. A low rumble of conversation drifted across the room, and Joe sipped the ice-cold water Giovanni brought him. He felt comfortable here, safe and easy.

He let his phone connect to the network, then answered a few emails from work. He'd had trouble concentrating after the funeral, and emails had piled up. His inbox was a giant conveyor belt. Stacks of messages just kept coming.

His mother was late, of course. He'd learned long ago that she was on time only for her performances. For everything else, the world could wait for her.

But he didn't want to wait. He wanted to ask her about his father. He picked up his spoon and stared at his big-nosed reflection—a face he must have inherited from the Smiths. So what if he was a Smith instead of a Tesla?

Did it matter?

It mattered. All Joe's life, his father had pressed and pushed him to be smarter, cleverer, quicker—to be a Tesla. His father's Tesla obsession had driven his parents apart, and it turns out they were never Teslas to begin with.

Joe was ten years old and sitting in the tiny booth at the front of the trailer. At night, the table leg folded to the floor and the tabletop folded down until it was level with the seats. His mother would take the bedding from its storage bin under the right booth and put it on the tabletop and seats, and Joe would sleep there.

During the day his bed turned back into a table where the family ate dinner and where he sat to do his homework. He always had a lot of homework—his father made sure of it.

Today he was supposed to draw the periodic table from memory using a blue pencil. He had to put in each element name, its symbol, and its atomic number. He drew the grid—18 columns (cyan, purple) and 7 (slate) plus 2 (blue) rows below. He knew the edges—the alkali metals on the left and the noble gases on the right—but then he had to slow down to think of the others.

"You must know this, Joe," his father admonished. "You are a Tesla. The world expects greatness from you: brilliance, wisdom, and courage."

"None of the other kids in the show know any of this." Joe set down the pencil and crossed his arms.

A muscle in his father's jaw throbbed, and Joe flinched.

"Let me get you a glass of milk." His father rose and went to the tiny refrigerator. "You'll think better with some milk."

Joe didn't see how milk could help his thinking, but knew better than to say so after his father made that face. His mother was away rehearsing in the tent, and he and his father were alone in the trailer. His father was meaner when they were alone.

His father filled the milk glass, a jelly glass with Barney Rubble painted on the front, but instead of bringing it to the table, he turned his back and hunched his shoulders.

Joe looked out at the red-and-white striped tent pitched several yards away. He'd be safer there. Farnsworth would let him feed Binky the elephant if he shoveled out her cage. Farnsworth was the veterinarian who looked after the circus's animals, and sometimes the people. Farnsworth drank like Joe's dad, but it didn't make him angry. It made Farnsworth funny.

His father set the glass next to Joe's work. The white milk shone against the pink scar in his palm.

"How did you get that scar on your hand?" Joe asked, as he had often before.

"Hubris." His father gave his usual answer. "Now drink up."

Joe took a sip. The milk was so cold it made his lips numb.

"Drink it up," his father ordered. "It's good for you."

Joe drank. His lips and tongue felt weird for a minute, but the feeling went away.

"Now, back to work," his father said.

Joe ran over the elements, their numbers a blur of colors in his head. He ran his finger across the elements he had completed: Hydrogen, Helium, Beryllium, Boron, Carbon, Nitrogen, and Fluorine. That was a good start.

His heart skipped a beat, then raced. He remembered all the elements at once. He had to get them down before they disappeared. His hand flew across the paper. He filled in square after square. He'd never felt so sure, so smart. His brain raced along like greyhounds he'd once seen at a track. They were nothing but gray streaks.

The door opened, and his mother came in. Her hair was up in a bun like it was when she performed, but she was wearing her old red leotard, the one she wore for practice. The tights had a hole in the left knee.

"What are you writing so fast over there?" she asked. "Secrets?"

"It's the periodic table of the elements," he said. "I've completed the first four rows, and I have three more to go, and then I'll be on to the man-made ones. Can you imagine doing that? Smashing together things to create a whole new element? One that never existed in the whole universe before, and one that will only be around for a tiny slice of time? But it would still be there, and you would know you made it."

She looked between him and his father, and her brows drew down like they did when she was angry. But why? He'd learned the elements. He was being a Tesla.

"Come see." He lifted the paper to show her, but he was moving too fast, and it ripped. Just a tiny bit on the edge. He could tape that back together. "I thought of drawing in pictures of what the elements actually look like in real life, but I only know it for a few of them, so I didn't do it because I thought they wouldn't all match."

His mother's cool hand cupped his chin, and she looked down into his eyes. Her eyes were clear brown, like the tea she drank every day with breakfast. Right now trouble shifted behind her eyes, but he didn't know why.

She let go of his chin and looked at his father. When she spoke, she used the super calm and deep voice she used when she was really angry. "What did you give him?"

"Just milk." His father looked at his scuffed shoes. Joe could tell he was lying.

"Men in this circus will beat you until you tell me," she said.

Joe jerked his head up. "I'm fine. I feel great. My mind is sharp and clear and fast and good. There's nothing wrong. Nothing at all."

"Coke?" His mother's calm voice was directed to his father. She ignored Joe.

But his father hadn't given him Coke. They didn't even have soda in the trailer. That was for suckers. You could charge them a fortune for sugar water. His father always said so.

"Tatiana—"

"How much?"

The question hung in the air, until finally his father's face crumpled up, and he spoke. "Maybe a quarter gram. Not much."

She touched Joe's shoulder. "We're going to see Farnsworth, Joe."

His father stood, too, as if he were coming along.

"When we come back," she said to his father, "you will be gone from this place."

"I don't have a car."

"If you are still here, I will feed you to Merle. And no one will stop me."

Merle was the lion Joe had been warned to stay away from. Not that he needed any warning. Merle spent his days pacing his cage, snaking his paw out whenever anyone came close, and peeing through the bars. They'd bought him a few months before and were looking for a sucker to unload him on. Merle would eat his father, no problem.

"Don't hurt him," Joe said. "He didn't do anything."

"Enough." She put her hand on top of Joe's head and pulled him in closer to her. He stopped arguing.

"You will vanish, George," she said to his father. "Or I will make you vanish."

Edison nudged Joe's shoe. He put down the spoon, packed away the memory, and petted the dog.

7

Quantum stopped at a park bench to stretch his calf muscles. He'd been keeping an eye on the entrance to the Waldorf Astoria hotel and on a suspicious gray-bearded hippie sitting on a bench in front of it. The guy had a *Wall Street Journal*, which didn't match his outfit, and he'd been pretending to read it while glancing at the hotel door every minute or so. Not subtle.

Quantum was here to watch for a certain woman to leave the hotel. After she left, he had orders to search her room for documents in Nikola Tesla's handwriting, and also for the Oscillator. Ash had given him the assignment, and he was thrilled to be trusted with something this important.

He leaned into the stretch, thinking about Ash. He hadn't managed to uncover much about him, but he was willing to bet that the guy was loaded. His Spooky actions always started with insider knowledge. Ash knew what happened off-line in the corridors of power and then used his online teams to screw things up. He was powerful in ways that Quantum only dreamed about. But maybe Ash would share some of that power and wealth. Whether he wanted to or not.

The old hippie shifted on the bench. He wore faded jeans and a gray NYU hoodie, and he had a beard like a wizard. He looked like Quantum had always pictured Geezer. What if he *was* Geezer? What if Ash had sent them both here? A prickling in Quantum's neck told him not to discount the possibility.

He'd lived through four foster homes, a violent older brother, and a couple of stints in prison. He knew to trust his instincts for danger. But that didn't mean he was going to wimp out.

Quantum wiped sweat off his forehead. More sweat replaced it. He didn't much mind. He'd spent every summer in New York, and he'd done without air conditioning for most of them. If he played his cards right, he'd end up living in air-conditioned splendor one day. He bet Ash lived in air-conditioned splendor all the time.

A bustle of activity drew Quantum's glance to the front of the hotel. His target had emerged from the building. She was a small woman, in her sixties, accompanied by a man in his fifties pulling a black suitcase. Both looked well-to-do, and the woman moved with a coordinated grace that made his awareness pop up a notch. She looked like she could handle herself. Probably a dancer, but she could just as easily be a martial arts expert. Not one to underestimate anyway.

Quantum might look like a nerd online, but in the real world he had a black belt in karate. Before she died, his mother had insisted on sending him to karate after kids started picking on him in grade school, like she thought he'd be a modern-day Karate Kid. After a couple of years, it started to pay off. He still ran from fights and didn't like to get hurt, but he was quick in the way that a little nerd on the streets had to be to survive. And when he had to stand and fight, he could actually kick ass. He'd given a kid twice his size a broken nose, been charged with assault a couple of times, and once beat a guy and left him for dead in the street.

He still didn't know if the man had lived or died, and he didn't much care.

The lady smiled up at the man in the business suit. He didn't look like anything to worry about as he kissed both cheeks and installed her in a bright yellow taxi, sticking the suitcase into the trunk himself. Only after the taxi pulled away from the curb did the man start walking briskly in the other direction.

Perfect. Both of them were out of their room.

In a piece of weird timing that couldn't be coincidental, the Geezer guy jumped to his feet and ran to the street. A taxi practically hit him, and he climbed inside. The hippie seemed to be arguing with the driver before it pulled away. Quantum debated following, but didn't. Ash had told him to search the room as soon as the couple left. He wasn't going to screw up such a simple assignment to follow some hippie.

He jogged across the street and looked right through the uniformed doorman. Quantum was a guest of this hotel, his room paid for through Spooky's petty-cash fund—another reason he thought Ash might be rich. Spooky always had access to plenty of money, either from Ash's pocket or stolen by him, each as good as the other as far as Quantum was concerned.

Since check-in, he'd ordered all the room service he could and had raided the minibar. Money was just a concept to someone like Ash, he suspected. And Quantum could resell those tiny liquor bottles.

He sauntered across the opulent lobby toward the elevators. Nobody said anything about the sweat he was dripping on the floor, because he had every right to be here. He was a guest. Refrigerated air wafted across his skin, and he took in a deep breath of it.

A quick smile in the concierge's direction, and he was already to the elevator. His room was beside the one he was supposed to search, and he had a card key to it in his wallet next to his own. If the card key didn't work, he'd have to improvise, but he bet Ash had come through. That guy didn't miss a trick.

A few minutes later he was in the hotel room of one Tatiana Tesla and Hugh Hollingberry, a tidy couple. He snapped on a pair of latex gloves and began his search. His mother called him The Accountant, because he was so meticulous in his habits—always putting things back as he had found them. He'd been like that as long as he could remember. A useful trait.

He finished the search and returned to his room, where he tapped out a message to Ash in a dark chat room, telling him he hadn't found anything, but the woman had left with a suitcase. Maybe the plans or the Oscillator were in there.

ash: she's at oyster bar in grand central. get suitcase
quantum: how do u know?
ash: tracking her. go!

It was spooky how much Ash knew. Quantum smiled at the pun. He only ever contacted Ash through a screen of false identities or with a disposable burner phone, so he wouldn't be easy to track, even for someone like Ash. Or at least he hoped not. His phone vibrated with an incoming text, reminding him that he was still on duty.

ash: get suitcase
quantum: any means necessary?
ash: do no serious damage. don't get caught

Quantum parsed those last sentences. What kind of damage did Ash deem to be serious? Tough to say. He'd have to use his own judgment. And no matter what, he didn't intend to get caught.

8

A flurry of movement by the door told Joe his mother had arrived at the Oyster Bar. Even in New York City, home to a fashion industry and full of beautiful women a third her age, something about Tatiana drew all eyes to her. She was always a star.

She still wore the black dress from the funeral, but she had taken off the hat, veil, and gloves. Her black hair, hair that would never go gray, was cut in a severe bob that angled forward, longer at the chin than at the nape of her neck. A new cut for her, and it looked good. She crossed the floor with easy grace.

He hadn't inherited any of her coordination.

A wheeled suitcase trailed along behind her. He jumped to his feet to take it from her.

She kissed him on each cheek and held his face in her hands for a second. "You look pale."

He kissed her on the cheek. "You look great!"

She waved her hand. "Always you say this."

"Always it's true." He brought her suitcase to their table and parked it before pulling out her chair. His mother was a stickler for manners. "What do you have in here, rocks?"

"You are closer than you think." She held her fingers down for Edison to sniff.

Edison refused, because he was wearing his vest. When he wore his vest, he considered himself on duty and didn't respond to anyone's overtures but Joe's.

"Such a serious dog."

"It's his training." Joe didn't bother to explain. She wouldn't have listened if he had. "What's in the suitcase?"

"We must speak of your father."

The waiter saved him from answering. His mother ordered a Brooklyn Summer Ale without opening the menu, and he ordered the same.

"So." She tapped the top of the suitcase. "You didn't come today."

"I can't. I explained before."

"Can't? Won't try? Who can say which this is?"

"I can say. I don't like it, but I have a real condition."

"But he was your father. You owed him such." She pushed back her hair on one side, and Joe saw the long scar it usually concealed.

His father gave her that scar. One night, she'd come back to the trailer late. His father, standing by the door with a whiskey bottle, had clipped her across the side of the head. If the bottle had been full, it might have killed her. As it was, it took Farnsworth nine (scarlet) stitches to close the wound. Joe was five years old, and when he sat holding her hand while Farnsworth sewed up her head, he had thought she would die.

He leaned over and touched the scar. "I didn't owe him a damn thing."

She took her hand in his. As always, her hands were warmer than his. "Your time together was more than those moments. Good moments, too. You owe him your life, the man you have become."

"I don't." Joe's voice rose. He brought it down. "Anyway, I couldn't go to the funeral. You know that."

She dismissed his agoraphobia with a squeeze of his hand. "Anything is possible. Always."

The waiter arrived with the beer. Joe ordered bluepoint oysters with steak fries, and his mother followed the waiter to pick out a lobster. Joe couldn't eat a lobster after he'd been formally introduced. His mother never worried about things like that.

He sat in his chair and wished that she was right, that anything was possible, and he'd be able to go outside again the minute he wanted to.

His mother returned and sat. "They fly the lobsters straight in from Maine. Imagine! I can see them sitting in little seats with their seat belts fastened, wishing they were allowed to smoke."

He laughed. "Maybe they let them smoke on those flights. The lobsters won't live long enough to get gill cancer."

Dinner was better after that. She caught him up on the happenings of the people in the circus. She kept in touch with them, although she hadn't performed in years.

When he got rich, he had bought her any house she wanted, and she chose a Victorian in San Francisco with a view of the sea. It looked much like the one where he lived, except that hers was full of old circus people and relatives from overseas.

"I suppose you are curious about my suitcase," she said after they had eaten.

"What's it for? You going on a trip?"

"It's for you, from your father."

"I don't want it."

"Not from him directly," she said. "From the Teslas, passed down."

"But Dad wasn't a Tesla, was he?"

"You knew?" She raised her sculpted eyebrows. "All this time?"

"I found out today at the funeral. Someone told Miss Torres, and I looked it up from there. Dad's real name was George Smith."

"Your Miss Torres is a pretty woman. Smart, too, and not one to be led about. Good for you, I think."

"She works for me. That's it." This was his chance to tell his mother about Celeste Gallo, but the thought of explaining their complicated relationship to his mother was too daunting. "Why did Dad lie about being a Tesla?"

"His name was officially changed with the government. He was as Tesla as you."

"But he always said we were descended from Nikola Tesla. That we got our mathematical minds from him."

"Perhaps you did."

"Not if we're not Teslas."

"Your father was born a Smith, this is true. But he did know Nikola Tesla. His father worked for the great scientist, and your father saw him often when he was a boy. That contact made George aspire to be a scientist—and so your scientific interest may come from Nikola himself."

"Dad told you that my grandfather was a scientist in Nikola Tesla's lab?"

"No scientist. Your grandfather raised racing pigeons, and he took care of Nikola Tesla's pigeons."

She'd verified everything he'd found online. "So, Dad pushed me to be like my ancestor Nikola Tesla, but not a drop of Tesla blood runs through my veins. I have pigeon-keeper blood in my veins."

"There is no shame in that." His mother gave a decisive shake of her head, as she always did when she considered a subject closed.

"There is shame in pushing a child to adopt a legacy that isn't his."

"Here you are. A famous man. A rich man. A computer genius. All because of that pushing. Is it so wrong now?"

"Yes." He had a hundred things he wanted to say, but none of them would change her mind.

"I am here, with my clever little suitcase, because of these connections. Because the famous Nikola Tesla trusted his pigeon keeper more than all the famous scientists he knew." She nudged the suitcase with her polished shoe. "Are you not curious?"

As usual, she had deflected the conversation down her own path. He was curious. But he didn't have to admit it.

"I see you look at it, Joe. I know. In this suitcase is a box that your father gave me to pass on to you when he was gone. So I do."

"It's probably a bunch of useless papers."

"Take it down to your hidey-hole and open it to see."

"It's a house, Mom, not a hidey-hole."

"Does it have windows that look out onto the sky?"

"If it did, I couldn't live there."

"Fine," she said. "Tell me about your house."

"It's Victorian, the same as yours."

She snorted. If it didn't have windows that looked out on the sky, it couldn't be the same as hers.

"It was built in the early 1900s, the same time as all this." He waved his hand around to encompass the Oyster Bar and the terminal beyond.

"Why would someone build such a house?" She sounded grudgingly curious.

"The lead engineer, the one who designed the station and its tracks, wanted a house to be built there so he could live in the tunnel system he designed."

"So they gave him a cave?"

"It's not a cave. You should come and see. The house sits in a hole blasted into the wall of a tunnel."

"This is a cave."

"But in that cave they built a two-story house—with a parlor and a billiards room and a kitchen and bedrooms, with wood floors and wallpaper and a fireplace with a mantel."

He pulled out his phone to show her pictures. He wanted her to understand about the house.

"It looks absurd, but…" The house had clearly caught her imagination, too.

"The engineer's contract specified that the underground house be deeded to his descendants in perpetuity, and I leased it from them." He didn't try to explain how grateful he was to the house. It had saved him from living out his days at the Grand Central Hyatt, where he'd been staying when his agoraphobia struck. In this quaint antique, alone underneath one of the most densely populated cities in the world, he'd felt at home for the first time in his life.

"Take my suitcase." His mother pushed it toward him with her foot.

He stared at the simple black case. On the one hand, it might contain Nikola Tesla's secrets, something any nerd in the world would like to see, including him. On the other, it came from his father, and he wanted nothing from him. Nothing.

His mother patted his arm, something she hadn't done since he was a little boy. "You have earned it, not because of who you were born to be, but because of who you became. Nikola Tesla would be proud to give this to my famous son."

Joe wasn't so sure. The company he'd created wasn't about bringing peace and light to the world. It didn't have the grandeur of Nikola Tesla's vision. Joe had created Pellucid to catch the bad guys, but he wasn't sure that's how it was used anymore. Nikola Tesla would probably slap him across the face with a glove if he were still around.

"If you don't take, what should I do with it?" His mother's eyes flashed. "Throw it away? Turn it over to the US government? They took all of Tesla's other papers. They might want these, too. This would then be on your hands."

In Pellucid, he had created something powerful, and he had sold it to the highest bidder. His life's work was out in the world, maybe doing damage. He wouldn't let these papers suffer the same fate, no matter how angry he was at his father.

He reached out and took the suitcase.

9

Geezer studied the figures through the Oyster Bar's arched windows. Tatiana sat across from her son at the corner table. She said something to Joe, and he laughed. He answered, and then she laughed, too. Clearly, they enjoyed each other's company.

Easy for Joe Tesla to laugh. He was recognized as a genius, written up in magazines and all over the Internet, a multimillionaire boy wonder. Geezer had worked his entire life and never achieved the recognition he deserved. But once he had the Oscillator, that would change.

He would take it apart and figure out how it worked, then he would draw up plans for it and present it to the world. He would be known as the one who found the Oscillator. The Oscillator wasn't doing the world any good locked away in some dusty trunk. It was wrong of George Tesla to sit on knowledge like that. It needed to be shared with the world.

He spotted the suitcase next to the table. Hoping that it might contain George's secrets, he'd wanted to grab it and run when he saw her come out of the Waldorf, but the sidewalk had been crowded with doormen and hotel guests, and he'd been across the street.

Instead, he'd hailed a cab and followed her. The cabbie hadn't wanted to do it, so Geezer had to pay him an extra twenty. Like the driver should care where the hell his cab was going—he should just drive.

They'd ended up at Grand Central Terminal, and Geezer had followed Tatiana inside. The terminal was crawling with cops and even armed soldiers, so he didn't dare make a move then either. But he couldn't let it get away, not if it contained his legacy. He glared at the suitcase. It was parked next to the table, as if it were an ordinary suitcase full of makeup and dirty underwear.

The sidewalks outside were busy. He'd find a place where he could snatch it. Later, he'd get all the recognition he deserved. He shouldn't have told Spooky about the Oscillator, but he'd wanted to brag. He wanted geniuses like Ash and Quantum to recognize him. He had been a fool.

But no more of a fool than George. One drunken night George had told him he had Tesla's Oscillator, but he wouldn't produce it. He'd gotten defensive when pressed, said he knew where to find it, but he didn't have it anymore. Said he had a map, but he kept it hidden. He said he wouldn't reveal it to anyone but his son, and even then not until after his death, which they'd both known was coming soon. He was an old man, and his heart was shot. Geezer sat with him for hours to get him drunk enough to forget they had talked.

A teenager with earbuds bumped into Geezer, and he nearly fell. "Hey!"

"Sorry, old dude," the kid said. "Didn't see you there."

Geezer watched him walk away. He wasn't surprised that the boy had run into him. He'd been invisible all his life, but that was about to change.

A flicker of light drew his attention to the Oyster Bar. He looked at the Tesla table, expecting to see Tatiana and her son still talking over coffee, moving in the synchronized dance of those who know each other well, laughing at half-finished jokes.

But their table was empty.

They hadn't come past him. He shifted from foot to foot, ready to run after them, but he didn't know where. The damn restaurant must have a second exit.

He pushed through the door at the Oyster Bar and sprinted through the dining room until he saw the other exit. He knocked a waiter on his ass when the guy tried to stop him and made for the door.

Everyone moved out of his way as he ran. The commuters weren't surprised to see a guy running in the terminal. Everyone had almost missed a train at some point.

He pounded into the main hall and saw Joe Tesla close to the clock, a yellow dog trotting along at his heels. Joe was pulling the black suitcase, and a man dressed in black was closing in on him.

Geezer sprinted toward the two men.

10

Joe tugged the suitcase behind him through the concourse. Edison walked on his left to stay out of the way, and he felt hemmed in. He shook his head. It wasn't Edison's fault that he was cranky because his mother had always known he wasn't a Tesla at all and had still let him be tortured because he hadn't been Tesla enough.

Now she'd brought him a box of secret papers from his paranoid father. They were probably Nikola Tesla's grocery lists, or notes about pigeon care and feeding.

Still, he was intrigued. His father had never given him presents, relying on Tatiana to remember birthdays and Christmases. This might be the first real present he'd ever received from his father. A present wrapped in all the mystery of Nikola Tesla himself.

Joe hurried toward the elevator, and his heart beat faster with anticipation. He couldn't wait to open the suitcase and see what was inside. She'd have known that, too, just as he'd known that she would love the house when she saw it. She'd thawed after she saw his pictures, agreed to come visit as soon as he could add her to the list of people cleared to use the elevator. He'd get Mr. Rossi to file the paperwork, and she'd be on the list in a few days.

Rush-hour travelers pushed by on either side. Grand Central, busiest place in the world, a cliché because it was true. He dodged left to avoid a gaggle of nuns in tennis shoes. They weren't exactly jogging, but they made a fast-moving undulating wall of black cotton.

His suitcase was yanked out of his hand—a quick, sharp pull, gone before he could react. Edison's reflexes were sharper. The yellow dog lunged forward and sank his teeth into the case's fabric. He braced his sturdy legs and pulled.

Joe had played enough tug-of-war with him to know he was deceptively strong. The guy stealing his suitcase hadn't. He slowed and tugged back. Joe charged him, but the man dodged, punching Joe in the side of his face as he went by. Joe saw a blur of black spandex, a black baseball hat, and sunglasses.

He lay sprawled on the marble. His cheek throbbed, and his hip hurt where he'd landed, but he scrambled to his feet, hands up.

Edison held on to the suitcase. Joe swung at the guy's face, but just a feint, instead using his real force to knee him in the groin.

But he hit air. Black Spandex was damn fast. Even more humiliating, he was fighting Joe while still holding on to the suitcase—basically winning with one (cyan) hand tied behind his back.

"Police!" shouted someone.

Joe didn't turn to see where the sound came from, and neither did his opponent. The man slid into a crouch, shot his leg out, and swept Joe off his feet. Again, he hit the floor hard.

From his new vantage point, he saw three men in military khaki and two cops in blue heading for them, a man and a woman. He stayed down. Better to make it obvious that he was the victim when they got here.

His attacker whipped his head around as if to take them all in, then let go of the suitcase. Edison held on to his end, growling. The cops closed in first—a tall blond guy and a shorter woman with black hair.

The guy in black went into a spinning frenzy, like an actor in a martial arts movie. He hurled himself straight at the pair of cops, striking with elbows and arms, bouncing from one to the other with a choreographed grace that impressed the hell out of Joe, even as he lay on the ground with the wind knocked out of him and his cheek throbbing.

The man knocked the largest cop down and spun to take out the second, but she had dodged to the side and was fumbling for her nightstick. She was quick, ducking and weaving expertly.

The soldiers had almost reached them when the attacker hurdled the fallen cop and sprinted toward the outside doors, dodging between commuters as if he'd rehearsed it.

The soldiers took off after Joe's attacker, but Joe doubted they'd catch up. He'd been attacked by freaking Bruce Lee.

Which didn't help his ego all that much. Especially since the female cop had held her own.

Edison dragged the suitcase over to Joe. He licked his bruised cheek. Joe gritted his teeth and pushed the dog away. Even such light contact hurt.

"Good boy," he said. "Give me some space."

Edison sat next to him and looked up to the woman reaching a hand down for Joe. She had shiny black hair and a nice smile. "I'm Detective Bailey. Are you OK?"

"I think so." He took the hand and pulled himself up, then grabbed the suitcase's handle.

He ran his tongue across his teeth. A couple felt loose, and blood filled his mouth. He wanted to spit, but couldn't exactly do that on the polished marble floor. He swallowed the blood and reached for a tissue in his pants pocket. "Thanks for your help."

"You should have let him have the suitcase," she said. "Nothing in there worth getting hurt for."

"Just some papers." He tightened his grip on the handle. He hadn't looked inside yet. What if his father had put some cocaine in there, for old time's sake? Surely his mother would have checked, wouldn't she?

His mother.

She'd had the suitcase first. What if the guy who'd come after him went after her?

"Need to call a friend," he said.

"We need to take a statement," said the cop who'd been knocked down. His truculent expression clearly showed that he held Joe at least partially responsible.

He had already speed-dialed Vivian.

"Torres," she answered.

"Tesla," he said.

The bloody-nosed cop glared at Joe, but the female cop put her hand on the guy's arm and said something in a low voice, hopefully calming him down.

Joe kept talking. "I need you to find my mother, make sure she's safe, and stick with her until you hear from me."

"Yes, sir," she said. "What's the nature of the threat?"

"Someone tried to take a suitcase she just gave me, and he was willing to use force." He hung up and texted his mother's phone number to Vivian. His mother was in the safest hands he could imagine—he'd watched Vivian take out a guy six inches taller than she was and armed with a knife without even breaking a sweat. But he wished he could go outside and look after his mother himself.

"We're going to need you to come down to the station." The male cop held a white tissue under his nose. "Give us a statement."

"That won't be possible," Joe said. "I can give you a statement here."

Detective Bailey reached for Joe's elbow. "It'll be quick."

His heart rate soared, and Edison stepped up next to him, his nose nuzzling against Joe's palm. "I will not leave this concourse."

"I understand you're upset, sir," she said. "You've had—"

"Mr. Tesla," called a voice from behind him. "Are you and that dog all right?"

Miss Evaline from the information booth hurried over. Commuters parted to make way for her round form. He bet even the nuns would have let the clerk through.

"He's fine, miss," said Detective Bailey. "He needs to come with us."

The cop with the bloody nose stood straighter. "He does."

"He most certainly does not," said Miss Evaline. "This is Mr. Joe Tesla, and he's not going anywhere."

Detective Bailey let go of his elbow and gave him an appraising look instead. "We don't need to leave the building, Mr. Tesla, if that's too uncomfortable for you."

Turned out, being a famous recluse, even if you weren't related to Nikola Tesla, had its perks. Joe felt angry everyone knew about his agoraphobia, even when it worked to his advantage.

"Thank you," he said. "How about we take a statement in the lobby of the Hyatt? It's quieter."

"That would do fine," she said.

"You all right, Mr. Tesla?" Miss Evaline asked again.

He realized he was shaking. All that adrenaline had no place to go. "I'm fine."

She knelt next to Edison and ran her hands over the dog, making sure he hadn't been hurt, something Joe should have thought to do himself.

"What a brave boy!" she crooned. "A good, brave boy."

Edison's tail wagged. He knew he was a good dog. Joe wished he could say the same about himself. He fished out a treat and gave it to the dog.

As Detective Bailey led the way toward the Hyatt, Joe trundled after her with his suitcase and Edison. He couldn't help but notice the detective's simple grace. She was coordinated and surefooted, walking with easy confidence and without a trace of her partner's swagger. She tilted her head to the side, her glance saying that she'd caught Joe looking.

11

Vivian was glad she still had on her formal suit from the wedding. Otherwise, they probably never would have let her breathe the rarefied air of the Waldorf. The doorman would have sensed, with his doorman radar, that she could never afford to stay here and tossed her out on her butt.

As it was, she walked through the white and gold columns unmolested, careful not to slip on the marble floor, and made for the elevators. Nobody in the lobby seemed like a threat—rich folks and their bodyguards and children. Nothing unexpected.

When Vivian had called her, Tesla's mother had given her the room number and promised not to leave until she got there. On the phone, she seemed more irritated than frightened. Only a few minutes after Tesla's call, Vivian knocked on Mrs. Tesla's door.

Hugh Hollingberry answered and showed her inside. He looked worried, and he locked the door behind her.

The suite was done in reds and silver, with a spindly looking table holding the television. She figured the table cost more than she made in a month.

"I'm sorry to be seeing you again under these circumstances, ma'am," said Vivian.

Mrs. Tesla gestured to a silver tray on the table in front of her. "I've ordered tea."

"I'd like to check that the suite is empty," Vivian said.

Mrs. Tesla raised her eyebrows. "I'm sure any killer would have had the sense to strike before we brought in a bodyguard."

"I understand, ma'am, but I still need to check."

Mrs. Tesla raised her shoulders in an irritated shrug, and Vivian took that as a yes. She went through the bedroom. When she checked the closet, she was surprised by how many clothes Mrs. Tesla had brought. Nothing hiding in there and nothing in the bathroom or under the bed.

Hugh Hollingberry was still standing next to Mrs. Tesla, his hand on her shoulder, when Vivian returned.

"My son is a little paranoid. He gets it from his father." Mrs. Tesla poured Vivian a cup of tea and handed it to her. "But I'm certain you know this already."

Vivian wasn't going to reveal what she did and didn't know about Joe Tesla. "What was in the suitcase the thief tried to take from Mr. Tesla?"

"Odds and ends his father wanted Joe to have. Papers, mostly."

There had to be more to it than that. "What kind of papers?"

"Whatever a father leaves a son," she said. "I'm certain Joe knows more about it than I do. He's an enigmatic man, don't you think?"

"I'm sure I don't know, ma'am." Vivian wasn't divulging anything, and neither was Mrs. Tesla.

"He's a very good son, but he worries too much about his mother." Mrs. Tesla smiled at Hollingberry. "It was kind of him to send you here, but unnecessary."

"I'm sure he doesn't think so."

"He is not the one who determines such things."

Vivian wasn't sure how to respond, so she kept quiet. Mrs. Tesla clearly didn't like being told what to do or being imposed upon. Vivian would probably react the same way.

"I need my privacy," Mrs. Tesla said.

"I understand, ma'am, and I will stay out of your way as much as I can."

Mrs. Tesla shook her head. "Please leave us in peace. I want no police, or security, or whatever you call yourself, watching me. I can look after myself."

"Mr. Tesla was very clear that I remain with you until he says otherwise."

"So I shall be very clear as well—he has no *say* here. He is my son, not my keeper."

Hollingberry twitched ever so slightly.

"I'll be outside if you need me." Vivian didn't need to sit in the woman's lap to protect her, although it'd be easier if she stayed close.

Mrs. Tesla crossed to the door, unlocked it, and opened it. "It was kind of you to stop by."

12

Joe was damn glad the elevator was working again. He pulled the doors closed and lifted the lever to make the cage move. The suitcase bumped against the back of his knee. Usually, the elevator made him nervous, but not today. He'd been through too much drama on the concourse to have any worry left about the elevator.

He looked at the freshly cleaned crystal chandelier above and the custom-made Persian rug on the floor. Shame to think that modern elevators weren't so fancy. This elevator was taking him home. Finally. Edison sat next to him, his eyes following the stone wall passing by outside the fancy wrought iron.

Detective Bailey had given him her card and told him to call if he remembered anything else. She'd written her personal phone number on the back. He touched the card in his pocket. Before New York, before Celeste, this would have been an invitation. But now that he was trapped inside, he felt neutered. It was meaningless for a woman to give a guy her phone number if he couldn't go outside.

The elevator doors opened onto the ever-cool air of the deep tunnels. Here, the hot outside winds had lost their battle with the cool, dank air from underground. At this depth, the temperature was always stable at around fifty. The sweat on Joe's skin turned icy. He ran his fingers through his sweat-dampened hair to let the cold soak in.

He checked the alarm he'd installed. All the lights were green—no one had opened the doors that closed off the ends of the tunnel on which his house sat, no one had moved inside the house itself, and no one had come out of the elevator before him. All clear. He'd worried a bit about the elevator inspectors, but they clearly hadn't ventured into the alarmed zone. Good.

He kept Edison at heel while he switched off his alarm, then he wedged the lever open that controlled the elevator's movement. Now no one could call the elevator up to the terminal level. No one could sneak up on him here.

His house was the safest place in New York City. But a shiver went down his spine as the suitcase's wheels bumped along the wooden planks that lined his tunnel, and he looked over his shoulder. Nothing behind him, and nothing in front of him but Edison.

He remembered the paranoid email his father had sent before his death. *I've said things I shouldn't, to people I shouldn't. I've set them on paths.* His father's paranoia wasn't crazy at all. Something in this box was worth stealing.

Just because you're paranoid doesn't mean they aren't out to get you, his father's voice rang in his ears. What if someone had been out to get his father? What if someone was out to get Joe now?

It wouldn't be the first time. He thought back to his last day in the outside world. He hadn't known it would be his last day, of course. He'd come to New York for what was supposed to be a victory tour. Pellucid had been set to go public, and he was supposed to ring the bell to open the New York Stock Exchange, but he had never made it there, too afraid to go out the Hyatt's front doors and into his waiting limousine.

At first, he had thought his condition came from a common change in brain chemistry. Agoraphobia came late in life to many, and the reasons were often unclear. His condition was no different than 1.8 million (cyan, purple, and a long row of black) other people who had developed the symptoms of agoraphobia out of the blue. Like them, he had no idea why he was suddenly unable to do something ordinary—walk out the front door.

But blood tests had revealed that his brain had changed because of chemical interference—he'd been poisoned.

He ticked off suspects in his head as he walked along the gray boards toward his house. First up: the flight attendant who had served lunch, Betty Bauer. Unlikely. He'd never met her before, but he'd checked with Virgin Airlines, and she'd been a flight attendant there for seven years. Probably not a hired poisoner.

For dinner he'd had a meeting with colleagues and a few members of the Central Intelligence Agency. The CIA had fought Pellucid in court and tried to prevent the company from going public, citing reasons of national security. He had been their chief opponent, but they had lost, so why bother to poison him? They had nothing to gain from crippling him, save revenge. Agent Bister had seemed like a guy who was willing to do a lot to take revenge, and his partner, Agent Dobrin, was a wild card. So, Joe had hacked into the CIA database and downloaded everything he could about them both, then hacked into their emails. Neither had ever been involved with operations where anyone was poisoned. They seemed to have given up on intimidating Pellucid after the IPO and moved on. Nothing indicated they might have done it.

If it hadn't been them, it might have been one of the others at that table: George Greenblatt, CEO; Sunil Sharma, CFO; Mary Mitchell, CMO; and a couple of investment bankers, Alvin Ross and Thomas Lee. Joe's crusade against the CIA might have cost them the fortunes they had all realized when the firm went public, but, again, by that day everything was already decided. They'd all won.

Still, he'd compiled dossiers on all of them and hired detectives to dig deeper, looking always for a hint that any of them might have had a reason, and access to the drugs that had poisoned him. Dead ends, so far.

His colleagues and the CIA made good villains, but they weren't the only ones who'd had access to his food and drink that day. That night his friend, Leandro Gallo, had invited Joe to a party. The Gallos were descended from the original engineer for whom the underground house was built, and Joe had always wanted to see it. He'd never imagined he'd end up living there when Leandro called. Joe had long since gotten the guest list from Leandro and had compiled dossiers on them as well, but all seemed harmless—rich socialites who would have had no motive to poison him. He checked this, too. None of the other guests had since come down with agoraphobia, or any other mental disorders.

No one seemed to have anything to gain from trapping him inside for the rest of his life. But that didn't change the fact that someone had poisoned him.

He unlocked the door, and Edison trotted ahead of him into the house. It was a real house, not a hidey-hole, no matter what his mother said, and he was grateful he'd found it.

With a sigh, he pulled in the suitcase, closed the door, and hung Edison's leash on the hall tree. He trailed a finger along the pale pink paint, called ashes of roses, which decorated his front hall. His mother would love the old-fashioned color.

He hadn't changed any of the house's details. He liked the feeling of stepping into a Jules Verne novel. He'd left everything intact, concealing his high-tech gadgets—a giant TV, high-speed Wi-Fi router, air filters, and an alarm system—in cabinets or gilt frames.

He lit the electric fire in the parlor, and faux flames glowed comfortingly under the carved black mantel. He rubbed his hands over the orange glow, although he was no longer cold, because that's what he always did.

While Edison lapped at the water in his bowl in front of the fireplace, Joe took off the dog's service vest. Then Edison flopped down in front of the fire. He dropped his head on his outstretched paws and closed his eyes. He was off duty and had earned a nap.

Joe sank into his favorite leather chair to see what secrets the great Tesla had entrusted to his pigeon keeper. He laid the suitcase on the marble-topped coffee table in front of him. He set his palm on top of the suitcase, drawing out the anticipation. His father had wanted him to have this. For better or worse, it was the last gift the man would ever give him.

Slowly, he unzipped the suitcase. Resting inside its black interior was a plain cardboard box held closed by four interlocking flaps on top. It was just like any other box. Nikola Tesla's secret wasn't even secured with a piece of tape. How important could it be?

Still, his heart beat faster as he lifted the flaps. Soft light fell on the contents—a neat stack of three folders. Joe drew them out slowly, almost afraid to touch their dusty surfaces.

The folders were each labeled in old-fashioned handwriting: Letters, Lists, and Long Term. Joe decided to exclude the most boring-looking papers first.

He opened the Letters folder. It contained about ten pages, all written in the Cyrillic alphabet, although he thought that Tesla's Croatia had used Latin letters. Still, Nikola Tesla had clearly known Cyrillic, or he'd had letters from someone who had. Joe would need to hire someone to translate these documents into English. He photographed each one carefully before returning it to the folder. He'd back them up somewhere safe, just in case.

Next up: Lists. This folder held sheets of paper in various sizes. He pulled out the first one. In the same careful handwriting: pigeon corn, new handkerchiefs, glass globes that will fit in the hand, copper wire. Joe paged through the others. Also lists of various items, some household and others electrical. He couldn't see anyone wanting these, but he diligently photographed each one.

He took a deep breath and opened the last folder: Long Term. It held four pieces of paper: three blueprints and a newspaper clipping. The top blueprint had a yellow sticky note on it. His father's small printing was centered in the middle. *Be afraid. Tread carefully.*

13

Ash flicked a bit of dust off his suit. The ribbon cutting was running ridiculously late. The police were working to clear out a crowd of protesters. Usually, protesters came down on his side, but this development was complicated.

He looked across the silvery surface of the Hudson River. The river looked so peaceful and clean that most people couldn't imagine the toxic soup in the water. It held everything from mercury to PCBs to raw sewage to anything else people had thought to dump into New York's giant toilet. The hand in his pocket tightened into a fist. Strides had been made—the bottom had been dredged of PCBs, mercury levels in the fish had gone down, mutations were less common—but it was nowhere near enough.

He had taken over the plot of land that protesters now stood on. It still held a ramshackle homeless shelter that had already been condemned. He intended to pull the building down and build a laboratory in its place, one that produced PCB-eating bacteria. The bacteria would be bred here and released into the river, eating away the toxins and excreting harmless waste in return. In fact, one of their byproducts was electricity, and he was working to harness that, too.

His intervention would allow nature to heal herself. The lab was an unquestionable good, but he had spent a fortune battling lawsuits filed by dimwits who thought that beds for a hundred homeless drunkards and addicts were more important than safe water and a clean ecosystem for everyone. How could they care about the comfort of a few people, when the future of the river itself was at stake?

He'd received hate mail and death threats and had been regularly blasted on the Internet. Now they were out there waving signs that said *Feed people, not bacteria* and *Wright is Wrong*. He'd been tempted to use Spooky to fight back, but he hadn't. His cause was big enough to absorb their vitriol. He was big enough. The Breakers took worse without blinking.

"Any minute, Mr. Wright," said his harried-looking assistant. She'd been talking to the police, demanding that the crowds be cleared far enough for the camera crew to get a good shot of the river.

His secure phone buzzed, and he took it out of his suit pocket, hoping for a distraction, and saw a message from Quantum: *suitcase not retrieved. in possession of joe tesla crazy millionaire.*

Ash smiled at the telegraphic summary. It was always nice to see Joe belittled. As much as he despised the Breakers, he didn't loathe them like he did Joe.

Ash had met Joe at a computer-security conference a few years before. Joe had worn jeans, sneakers, and a T-shirt with a mushroom cloud on the front like any other paranoid techy. But while he'd looked like everyone else at the conference, he'd been sitting on a company that was soon valued at a billion dollars. A company, ironically, that was working to help law enforcement at the expense of privacy and security. How Joe reconciled that with his own staunch ideas on privacy, Ash never understood. Ash hated Pellucid. It put unprecedented power in the hands of the government and made it even harder for disruptive forces, forces that were not necessarily even illegal, to move unchecked. But Joe seemed not to have such qualms about the few repressing the rights of the many.

Ash had been at the beginning of his divorce then. He'd hoped the marriage would simply end, like a flopped business, and they would move on. But the divorce had drawn out over months as they battled for custody of Mariella, their profoundly autistic daughter. He lost his bid for full joint custody and instead was granted visitation every other weekend. She paid less and less attention to him every time he saw her.

After she'd been diagnosed, he'd funded research into the causes of her condition. Genetics loads the gun and the environment pulls the trigger, he'd been told. What a terrible metaphor to use for a parent whose child had been shot in the brain by an incurable condition.

One of the triggers was PCBs. That was why he was standing here today taking them out of the environment—for her. And she would never even notice.

The protesters' angry chanting reminded him of his ex-wife, Rosa, and their arguments, more about angry tones than real content. In the midst of that strife, he'd met Joe Tesla at a bar near San Francisco's Moscone Center. After a few drinks, Joe called him a "sad sack," and Ash saw pity in those intelligent eyes. That was when he started to truly hate him.

Joe took him to the Golden Gate Bridge. Not, it turned out, to throw the pitiful Ash over the side, but to distract him with a climb to the top of the north tower in the middle of the night. Joe had climbing gear for both of them and a key to the tower.

He never learned how Joe got the key, or how he'd managed to get them up without being caught, but he would never forget staring down at the orange span glowing in the fog below him. The sight gave him a moment of peace and clarity, and a reminder that the rules didn't apply to him. On the bridge, and in life, he had a perspective on the world that no one else did, and that gave him the right to bring his visions to reality. Just as Joe did. In fact, more of a right, because Ash's vision would heal the world.

When he heard Joe had moved to New York, he expected a call. Ash had learned how they could get to the top of the Empire State Building and touch the antenna there. It was a simple matter of money. To show off, he had sent Joe a coded invitation to join him on his adventure, but the man never responded.

All Ash's emails and calls went unanswered. When he saw the *Forbes* article about Joe's agoraphobia, he knew why. Shame had driven his old acquaintance into a deep, dark, and lonely hole, and he didn't want company. Joe deserved pity now, not Ash.

But even a trapped Joe was clever. Maybe they could work on Nikola Tesla's device together. But what then? Joe wasn't interested in disrupting the system, and he cared about human life.

He wouldn't put people in danger. He didn't share Ash's big picture. That was why Joe had never turned up on Spooky. He wouldn't be part of that kind of game. He would have left the homeless shelter there, left the PCBs in the water, let them eat away at the brains of toddlers.

Ironically, only the Breakers would understand his actions. Even if they were on the other side of the spectrum, they had a global perspective. They, too, were above the law.

No, Joe wouldn't give him unfettered access to the plans for the Oscillator, so he would have to get them from him. If Joe came to grief over it, all the better.

He would track him, and he would take the device from him. Because of his illness, Joe was easier to track in the physical world than most. Since he lived near Grand Central Terminal and never went outside, he'd be easy to find. It would be like the proverb—like taking candy from a baby.

Ash tapped his thumb against the phone's tiny screen, the grand view from the riverbank forgotten. He could hire surveillance teams, but that was too obvious. He'd tried to track Joe online over the years, just for fun, but the man was practically a ghost. Even his cell phone popped on and off the grid sporadically, showing up at Grand Central Terminal but nowhere else. He'd taken paranoia to a whole new level.

Glancing up to make sure that the event wasn't ready to start, Ash returned his secure phone to his left pocket and took his regular phone out of his right. He typed up an email explaining he had heard about Joe's father's death "through the grapevine" and suggesting they meet for drinks at The Campbell Apartment. The bar was inside Grand Central Terminal, so that shouldn't be a problem for Joe, although he didn't mention that.

What would Ash do once he had the Oscillator? Maybe the device could be sent into space, attached to an asteroid on a collision course with Earth, and deployed to save the world. Maybe it could destroy the Breakers' fracking equipment, collapse their boreholes with what looked like fracking-induced earthquakes. That was a good start. Come to think of it, targeted earthquakes could also shake loose enough people to let the planet truly heal, since seven billion was not a sustainable population. He'd save his grandest ambitions for later and start small—with the Empire State Building.

His office there was overinsured anyway, but not by enough to be suspicious. He might start there, but he wouldn't stop there. He realized he was smiling. The Oscillator was a powerful destructive force. He looked at the crumbling homeless shelter that would be leveled soon. The seeds of its destruction would grow into newer, better creations.

Who knew what the Oscillator might create in the world? It would have to be found. It would have to be tested. But the potential was there.

He must have it.

Only he would dare to use it properly, and to its full potential.

14

Joe stood at the billiard table with pages spread out across the green baize. The blueprint with the sticky note on it was for an unnamed device. There was no picture of it fully assembled, but it didn't look as if it would turn into anything sinister. It looked like a tiny articulated figure run by gears and racks.

Nowadays it would be called a robot, but Nikola Tesla would have called it an automaton. Whatever it was called, it didn't look worth all the trouble. Its harmless looks must be deceiving.

He read the newspaper clipping, learning about the collapse of a bridge in Connecticut a few months before he was born. Three (red) people had died. The article speculated that metal fatigue was responsible for the disaster. His father had stuck another yellow note on the picture of the broken bridge. On that one he wrote: *I was responsible for this. May God forgive me. Show the wisdom I did not and have the courage to destroy it.*

Joe had no idea what his father wanted him to destroy. He was hoping that the automaton would give him a clue, because he knew that he would follow his father on one last, crazy adventure and try to do as he asked.

Maybe it would help him to make sense of the man. Maybe it would help him to make sense of himself. Or maybe it was another wild-goose chase. Whatever it was, it was the last thing he had from a father he'd ignored too long.

He studied the newspaper clipping. How like his father to give him this as his final gift—guilt and a confusing request to show wisdom without an explanation as to how or why. Could his father have knocked down the bridge? If so, what did that action have to do with the plans for a tiny automaton?

Joe pored over the plans, making a list of items he would need to build the tiny creature. By the time he finished, his list looked a lot like the lists in Nikola's folder.

His neck cracked when he straightened up. Too long bending over the billiard table. He rubbed his eyes and yawned. Time for bed, but he still had stuff to do.

First, he gathered the original plans and put them in the old cardboard box his father had saved for him. Even though he'd photographed every scrap of paper in the box and backed up the photos, he felt as if he ought to lock the box in a safe, just in case.

But he didn't have a safe. He didn't need one, because his entire house was more secure than most banks. He took the box upstairs to his office and stashed it in a closet behind boxes of turn-of-the-century Christmas decorations. It seemed like the last place anyone would look.

He stuck his parts list in his pocket and went down to the kitchen to make a cup of chamomile tea. Some previous inhabitant of the house had purchased an electric kettle made out of copper. Based on the wiring, he thought the device had been created in the 1930s. So far, it had always worked, and it had never threatened to set the house on fire, but he reminded himself, again, that it might be a good idea to take it apart and replace the electronics. He had no intention of parting with the dinged kettle itself. It belonged to the house.

Tea in hand, he headed to the parlor. His upstairs office was fine during the day, but he preferred to spend his evenings working on his laptop in the parlor. He liked the warmth of the fireplace. Edison did, too. The dog was stretched out in front of the artificial flames, snoring away.

Joe set the teacup on the marble-topped coffee table like a Victorian gentleman. This was a room his non-ancestor Nikola Tesla would have understood. Except for the laptop on the ottoman, everything dated from Nikola's era, and the inventor would have recognized the laptop as a device he had predicted over a hundred years before, one that could wirelessly send and transmit information across the globe.

Nothing here would shock Nikola. For all Joe knew, Nikola Tesla might have visited this underground house and sat in this very parlor. He might have known the designer of one of the largest electrical underground rail systems in the world—one that ran under his very feet. If so, why wouldn't the man have invited the famous scientist here for tea?

Joe pulled the leather armchair closer to the fire and set his shopping list on the arm. It wouldn't take him too long to order the parts. He'd have them sent to his lawyer's office. Mr. Rossi would forward them by bike courier to the information booth. That was how Joe got all his mail.

Before he started ordering, he needed to check his email. He'd been off the grid for most of the day, other than a quick note to his administrative assistant to tell everyone he'd be unreachable.

One (cyan) email had been sorted into his Private folder, and he went there first to see an email from Alan Wright, CEO of Wright Industries. Joe paused before answering it. Alan had sent him a few emails over the months he'd been in New York, and he hadn't answered any of them. He hadn't wanted Alan to see him penned up in the tunnels like a hamster.

He skimmed the email. Alan had heard of his father's death and wished to express his sympathy. How had Alan heard, and why did he care?

Joe hadn't told anyone but Celeste and Vivian about his father's death, but the Internet was a giant tattletale, so presumably the whole world knew. Anyway, Alan wanted to meet tomorrow for a drink at The Campbell Apartment—a trendy cocktail lounge in Grand Central Terminal. That couldn't be an accidental choice. Alan must know he was trapped here.

In some ways, Alan was as trapped as Joe. He could move around the world, but he couldn't escape from his role as a billionaire CEO. Joe knew the trap of being surrounded by people suddenly afraid to tell him the truth, afraid to open up to him, ready to lie to make him happy, certain his life was far too glamorous for them and their concerns. He wondered if Alan missed being ordinary as much as he did. He tapped out a quick answer, arranging to meet him the next evening at eight (purple) for drinks.

Then he switched over to his Work folder which contained bug reports and a couple of questions from the young software architect he'd been grooming to take over maintenance of the facial recognition engine so that Joe could switch to working on gait recognition.

Gait recognition was new and interesting. In gait recognition, the computer tried to determine a subject's identity from the way he or she walked. Gait recognition enabled identification from a much farther distance than facial recognition. It was surprisingly effective.

He dealt with those emails before moving to his newest folder, RRT, an abbreviation for Recognition Request Tracking. He whistled in surprise, and Edison lifted his head.

"It's OK, boy, go on back to sleep," Joe said.

But it wasn't OK. Just the opposite. In the last few hours, a million more requests had been made than the week before. That didn't make sense. Either his software had a bug, or all the governmental agencies in the United States were experiencing a massive crime wave, or something new had come online, probably something automated. His stomach clenched.

List forgotten, he logged into the system and began tracking the requests down, compiling reports of where the requests originated and the reasons why. So far, they all came from a single source.

Edison nudged his knee, but Joe pushed him away. "Busy, Edison."

The dog dropped his head into Joe's lap, blocking his view of the screen.

"What do you need?" He looked at the clock on the corner of his computer. He'd been sitting here for hours. "Bedtime?"

Edison wagged his tail and looked meaningfully at the door. The dog didn't think it was healthy to sit here this long. He was right, of course. But he didn't have to go to the bathroom. When he did, he stood by the door and gave a bark to let Joe know it was important. Just a single bark, because Edison, or Joe, was well trained.

"It's going to be a while, buddy," Joe told him. "Sorry."

Edison gave him a skeptical look and wandered out toward the kitchen. A crunching sound indicated he had found a midnight snack.

Joe scrolled through the reports he'd just generated. It was unmistakable. The National Security Agency was submitting millions of match requests.

What was their source material? He found that, too. They'd submitted surveillance footage from all across the country—people going into stores, people crossing the street, people leaving church, people eating at McDonald's. Any of those requests would have been normal, but so many of them at once meant they had tapped into thousands of surveillance cameras and were looking for automated matches of the millions of people who appeared on the videos. Those people couldn't all be criminals or terrorists—the vast majority of them were innocent. But they were still being tracked.

Millions of innocent people were being tracked.

And Joe had created the monster.

15

Vivian checked her phone. She'd been pacing the corridor outside of Mrs. Tesla's suite for hours. The woman hadn't come out, although a room-service cart had gone in. Vivian had intercepted it outside the door, searched it, and patted down the bewildered Hispanic waiter.

The elevator dinged, and she tensed, as she had about a hundred times over the course of the evening. So far she'd watched a drunken couple practically have sex in the hall, a bored businessman with a briefcase head straight to his room, four guys in black T-shirts who smelled like pot and couldn't stop laughing stumble to their room, and a guy lugging what she swore was a monkey in a dog carrier.

Dirk stepped out of the elevator, and she relaxed. He was here to replace her, and she had trusted him with her life for years.

A police officer by day, he sometimes moonlighted for Mr. Rossi's security company. Mr. Rossi was Tesla's lawyer. She'd met Tesla when Mr. Rossi had hired her to protect him. But Tesla had given her the slip and disappeared underground—reappearing with the agoraphobia that still plagued him. If she'd kept an eye on him as she should have, he'd be fine today.

"Yo," Dirk said. The circles under his eyes looked darker than usual, and his jeans and white shirt looked as if he'd slept in them. Not his usual dapper self.

Dirk looked that way only when he had girl trouble, a condition that cropped up about every six months. Dirk had commitment issues.

"Long day?" she asked.

He shrugged and looked around the empty corridor. "Better than yours, by the looks of it."

She filled him in on the situation, then took the elevator down. This time she didn't feel so awed by the lobby. The people here weren't different from anyone else, except they had more money to burn.

She turned up her collar and started walking toward Grand Central in the warm night. Even though it was late, people swarmed around her on the sidewalk, some dressed in formal evening wear, others in grungy torn jeans and covered in piercings. Lucy would look like that if their mother weren't so strict.

She tapped out a text message to an informant she'd been cultivating at Grand Central. If she didn't get a response, this was likely a wasted trip. Still, it felt good to be walking and actually getting somewhere instead of just wearing down the carpet.

A few blocks later, she got an answer.

Good. He was sober enough to type, and he hadn't lost or hocked the phone.

She arranged to meet him in front of Pershing Square restaurant. She was starving, and he likely was, too.

Then she hailed a cab, remembering to ask for a receipt. This was definitely a business expense, and Tesla would have to pay for it.

She climbed out in front of the terminal and jogged across the street. The green Pershing Square sign was turned off, the chairs up on the tables inside. They were always closed this late, something she should have remembered.

A gaunt figure in an Army green jacket emerged from the shadows next to her and grabbed her elbow. She resisted the impulse to smack him because she recognized him from the smell. "Rufus?"

"The same, baby."

She looked at his thin, leathery cheeks, faded brown eyes, and scraggly black beard. "Not your baby, Roof."

"You might be, you find out what I have to tell."

"What you got for me?"

He rubbed his thumb against his fingertips in the universal sign for money.

"Let's get some food into you first." She worried about him, even though she knew she shouldn't.

Once, he'd told her that at night he slept on a bench in Central Park in the summer and next to a warm subway grate in the winter. He slid around the city on his own paths, always one step ahead. At least tonight he looked mostly sober.

A few minutes later they were at an all-night diner, drinking coffee and waiting for two orders of bacon and eggs.

Under the fluorescent lights, Rufus looked even more bedraggled. Grit had settled into the deep lines on his forehead and cheeks, and what was left of his hair didn't look as if it had been washed or combed since Obama was first elected president.

He'd seen some hard living, had Rufus. But that was why she needed him. He'd been panhandling around Grand Central so long he was practically invisible, and he knew everything that went on there. For a price, he'd share.

"What you got?" She fell into his rhythm of speech.

"Your man was attacked today in the terminal."

She knew that. "What you know about it?"

"He had moves." Rufus made a karate-chop motion in the air.

She slid a ten across the table and resisted the urge to ask for a receipt. So far, he hadn't told her anything she didn't already know, but it was good to keep him on the payroll so he'd keep trying.

"Word in the station is, he took out two cops and ran off."

"Has he been around since?" she asked.

"Maybe." Rufus leaned back so the waitress could set a loaded white plate in front of him.

Vivian gave him another ten.

Rufus scooped up the bill, then cut his bacon in half with his fork and ate it, his movements surprisingly dainty.

Vivian usually ate bacon with her fingers, but she decided she'd better up her table manners if Rufus was more refined than she was.

"Saw a guy go into the tunnels." Rufus took a long sip of coffee. "Not a homeless guy. He dressed in black, clean-shaven. He went down in the tunnels off Track 42, smooth as you like. Never came back."

Vivian stifled a curse. This was definitely about Tesla.

Too late to call, but she texted Tesla a warning and told him to be on the lookout for a guy dressed in black, maybe the one who attacked him, in the tunnels.

Tesla didn't answer, but she didn't expect him to. He kept his phone in that stupid pouch, and collected his messages whenever he felt like it. Besides, he was probably asleep. Like she should be.

But she still worried.

16

Joe's phone rang. He groaned and rolled over in bed. Too early. It rang again, and Edison nudged his arm. Time to get up.

Could the bike couriers be delivering his parts already? If so, he had to get up to the clock to meet them quickly, or they'd take the delivery back. Bike messengers waited for no man.

He yanked the phone off its charger. "Tesla."

"Still sleeping?" Celeste's breathless voice sounded surprised. Joe had taken to waking up early since he'd moved underground.

"Late night." Joe rubbed the stubble on his chin and yawned.

"Carousing?" She laughed.

He filled her in on the near mugging. With his luck, it was probably already in the newspapers or on a blog somewhere, so lying wouldn't do any good.

"Tell me about this Detective Bailey," she wheedled.

Celeste was never jealous, always urging him to find a partner, as if it would be easy to find a woman who wanted to live underground with a man who couldn't go anywhere. As if he wanted anyone but Celeste—the Celeste of his twenties, when they were both young and healthy and easily in love. "Not much to tell."

"Don't be like that. I want details."

"She just took my statement." Joe checked the time. Already ten. He needed to get showered and shaved.

"Is she cute? She sounds Irish. I bet she has a great accent."

"She's a cop."

"Cops can be cute. Like Beckett on *Castle*."

"Beckett's not a cop—she's an actress." He didn't know where this was going, but he was plenty uncomfortable along the way.

"Is Detective Bailey cute like Beckett?"

Edison barked from the front door. He needed to go outside, and pronto by the sound of it. Joe stuffed his feet into a pair of slippers. "I have to take Edison out."

"Poor baby!" Celeste said. He wasn't sure if she was talking about him or the dog.

He thudded down the stairs to where Edison waited by the front door. He pulled on a sweatshirt, slipped into his running shoes, and took the dog out.

Edison raced ahead of him to the door that led out to the long tunnel. That's where they usually went. Joe trotted along after him, stopping to enter the long string of numbers that would open the door.

With a grateful bark, Edison bounded through the door and out into the dimly lit tunnel. His silhouette paused at the end of the tunnel, before he veered off to mark the side of the tunnel, the beginning of his outside territory.

Joe yawned and trudged after him. He picked up the bottle of odor remover that he kept right at that spot and sprayed it onto Edison's pee. He wasn't sure if he believed that it broke down the odor on a bacterial level like it said on the package, but he had to admit that it kept the smell at bay.

Edison stopped to sniff the ground. His ears perked up. Probably rats. The dog could track a rat for a mile, but he never attacked them. Joe was grateful for that. He kept Edison's rabies shots up to date, but you never knew what other diseases tunnel and sewer rats might carry.

He whistled for the dog. Edison barked once, a sign that he wanted to be taken seriously. He probably wanted more time to run around.

"Not in the cards today, buddy," Joe called. "Come on."

Casting a glance over his shoulder, the dog loped to Joe's side.

Joe followed Edison's look, but he didn't see anything. But Edison often saw things he didn't in the tunnels. Dogs had much better low-light vision than people.

Probably a rat.

But the back of his neck prickled while he stood at the end of his tunnel, entering in his security code. He and Edison went through, and he swung the door shut. Just before it closed, a faint crinkling sound came from the tunnel.

Maybe a stray breeze blowing an empty candy wrapper across the tracks, or maybe something more. He was glad the door was closed, and they were safely on the inside.

He checked his phone messages. Vivian had left him a warning about a man who might have followed him into the tunnels. That would have been handy to know a few minutes earlier and made him feel even more worried about Edison's reaction. Maybe someone was lurking outside his back door.

His phone buzzed, and Joe jumped. It was the bike courier. Joe had to be at the clock at 11:30 (cyan, cyan: red, black) to get the various metal bits he'd need to use to assemble Nikola Tesla's automaton. Joe grabbed a quick breakfast, then got some actual work done before taking the elevator up to meet the man with his parts.

Evaline gave him a quick wave when he came into the information booth. She was with a customer. Joe let himself out into the busy concourse. Lots of folks hurrying around, out for their lunch breaks. His heart beat a little faster when he glanced at the spot where he had been knocked down, and Edison crowded closer as if he sensed it, too.

He leaned against the booth to wait. Edison sat next to him. Joe looked around the giant room. His gaze lingered on the blue ceiling. He loved the constellations. He'd read they were painted in mirror image, either an artist's error or a representation of divine perspective—God looking down from the other side. Today he couldn't enjoy the graceful constellations. He felt as if he were being watched. Hundreds of people walked and stood in the giant room, and any of them might be watching him or not watching him. Maybe his feelings were just his body reacting to being back where he had been attacked yesterday. Or maybe they were serious. Nothing much he could do about them either way.

A sweaty guy in spandex clomped in. He wore specialized biking shoes that rang against the marble. Under his arm was a cardboard package. Joe's parts. Joe waved him over, signed for the package, and retreated down the elevator.

He had work to catch up on and the GCT video surveillance archive to hack to see if he could get a good look at the guy who tried to take his suitcase. But he knew he wasn't going to do anything until he'd taken on his father's challenge and assembled Nikola's automaton.

He had to know what his father had left for him.

17

Ash liked The Campbell Apartment with its tall, open-beamed ceilings, bank of windows looking out onto the station, thick patterned carpet, and the air of old New York that hung like an invisible fog. He ordered a Prohibition Punch—a brandy snifter full of rum, Grand Marnier, fruit juice, and champagne. Prohibition couldn't have tasted this smooth. It would have been harsher, forbidden, dangerous.

Joe Tesla walked in with a leather satchel slung over his shoulder. He looked harmless, like a bike messenger or a college student. His yellow Lab walked next to him. The animal wore a blue vest, like a seeing-eye dog, reminding him of Joe's disability.

Even in the soft golden light of the bar, Joe's skin looked white as milk, underlining again the reality that he never got out into the sun. It was hard to remember the tan young man who had climbed to forbidden heights on the Golden Gate Bridge.

Joe exchanged glances with the bartender and took a red velvet chair opposite Ash. The dog sat next to him, its yellow muzzle raised as it studied Ash alertly, clearly sizing him up as friend or foe. It didn't growl, but it didn't wag its tail either, so he didn't know where he stood in the dog's estimation.

He voiced his condolences, and Joe thanked him politely, clearly as eager as he was to get through the formalities.

"Nice dog." He petted the dog's head and neck, sliding his fingers under the animal's collar and back out again. The dog didn't move or object. Good.

"His name's Edison," Joe said. "Probably named in honor of all the dogs the great man electrocuted."

Ash was familiar with the rivalry between Nikola Tesla and Thomas Edison over the safety of direct current, Edison's baby, and alternating current, Tesla's idea, the one that ended up being adopted around the world. Edison had tried to show how unsafe alternating current was by electrocuting animals with it, including dogs and cats captured off the streets.

"You can't make an omelet without breaking eggs," Ash said.

"Dog omelet?" Joe grimaced. "I thought you were always on the side of the natural world."

"Domestic dogs aren't any more a part of the natural world than PCBs. Or overpopulation," Ash said. Joe was hopelessly naïve.

The waiter arrived with a drink and a plate of sliders. The waiter grinned at Joe like an old friend, then hand fed a meat patty to the dog after setting the plate on their table. Apparently, Joe was so well known here that he didn't even need to order. They knew what he, and his dog, wanted. He probably didn't need money here either, probably had an open line on his credit card at the bar. Ash felt a stab of envy.

Joe gestured to the tiny hamburgers, but Ash, a vegetarian, shook his head.

"I read about your ribbon cutting online," Joe said. "The plant sounds like a worthy cause."

"All my causes are worthy." He palmed a GPS tracker from his pocket. Smaller than his thumbnail, it should provide him with data on the dog's location for up to two months. It was even waterproof. From what he'd heard, the dog went everywhere Joe did, so tracking one meant he'd have tabs on the other as well. "If I don't work to clean things up, people like the Bakers are going to wipe out this world. A few inconvenienced homeless people here or there are insignificant compared to that."

Joe took a long sip of his drink as if he were swallowing his response to Ash's words, which he probably was, because he did not have a long-term perspective. He was a small-minded thinker.

Ash kept his hand under the table and worked the chip down to his fingertips, peeling off the strip that covered the adhesive side. Under the guise of petting the dog, he stuck the chip to the inside of its collar. Even if Joe found the little device, he'd have a hard time tracing it to Ash. Lots of people probably petted the dog in the course of a day.

"What's in the bag?" Ash picked up his drink again.

Joe's blue eyes shone as they had before he dragged Ash up the Golden Gate Bridge. "Surprises."

Ash's heart beat faster, but he kept calm and waited him out, which took all of a minute. Joe was clearly bursting to tell someone his news. He was like a child, although not, sadly, like Ash's child. Mariella was never excited to tell him anything.

"I acquired plans from my father for a mysterious device." Joe sipped his drink and wolfed down a slider.

Ash held his breath. Was Joe going to pull the Oscillator out of his bag? He could offer to buy it, or take it and run. Once he got outside, Joe couldn't follow. "What kind of device?"

"One that hasn't seen the light of day in quite some time, I'll warrant." Joe unbuckled his satchel and took out an object the size of a small flashlight.

Ash stared at it for a moment, trying to make out details in the dim light. It didn't look like the pictures he had seen of Tesla's patented Oscillator. He leaned in for a closer look.

The object looked like a tiny man made of metal. The man had a round stomach, a round head with a painted handlebar mustache, and short metal legs that ended in feet clad in metal spats. It wasn't the damn Oscillator. It was a doll. "It looks like Tik-Tok of Oz."

Joe grinned. "I thought I was the only one who read that book."

"Mariella likes the Oz books." Or at least she sat still during them. Ash wasn't sure what she liked and disliked. It was hard to tell. And, like Mariella herself, this tiny man wasn't what Ash had hoped for. Trust Joe to disappoint.

"It winds up." Joe turned a crank on the contraption's back, and it produced clicking sounds.

Then he let go of the lever and watched the automaton. Ash was struck by the enthusiasm and energy in his gaze. Joe might be down, but he definitely wasn't out. Ash found that this simple optimism made him hate Joe even more.

Maybe this doll wasn't the Oscillator, but it was a curious object, one Ash hadn't expected. A surprise now and then was a good thing, he told himself even as he clenched and unclenched his hand under the table. But where in the hell was the Oscillator?

The figure lifted its metal hand. Its tiny fingers were curled around a stick. At first he thought the man was brandishing a gun, but it didn't have a stock or a barrel. "What's he holding?"

"I think it's a pointer, like teachers use." Joe's eyes danced.

The end of the pointer lit up red, and the stick made a series of precise movements. Then the automaton's stored energy ran out, and it stood still.

Ash marshaled up his politeness and asked the obvious question. "What's he pointing at?"

Joe laughed. "I have no idea. That's the best part."

Ash didn't think so. The best part would be if he actually had the Oscillator hidden in his fat little belly, but there simply wasn't room. "Did you build him yourself?"

Joe took another sip of his drink before answering. "I did. My father left me detailed plans for it, but they weren't his. They were drawn by the great man himself."

"Nikola Tesla?" Ash asked before he could stop himself.

Joe's lips pursed as if he wanted to say something, but he didn't. He'd always hated being a Tesla.

"So, you have plans drawn by Nikola Tesla?" Leave it to Joe to have built the most useless device first.

"Just plans for this." Joe wound the automaton up again.

Either Joe was lying, or he had no idea what he had.

The metal figure waved its pointer again and then fell still. Disappointment washed over Ash, replacing the anger. He'd reached a dead end. He'd spent the last few days searching for a windup doll. No matter how intriguing the little figure was, it didn't have possibilities.

The dog cocked its head and stared at him intently, as if sensing his distress. Hell, it was probably trained to do that.

He was damned if he was going to let a dog read him. Besides, he had no reason to give up hope. If he hadn't been misled, then Joe must have been. There must be more possibilities than Joe had originally seen.

"Fascinating man, your ancestor. Did you know he liked Grand Central Terminal quite a lot?" Ash imagined the eccentric inventor standing alone in the concourse, talking to the artificial stars. Those were the last years that Earth had a sustainable population, so what had old Nikola had to worry about? "Used to come here at night."

"Really?" Joe looked uncomfortable.

Ash knew that he'd never liked talking about the genius in the family, so he kept going. "The concourse was his favorite sanctum. It's said he came late at night, when he could be alone, to bounce ideas off Pegasus, Hercules, and the other heroes."

"Did he?" Joe raised his hand to order another drink.

Ash had never understood this casual disregard for his famous ancestor. "Of all the drawings to have in the family, why pass down a drawing of a toy?"

"Maybe it's more than a toy."

Ash picked it up and examined it. A simple hook latch on one side held the body together. On the other side was a hinge. He lifted the latch and opened the tiny man's round stomach. Gears and cogs filled the space inside. He saw, in a rough way, how they led to the actuators that moved the arms. A clever piece of machinery, but it wasn't the Oscillator—it was a toy. He closed it up, latched it, and handed it to Joe. Nothing interesting there.

"I can't stay long," Ash lied. "I have to get home to Mariella."

"How is she?"

"The same," Ash said. "I spend a fortune on therapists and teachers and God knows what all, but she just sits there with her broken brain and rocks."

Joe downed his drink in one long swallow. "It's not necessarily broken. Just different."

The crazy man was sensitive about broken brains.

Ash kept going. "Her brain is broken. We broke it. We brought her into this polluted world with all her other risk factors, and we broke her brain." He had read enough studies on autism and pollution, autism and genetics, autism and parental age, autism and preterm birth to know what had happened to Mariella. All that knowledge didn't help. "Broken brains can't be fixed."

Joe slammed his glass onto the table. Ash felt good that he had provoked him. Joe was usually an even-tempered guy, but clearly he'd found a soft spot.

The dog nudged Joe's knee, and he dropped his hand onto its head, fondling its ears and running his hand down its back. He might pet the dog's neck and find the GPS tracker. Ash would have to act properly shocked if he did, but he was more than up to that challenge.

Joe packed his automaton into the satchel, stood, and exchanged a hand signal with the bartender that seemed to indicate he wanted the drinks put on his bill.

"I don't want to keep you from Mariella," Joe said stiffly. "She needs her father."

Ash rose, too. "I hope to see you around more, Joe."

Joe shook his hand. "You know where to find me."

Ash watched him walk out the door with the dog at his side. He knew where to find him.

Every minute.

He took the secure phone out of his pocket. He'd assigned Quantum to watch by the clock in the concourse and wait for instructions. A hopeful part of him had thought that Joe might have brought the Oscillator or its plans to their meeting, and he could have had Quantum steal it from him. Instead, he'd brought a doll.

It wasn't much, but there must be possibilities there that Joe hadn't realized and that Ash himself hadn't seen in the few minutes the automaton had capered about in the dim light of the bar. Even if it didn't, Joe liked it.

He texted Quantum: *take his bag*.

18

Joe walked out of the bar without looking back. Alan Wright hadn't changed a bit with his crack about broken brains and how they couldn't be fixed, and it pissed him off that the man would use those words to characterize his own daughter. With a father like that, the kid didn't stand a chance.

Alan had always been a survival-of-the-fittest guy. Joe suspected his compulsion to save the world was driven by misanthropy. Alan thought that Earth would be better without humans on it, or at least everyone but Alan himself. Joe had once listened to a long lecture from Alan about the "sustainable carrying population of the planet," and it had left him wondering if Alan would be happier if five billion (brown and a long row of black) humans suddenly died. Joe didn't want anything more to do with him. He didn't know why he'd even agreed to meet him.

Edison nosed Joe's hand—a gesture designed to calm him down. Joe petted his muzzle. Edison was right. He shouldn't let Alan get him riled up, and he ordinarily wouldn't, but his father's funeral had put him on edge and reminded him of his prison sentence underground.

Edison looked at the satchel and wagged his tail. He'd seen Joe put a tennis ball in there. "We'll take a walk through the tunnels, play some fetch soon. Would you like that?"

Edison's tail wagged again, and he bounded a few steps ahead of Joe. It was as simple as that to keep him happy. Joe needed to take a cue from him. Who cared what Alan Wright thought?

Edison was leading the way down to the concourse. Should they take the elevator and hike out to the tunnels from the house, or should they head for a platform and walk out from there? Track 36 (red and orange) was free right now. They'd be able to climb down there and hike over to Edison's favorite spot, where a bunch of tracks converged at once. It had a large section of unused, and un-electrified, tracks so that Joe could throw the ball fairly far.

Decision made, Joe followed Edison down another flight of stairs into the concourse. He paused at the balcony and looked out over the vast room. Passengers checked out the boards, milled around the clock, and rushed off to the platforms. A guy leaning against the information booth looked familiar. He was about Joe's height, with straight black hair. He wore jeans and a black T-shirt. Joe struggled to place him.

Then the man moved.

Joe's research in human movement had made him aware of how people stand, how their joints move relative to each other, how they carry their heads. This man was familiar. He reached for a train schedule, pulled it out of its slot in the side of the information booth, and pretended to read it.

But he was pretending. His eyes didn't rove across the numbers. He folded the schedule again and took a single step to return it to its original position. That step was enough for Joe to recognize the athletic grace and purpose, each movement precise and fluid. He had moved just like that when he grabbed Joe's suitcase the day before.

"Edison," Joe called in a low voice.

The dog caught his tone and came to heel, his bouncing joy gone.

He hesitated another moment, trying to decide where to go. Upstairs was isolated this time of night. Someone might come down out of The Campbell Apartments as they had done, but most would take the front door onto the street. If he and Edison backtracked, the man might catch them completely alone. Joe had no illusions he could best this guy in a fight. Joe wasn't a total wimp—he'd fought as a kid and teenager at the circus. But not for years and never against anyone who moved like the man by the information booth.

He thought of calling someone but dismissed the idea. It would take too long for them to arrive, and he'd look like a paranoid fool, afraid to walk down to his own front door without an escort. He couldn't call for help every time he had a feeling. As a crazy person, he already had so little credibility that he didn't want to squander it.

If he couldn't call for help and he couldn't go back, forward was the only way. The 8:52 (purple: brown, blue) southeast train was leaving in two (blue) minutes from Track 42 (green, blue). Even this late the platform would be pretty full. That train halted for about a half a minute at an underground signal not long after it left the platform to let another train go through. When it stopped, he and Edison could get off at the last second and disappear into the underground darkness. No matter how clever this guy was, Joe could lose him in the tunnels.

But if he and the dog didn't get off the train in time, it would carry them out of the station and outside into the night. Outside. Blood rushed in his ears, and he imagined his house, waiting far below with its porch light on. This seemed like his best chance of reaching it.

The clock in the middle of the concourse always ran a minute fast, and the train would leave a minute later than its scheduled time. This was standard Grand Central policy. Giving passengers that extra time relaxed them enough to make Grand Central Terminal the train station with the fewest slips and falls in the US, in spite of the smooth marble floors. Joe needed to build the time discrepancy into his schedule.

He waited the extra minute, pretending he was still surveying the vast room and the iconic ceiling. What could the guy possibly want with him? The box hadn't contained plans for any extravagant Tesla device. While the doll had been fun to make and was fascinating to watch, it didn't seem worth going to all this trouble for. But clearly someone else thought differently, which meant that he was missing something. After he got out of this situation, he'd have to give that more thought.

He glanced once more at the clock and said, "Heel."

Edison stayed close to his heels as they went downstairs. The dog had understood his tone and was on guard. His yellow muzzle was raised, and his alert brown eyes roved over the people in the station. He was clearly trying to figure out who had Joe worried.

Joe tried to set himself a brisk pace, like a man who was late for a train, not like a man who was trying to outrun an assailant. He skirted the side of the room as he made his way toward Track 42 (green, blue). The man by the clock made no move to follow. He slouched against the information booth as if his train wasn't leaving for a good long time.

Joe walked onto the platform, stepping into the heat and noise produced by a train getting ready to disembark on a hot summer evening. About forty people stood on the gray concrete, saying good-bye, getting in a last kiss, a last sip of coffee, before boarding. Nobody here seemed suspicious either.

He turned around, ready to return to the clock and go home. No need to go through with his plan. But his sigh of relief caught in his throat. The man in the jeans and the black T-shirt stood at the entrance to the platform, dark eyes scanning the crowd.

He'd followed Joe after all. That didn't mean he had malicious intent. Lots of people waited by the clock for their trains. New York was full of dancers and martial artists and just plain graceful people who moved like this man did.

Recognizing his comforting patter as denial, Joe walked to the second to the last car and boarded at the last second. Out of the corner of his eye, he saw the man jump on board a few cars behind. Joe held his breath as the doors closed, and the train pulled out.

He counted in his head as the train approached the signal. If it didn't stop, like it usually did, he would pull the emergency brake lever. He wasn't sure that would actually stop the train or if it would signal the driver to think about stopping the train, but it gave him something to focus on, a backup plan.

Fortunately, the train slowed where he expected it to. He counted to twenty in his head, each color flashing, then stepped to the door. He reached up and pulled open the silver hatch housing the emergency door controls. Hoping that it would actually work, he pulled the red handle down and tugged on the door handle. The door slid open halfway.

He pushed through sideways and jumped, bending his knees when he landed to take some of the impact. Hot pain shot up from his ankles, but nothing felt broken. Edison looked out at him through the half-open door as the train released its hydraulic brakes and got ready to move.

"Jump, boy!" What would he do if Edison stayed on the train? What if the guy took his dog? He should have made Edison jump out first. Joe pursed his lips together and let out a shrill whistle.

Edison jumped, landing next to him.

He pulled the dog behind the signaling tower and crouched as the train pulled away. If the man following him wasn't looking directly at them, he'd never know they were here. Once he came up to Joe's car, he'd know, but that would be too late.

After the train clattered away, he checked Edison's paws and legs. The jump from the train hadn't hurt the sturdy dog. They'd both come through it all right.

He struck out at a brisk jog. He could evade anybody down here. Nobody knew the tunnels better than he did. But he and Edison should get behind the security door as soon as they could.

His satchel banged against his hip as he ran, reminding him about the little automaton inside. This figure was the first part of the complex secret that his father had left for him. He had an idea, but he couldn't put it into action until later that night.

Edison ran ahead of him, his bright yellow coat shining under the orange lights.

Later, the three of them were going on an adventure— Joe, Edison, and Tik-Tok.

19

Ash was sitting in his limousine on the way to Rosa and Mariella's apartment when he got a text: *subject did not enter clock. took a train. bailed out in the tunnels.*

He tightened his lips. Joe had known he was being followed, and he still had the automaton. Quantum had failed. Maybe he should see if Geezer might be more useful.

The bright lights of the city on the other side of his rain-streaked windows promised warmth and food and fun, but he chose to stay in the luxurious privacy of the car. He logged into the dark chat room where he sometimes met Geezer.

geezer: About time, ash.

He was taken aback. Geezer was usually tentative, wanting approval and recognition. He just wanted to run with the big dogs.

geezer: I know you're here.
ash: hi
geezer: You sent that man to take the suitcase from Tesla, didn't you?

How could Geezer know that? He must be tracking Tesla, too, but how would he make that connection?

Ash had been unable to track Tesla online, so he'd hacked his mother's email. She'd sent her son a note saying she was running late, and he should order oysters without her. Ash guessed, correctly, that the most likely place for them to meet in Grand Central Terminal was the Oyster Bar.

Since it had two exits, he'd sent Quantum to wait by the clock on the theory that Joe would use that entrance to return home. But how could Geezer know any of that? Had he been in Grand Central and seen Quantum attack Joe?

ash: ??
geezer: it's mine. i found out about it. if you try to take it, i'll go public, call you a thief. i want credit for this one little thing. you don't need it. you have enough.

Ash stared at the screen for a second. How did Geezer know what he did and didn't have? He wondered what Geezer meant by going public.

ash: don't want ur plans dude relax

A lie, but Geezer couldn't know that.

geezer: no such thing as coincidence
ash: paranoid much?
geezer: you're not as young as you're playing

Ash didn't like the sound of that. Geezer seemed to know more than he should.

ash: whatever
geezer: let me keep what's mine. AW AW AW

Ash left the chat room before Geezer had a chance to say anything else. Ash stared at his own initials on the screen: Alan Wright, AW. Geezer knew who he was. That could not stand.

Rain ran down his window, turning the car into a lonely pod. A quick glance told him that the glass partition was up. He usually left it that way. The chauffeur didn't need to know all his business, especially not tonight.

Ash made a call on his secure phone, one he'd hoped he'd never have to make, but Geezer had brought this on himself. He entered Geezer's real name, his address and the number zero. The man on the other end would eliminate Geezer, and it would look like an accident. An extreme measure, but he couldn't let his connection to Spooky become public knowledge.

The car was stuck in traffic, barely inching along. If he didn't mind getting wet, he could walk faster. But he did mind getting wet, so he stayed put.

With a few quick movements he brought up the tracking app on his phone. The tag was working. A strong green dot dashed forward a few meters, then back again. The app said it was in the concourse of Grand Central, but the dog was probably a hundred feet below playing fetch. How pathetic—Joe Tesla, multimillionaire, was playing fetch with a dog in a tunnel.

Maybe he'd join the Vanderbilt Tennis and Fitness Club at Grand Central and invite Joe to a friendly game. They could go out for a juice after, talk about things. Joe hadn't been secretive about the automaton—he trusted Ash.

Ash intended to keep it that way.

His driver stopped in front of the 72nd Street entrance to The Dakota. The old stone building looked grand in the fading light. Because Ash loved it, Rosa had taken it in the divorce. She'd had other options, of course, but had taken his favorite apartment as a matter of course.

"Give me an hour," Ash said. Mariella fell asleep early.

The doorman nodded to him as he hurried by on his way to the elevator. He was watching the numbers flicker by when he got another text, this one on his non-secure phone, from Rosa.

Mariella went to bed early. No bedtime stories tonight.

He sighed. The simplest thing to do would be to take the elevator right back down to his car, but he never did the simplest thing.

A minute later he stood in front of Rosa as she lounged on the sofa. The housekeeper who had seen him in mumbled an excuse and backed away, clearly not wanting to be part of whatever came next.

"Were you in the elevator when I texted?" Rosa tucked her waist-length hair behind her shoulder.

"Based on the timing, you knew that before you texted."

"Mariella is asleep," Rosa said. "Surely you don't wish to wake her."

He very much wished to wake her, so that he could at least say good night, but Mariella was a poor sleeper and might be awake for hours if he did. He couldn't let her suffer—something else that Rosa knew.

"She's been unavailable for the last three visits," he said.

"A cold, a meeting with her therapist. I told you the reasons." Rosa's brown eyes opened wide and guileless. That look had gotten her full custody from the male judge. He couldn't blame him. It had gotten her a lot more out of Ash.

"You did." He'd logged each missed meeting with his lawyer, in the hopes that he might be able to use them as evidence that Rosa was deliberately keeping him from his daughter, but it would be a hard sell. Colds, therapy, early bedtime—those were all reasonable excuses, even if they did pile up. "But if I go a month without seeing her, she barely seems to recognize me."

"There's nothing I can do about that." Rosa set her book down on the green velvet and crossed her arms. "Maybe you shouldn't skip visits."

The last visit he'd missed was six months before. Like him, she'd probably logged it. "No matter how busy I am, I almost always keep to my scheduled visits."

"Such a busy man you are." Her eyes narrowed. "Cleaning up the whole wide world."

"I'm trying to protect other children, so they don't end up damaged like Mariella." He was going to make the world a better place for his daughter. Even if she would never know or understand it.

"She is not damaged!" Rosa lowered her voice. "She is who she is. She's not some kind of rifle sight—something you can use to aim yourself at a cause."

Ash didn't bother to respond.

Rosa unfolded her long, slim legs and stood in front of him. "You use her as an excuse to be ruthless, a way to justify not caring about anyone or anything that might get in the way of your goals."

She must have seen the homeless-shelter protest on the news. She claimed to care about the fall of every sparrow, never once stopping to take in the big picture. Hard to believe that he'd once found her so appealing.

His secret phone buzzed in his pocket, so he cut the familiar argument short and retreated to the elevator, texting his driver on the way down.

Spooky didn't disappoint him. Spooky understood about disruption, about risk, about sometimes sacrificing the proverbial sparrow to the greater good.

20

Joe set his teacup on the coffee table, then plopped next to Edison in the parlor, watching the dog snooze in front of the fire. They'd played for a long time, and the dog was worn out. They'd stayed inside the tunnel in front of the house because Joe hadn't felt safe enough to go play in their usual spot after the incident on the train.

He cracked open his laptop and wrote up the details of his encounter with the man by the clock—how he reminded Joe of the man who'd attacked him, how he'd followed him onto the platform and boarded the train. He didn't mention when he'd gotten off the train, just that he had. Deciding that was enough, he sent the email to Detective Bailey and blind copied Vivian. They could track the man in the outside world, and he would track him underground.

Time to get started with that. He took a sip of tea and hacked into the surveillance footage for Grand Central. He'd done this often enough in the past that he could get in, back out, and cover his tracks in his sleep. He pulled up footage from Track 42 (green, blue) and followed the man back in time across other surveillance cameras. He had been wandering around in the concourse for hours before Joe spotted him. But he seemed to know exactly where the cameras were placed, and every single shot caught him looking away—head turned so far that his face was unrecognizable, or head tilted so far down that his face couldn't be seen. The guy was clever.

Joe pulled up the footage from the evening when the man had tried to take his suitcase. That man wore large sunglasses and a hat, plus he was moving too quickly to register properly. Pellucid's facial recognition software wouldn't be able to produce an identification.

That left his experimental gait detection software. He loaded up clips of the man walking calmly, before he grabbed the suitcase and compared them to the man walking toward track 42 (green, blue). A match—both men had identical stride lengths and leg lengths, and their arms and feet moved in the same way when they walked or ran. Not enough to hold up in court, but enough to tell him that he hadn't been paranoid—he'd been in danger. Still, an identification would have made everything a lot easier.

He carried the automaton into his billiards room, the spot where he had built him, set him on the table's green felt surface, wound him up, and watched him wave his pointer around. This creation was at the center of everything. His father's warning had been attached to its blueprints, and the man on the train had come after him twice. But why?

The automaton wound down, and Joe wound it up again, watching his waving arm. What if he was pointing at something, like a teacher at a blackboard? If Joe could figure out what the tiny man was pointing at, maybe he could figure out why his father had wanted him to build this automaton in the first place.

First, he needed to make the movements clearer. Nikola Tesla claimed to have extraordinary eyesight, but Joe's wasn't that great. He took out his set of small screwdrivers and removed the automaton's delicate arm. Soon, laid out on the table were a dozen tiny parts.

Looking at the pieces gave him pause. He was altering Nikola Tesla's original design on a hunch. That was practically the definition of hubris. He laughed, then remembered the scar on his father's hand, the one that he had said was caused by hubris. Hubris, another word in the Tesla family lexicon.

His hands moved as if they had a mind of their own as he plucked tiny pieces from the green felt and fitted them into the tiny arm. At the circus he'd worked with Jackson, a quiet man with long fingers who always smelled like engine oil and Brut aftershave. Jackson was responsible for keeping the carousel and the rides running. He'd taught Joe about machines. Before he'd gotten the scholarship from MIT, Joe had thought of leaving the circus to become a watchmaker, particularly because he knew that it would horrify his father. The Tesla genius thrown away on watches, even if Tesla himself had been a mechanical genius.

His life would have been different, maybe better, if he had. He loved the contemplative nature of assembling simple, tiny pieces into intricate designs. Manhattan had watchmakers, too. Maybe he could find one who'd take him on as an apprentice. Or maybe he'd buy broken watches online and fix them so that they could be resold and go back to work in the world. He smiled at the headline: *Multimillionaire Software Recluse Turns to Watch Repair.*

A quick glance at the grandfather clock told him it was two a.m. (blue). The concourse was officially closed. It would take a while to get everyone herded out, clean up the worst of the mess, and leave the hall empty and quiet. He would wait.

He left the reassembled Tik-Tok in the center of the green felt, like a professor waiting for his class to arrive, and went to the kitchen to make himself a sandwich. Edison, never one to sleep through the creak of the icebox's door, trotted in. Joe had removed the interior and replaced it with a modern fridge to keep the period look but still have proper refrigeration. Considering the sound of that door was such a siren song for Edison, he wondered if he ought to replace the whole refrigerator.

"Here to see if you can beg some food?" Joe asked him.

Edison's eyes went straight to the open refrigerator, and his tail gave a tiny wag. That was a yes.

Joe laughed and pulled out a white paper-wrapped packet of shaved ham. Edison licked his lips. He gave the dog a piece before making himself a ham on rye with a pickle. They both went upstairs to the library, Joe to catch up on some mindless TV, Edison to look mournful until he got more ham.

21

Vivian dragged herself out of bed. She stumbled into her clothes as quietly as she could so as not to wake Lucy. Lucy shared her apartment with her, and she had an early class in the morning. Lucy woke up like a grizzly bear, a good reason to let her sleep.

Vivian made it to Grand Central Terminal right before two a.m. The place had just closed up for the night, and a few people still milled around on the front steps. If she was lucky, Tesla's credible threat might have hung out in the terminal until closing time, hoping to get another glimpse of him. If so, she intended to follow him home, maybe get his identity. Then she could turn the information over to Tesla and recommend that he give it to the police to follow up. He might not ask them for help, but she'd at least give him all the information she could.

She hadn't been waiting long when a man matching Tesla's description and photo—tall, Asian, coordinated, wearing black—strolled out the front doors. She was across the street, half-hidden by the doorway of Pershing Square. Lots of men might fit that description, but she had a hunch that this was the guy.

He looked both ways, then turned left. She intended to let him get a good lead on her, but he went right into the Chrysler Building. Interesting.

She jogged over. She didn't need to get close, because the lobby was lit up. Her guy chatted with the security guard as if he knew him, then swiped a card and headed for the elevators. So, he worked here. Even if she lost him, she could come back and stake out the building. Good. While she waited for him to return, she typed what she'd found into an email and sent it to herself. Nothing looked more natural than someone standing around texting these days.

The man returned a few minutes later. He loped down the street like someone with no place to be. As the streets emptied, she had to leave more and more space between them. She was reaching the point where she'd have to close up the distance and risk being caught, or let him go.

She decided on the latter. A few expensive cars were on the streets, but this wasn't a friendly neighborhood. She cut over a block and headed back. She had a couple of miles to put behind her before she was home.

The deserted streets kept her from dropping her guard, and she saw his shadow from half a block away. He'd doubled back, too. She slipped into an empty doorway, but she knew the game was up. Not a good place for a fight either. Nothing stirred on the street except for her and the man she'd been following.

Near as she could tell, he hadn't been carrying a gun, except maybe something small in a shoulder holster. It was too warm outside to wear a jacket without looking conspicuous, and he was dressed in jeans and a black T-shirt that was too tight to hide anything underneath.

She had a gun. She wore a loose blouse with a ruffle along the bottom that was the perfect size to hide a flat gun tucked into the back of her waistband. Cop-fashion, her sister called it. Vivian hated to use the gun, but she wasn't going to take any crap either.

With one sweaty hand, she reached back and pulled it out. She released the safety. He hesitated at the sound. He knew what it meant. Hopefully that would be enough.

It wasn't.

He kept coming, but he raised his hands in the air. "I don't know why you're following me, lady."

He had a slight accent she couldn't place. East coast, at least. "From where I'm standing, it looks like you're following *me*."

He moved closer. "I'm trying to get home."

She stepped out into the light so he could see the gun, assess her stance, and know she meant business. She was in the middle of the sidewalk now, the streetlight full on her. "I think you'd better find a different way home."

He glided forward another step. If he came in any closer, she'd have to shoot. Life wasn't like the movies where you could let someone get an arm's length away from you before shooting. A gun was most useful as a distance weapon.

If she pulled the trigger, she wouldn't have time for a warning shot. She'd have to hit him. And, if he kept coming after that, she'd have to kill him. He didn't look like someone who'd let a gunshot stop him from killing somebody. He looked like somebody who might just get pissed off.

She kicked out, and her quarry slowed in surprise. He wasn't close enough for her to kick him.

But she wasn't aiming for him. Her foot crashed against the side of a blue BMW M5. Its alarm wailed. People mostly ignored car alarms these days, but this was a damn expensive car on a street where its owner was probably nervous.

Her assailant looked up when lights went on in the building next door. She could see him weighing his options. He might take her before she shot him, but he might not, and the appearance of someone else on the scene changed the odds.

He shrugged and backed away. She didn't lower the gun until he was around the corner. Then she stepped away from the BMW and tucked the gun under her shirt.

A man in silk pajamas appeared in the doorway she'd just vacated. He brandished a baseball bat.

"I saw the guy who kicked your car," she said. "Do you want me to stay so you can file a police report?"

His eyes flicked to the dent she'd made in his fender. She felt a pang of guilt, but better his insurance company covered the damage than that she had to shoot the guy she'd been following.

"Did you get a good look at him?" he asked.

"Better than you did." She called a cab while he thought that over. At least he'd lowered the bat.

She gave him a quick description of the guy. Maybe she'd get lucky and the cops would pull him in for damaging the car. Yeah, and maybe Santa Claus would give her a ride home in his sleigh.

She took the cab.

22

At three a.m. (red), Joe gathered up the automaton and took the elegant elevator up to the concourse. He hoped the guy who had been following him hadn't somehow managed to evade Grand Central security and was still inside. Joe had kept an eye on the surveillance cameras while watching TV, and he'd seen only the regular nightly cleaning crew moving about the terminal.

A few minutes later he and Edison were alone in the vast room. Illuminated stars on the ceiling glowed softly. He had read that the LEDs installed in 2010 were equipped with special light-blocking filters so that each star glowed with the same relative brightness as its counterpart out in space. He liked that.

He carried Tik-Tok over to the corner under the constellation for Cancer the crab. Nikola Tesla was born on July 10 (cyan, black), which meant his astrological sign was Cancer. If Alan was right, and Nikola had spent nights here, walking the concourse alone, maybe Cancer would have special meaning for him, and maybe Joe's father would have known that. Edison's claws clicked against the marble as he walked, a sound Joe never heard during the noise and bustle of the day.

With a clink, he set the metal man on the polished floor and lined him up with Beta Cancri, the brightest star in the constellation. He wound him up, each click loud in the empty room. Tik-Tok raised his arm. Joe had changed the simple red bulb on the end to a laser pointer. He hoped the little man's arm might point to the Oscillator.

But it didn't.

He moved the man to various locations around the terminal, trying all the stars of Cancer, then Hercules, and then each constellation in turn. He even climbed the information booth and positioned the man atop the clock, trying not to think about the fact that each face of the clock was made of high-grade polished opal and that Sotheby's had put a replacement value on each face of between two and a half and five million dollars. He'd also heard that the clock faces were made of opalescent glass, which would make them significantly cheaper. He hoped the second explanation was true.

Roger, the older gentleman who washed the floors, raised an eyebrow when he saw Joe crawling around with a doll, but he didn't say anything. Joe officially had the run of the place, so he was allowed to be there, and he was considered eccentric enough that nobody questioned him. Perks of being a crazy rich guy.

By the time 5:30 a.m. (brown: red, black) rolled around, his knees hurt from kneeling on the cold Tennessee marble, his fingers were sore from winding up the little man, and Edison was sleeping on the bottom stair of the East Staircase.

The station would open to travelers soon, and he'd accomplished nothing. He felt as if he'd betrayed his father's memory by not being smart enough to solve the puzzle left for him. More was expected of him, even if he wasn't a Tesla after all.

23

Joe woke up late and grouchy. He fed Edison and put on a cup of coffee. His coffee maker was a work of modern-day wonder, even if it didn't match the décor. Some compromises he was willing to make.

He switched on the flames in the parlor and stared into them until he had enough caffeine in his system to think about his email. Regular work stuff, more surveillance matches from what had to be the most massive government surveillance program ever, and a few private emails.

One from Alan Wright inviting him to play tennis later in the week. Did Alan even play tennis? Maybe he was reaching out because Joe's father had died, but that didn't mean Joe had to play tennis with him, did it? Plus, Alan didn't strike him as a reacher-outer. He must want something. But what?

One from Vivian saying she'd followed a man matching the description that Joe had given her to the Chrysler Building, where he seemed to work, but had lost him afterward. She must not have gone to bed. She didn't ask any questions about why he wanted to have the man followed, which was good given that his best answer was a bunch of paranoid worries about a box of papers from Nikola Tesla that only had instructions for how to build a windup toy.

The toy stood on the mantel next to a human skull and a black statue of the Egyptian cat-headed goddess Bastet. It looked right at home among the other Victorian-era collectibles.

Joe admired the toy's clever design, then took a long sip of coffee and braved the surveillance folder. More requests. Hundreds of thousands from computers that he'd traced to the National Security Agency. Someone was fishing, and they'd scooped up all the fish they could find.

What could he, Joe Tesla, do about it? The National Security Agency had enough lawyers on its payroll that he'd never be able to prove the volume of requests was illegal. He could leak the results to a whistle-blower website like WikiLeaks, but that wouldn't do more than spark a month of outraged navel-gazing.

Doing nothing wasn't an option either.

He took a shower and got dressed, but when he returned to the parlor, his laptop was still there with its millions of facial recognition match requests next to the stubborn little automaton. Neither was showing him the way forward.

With a sigh, he sat down and stared into the flames again. Edison inched closer to him, brown eyes watching his every move. That helped Joe make his decision. It was no good to have your every move watched unless you knew the watcher and loved him.

So, he would have to deal with the NSA. First, he'd have to remove any traces that he'd logged its activities. The government agency shouldn't know that he had been watching it watch everyone else. That took only a few minutes. He'd written the underlying code, after all, and he knew what to tweak.

His next actions were straightforward, but the consequences were profound. If caught, he'd go to jail—probably some nasty federal jail where they'd arrange for him to be housed in a glass cell staring out at nature on all sides. Sweat filmed his palms just thinking about it.

Even worse, he would have to break his greatest creation. He would have to sabotage the facial recognition engine that underpinned everything Pellucid did. And it wouldn't be enough to just break it. If the software stopped working, they'd roll back to an earlier version. He had to create an algorithm that would slowly decrease the number of possible matches across time. It would have to be so gradual that no one would be able to pinpoint when it started, and so subtle that it would look like a scalability bug that crept in when the system was stressed beyond its original design parameters. And it had to be so pernicious that it could never be fixed.

He had to create a digital version of Celeste's ALS—barely recognizable symptoms at first, then incurable creeping paralysis. The system had been his life for years now—the last thing he thought of before he went to bed and the first thing he thought of when he woke up. He dreamed the numbers and colors that made it run. And now he had to turn all the colors to black.

Edison sensed his mood and dropped his head in Joe's lap. His tail wagged once.

"You can't help me with this one, buddy," Joe said. "I've got to do it."

He connected to the darknet to hide his IP address, then logged into Pellucid's system using the account of an intern who had left the company. With any luck, his actions would never be traced back this far, but if he was, she'd have an alibi—she was trekking in Tibet and completely off the grid.

Hours ticked by as he skipped through the code, changing tiny pieces here and there, hiding his intent in hundreds of places across thousands of lines of code. Colors flashed through his head as he calculated numbers and percentages, but the colors were muted and dark. He'd never experienced this before, but he knew they had changed their color because they were sad.

He was crippling something bright and amazing because it was too powerful, too dangerous, and always in the wrong hands. He had created this monster with the best of intentions, but as his father always said, *the road to hell is paved with good intentions*. He was going to have to kill his creation, not quickly, but with a thousand tiny cuts, until its colors and numbers had bled out.

Andres Peterson called in the afternoon. Andres was his dog walker—the man who made sure that Edison got the fresh air and sunshine he deserved. Celeste had recommended the Estonian artist when Joe was looking for someone, but she had warned him that Andres would be very famous someday, and he'd have to get another dog walker.

Joe's mind was still connected to the lines of code that he had created as he took Edison up the elevator. He greeted Evaline in a daze, barely spoke to Andres, and went back down to his work.

By the time Andres's next text reached him, Joe's latticework of deceit was complete. But he didn't have the heart to put in the final line of code, the one that would set it all in motion. It would destroy his creation, and it could destroy his life.

He scrolled through the surveillance reports one last time. He thought of the millions of dollars that he and his colleagues would lose when his changes reached full effect and Pellucid's stock tanked. They'd all sold enough to be comfortable for the rest of their lives, but that didn't mean they wanted to lose the rest.

He thought of the millions of people who had lost their privacy to his machine. He weighed their rights against the people who might be harmed if the NSA could no longer use the software. The innocents who might die because his software didn't identify those intent on doing harm.

And he didn't write that final line.

Instead, he went up to collect Edison. The dog panted happily next to the information booth. When Joe bent to pet him, he smelled like grass and dog. He'd been soaking up summer, just as Joe's father would have wanted. What if Joe had tried to forgive the man, and they'd spent one last summer together? Would that have been so wrong?

Andres wore ripped jeans and a rust-tinged cotton shirt. His curly hair was disheveled from the wind, and he was sporting the beginning of a tan. Joe suspected the only time he spent outside was with Edison and otherwise spent his days in his studio crafting his giant metal sculptures. They were gloomy, but Joe liked them. Celeste adored them.

"Edison runs like a champion," Andres said. "Even in the heat he could not be stopped. We went to Central Park so he could roll in grass. He loves grass."

"Were you a good boy?" Joe asked Edison. Somebody ought to be.

"He is always good," Andres said. "You are lucky to have such a fine animal."

Joe nodded and handed Andres his money. He always paid Andres in cash. Andres was one person he interacted with for whom there was no paper trail. He even had Andres text and call him using an app that kept his location secret and deleted the texts every twenty-four (blue, green) hours. Anyone who hung around Grand Central would know of their connection, but they weren't linked online. That anonymity had saved Edison's life once when Joe was under electronic surveillance and the dog was wounded. It was worth preserving.

Andres crumpled the bill and pushed it into his front pants pocket. "In my country I had such a dog once, a fine, brave fellow, but the neighbor said he ate her chicken, and he had to be destroyed."

"I'm sorry to hear that."

"He did not eat the chicken, of course." Andres's pale blue eyes flashed. "But everyone knew that this neighbor was an informer for the government, and we could do nothing. Her husband shot the dog in front of my house. I was seven years old."

Joe dropped his hand to Edison's shoulder, touching the scar where Edison had been shot a few months before. He imagined a seven-year-old watching his dog get shot and die in front of him.

"I'm sorry." It seemed so inadequate.

Andres shrugged. "It is over now, and I can play with your Edison every day, even get money for that. In this country that is so free. Those are good things."

Andres patted Edison one last time and slouched off toward the giant front doors.

Joe watched him go, out into a country that he thought was free, but wasn't.

24

Quantum liked his borrowed apartment. After being confronted by that woman, he didn't feel safe going home. Who knew how long she'd been following him before he noticed her?

So he'd done what he usually did when he went to ground. He found an apartment marked as empty on Airbnb, using an algorithm he'd invented to search the database for unrented temporary apartments. Once he found one that he liked, he'd hack the owner's email account and find out how he had tenants pick up keys. Then it was an easy matter to show up at a convenience store with fake ID and pretend to be a renter or to retrieve the key from under a mat or a coded mailbox.

This apartment was particularly nice. It had a widescreen TV and Wi-Fi, and the last tenant had left the fridge partially stocked. Quantum was settling in when his phone buzzed. Ash. It had been hours since Quantum told him that he'd lost Joe, and he knew Ash was furious. He was going to have to take his lumps and smile. If he could manage it.

ash: details
quantum: he jumped off train in tunnels
ash: u didn't pursue?
quantum: train moving before i could
ash: device worth risk

Said by a man who was not down in the tunnels on a speeding train, knowing that if he jumped he might get his legs cut off or he might land against the third rail and get electrocuted. Not on Quantum's list of ways to spend the day. He gritted his teeth.

quantum: sorry
ash: more risk, more reward

That sounded promising. It was the first mention of reward. He'd been doing this as a freebie, even blowing off his regular freelance IT work, just for karma points. But cash would be better.

quantum: ??
ash: get what i want any means necessary i'll make it worth ur while

That sounded pretty vague, but it was a start. Quantum rested his feet on a blocky coffee table that looked as if it came from IKEA.

quantum: any means necessary?
ash: don't want to know just want results

That meant he didn't care whether Joe Tesla lived or died.

Sometimes Quantum wondered if Ash was a CEO or a Mafia don. He wanted things done, and he wanted plausible deniability if they were. Would he have businessman loyalty, which was to say none at all, or would he reward loyalty like a Mafia don?

quantum: how much?
ash: bottom 6, u know how and where

Quantum did. Bottom six meant bottom six figures, or $100,000. How and where were easy too—Bitcoins from Spooky's petty-cash account, simple and untrackable. But he didn't trust Ash.

quantum: i'm a hacker. i can snatch something, but i don't do any means necessary
ash: not true

Quantum's stomach did a backflip.

quantum: ??
ash: i've seen ur record, mike pham. i know it's not complete

Quantum's stomach went straight from backflip to full-on spinning. Ash knew who he was. He knew about the identity Quantum had abandoned years ago. Nobody in his new world knew his real name. Except Ash.

ash: do this for me and u get the carrot not the stick

He took a deep breath. He didn't owe Joe Tesla anything. Best plan was to get the device, get paid, and then dive down so deep that Ash would never find him. He sat up straight on the anonymous couch and decided how to play it. Matter of fact.

quantum: i like carrots

Ash would know that was a yes.

ash: then earn them

Quantum looked around the comfortable apartment and sighed. He'd have to be up early. Grand Central opened at 5:30 a.m., and he'd have to stake it out again, but he needed a disguise. He decided to go for beggar. He'd need to skip shaving, buy a filthy jacket off one of the homeless who haunted the terminal, smash up a fedora so he had a battered hat to shield his face from the cameras, and make himself a cardboard sign. If he put a mirror on his begging cup, he'd be able to sit with his back to the clock and still watch it. Hopefully, a clever position and the disguise would be enough to conceal him if that hot Hispanic woman from last night had been sent by Tesla.

If not, he'd have his gun.

25

Joe paced around his house—front hall, parlor, billiards room, kitchen, and library. Edison trotted along at his heels. But the yellow dog didn't have the solution to Joe's problems.

He made a round of the parlor. The automaton's metal surface gleamed enticingly in the firelight. The little creation had answers to something, even if it wasn't his current dilemma. Maybe what he needed was a distraction. He picked up the automaton. "Why was my father scared of you, little fellow?"

The toy didn't answer.

"And why does it feel like somebody else wants you? Somebody scary."

Predictably, the toy didn't answer again.

It couldn't, being only a toy that didn't even have a voice box.

Deciding to talk to someone who did, he called Vivian.

"Torres." The name was clipped and economical, a military greeting.

"It's me," he said. "Is my mother all right?"

"Fine," she said. "I just checked in with Dirk. He's on shift right now."

"Do you have some time today?"

"I can make some," she said.

"Could you meet with those professors from the funeral?"

"Egger and Patel?" Trust her to remember the names.

"Them. Find out if they know who might have wanted to take that suitcase. It had papers that my father left me in it."

"What kind of papers?"

Joe tightened his grip on Tik-Tok. "Just papers."

"I'll get right on it, sir." Vivian hung up.

Joe looked at the automaton in his hands. Maybe he'd missed something last night in the concourse. Maybe Tik-Tok was trying to tell him something, and he hadn't seen it. He tucked his feet up in the leather armchair and went over the surveillance footage of the previous night's adventure under the constellations. A tiny Joe Tesla walked onscreen with an even tinier man and a cheerful-looking dog.

The Joe Tesla of last night had known he was being filmed, but he hadn't bothered to hide from the camera, even though he was doing unusual things. He carried the toy around, placing it in various locations, watching the little arm paint with light on the walls. Again, the arm never pointed at anything that seemed significant.

Still, something looked familiar in the movements of the arm. They weren't random. Too much time and care had gone into those movements for them to be random. Nikola Tesla had an extraordinary visual memory. He built all his machines in his head first, not bothering with blueprints, and watched them turn and move, studying them for inefficiencies and improper wear patterns. He spent hours on the models in his head before he built them in the real world.

A man like that would think it child's play to watch the motions of the arm and remember where the arm had pointed moments before. Joe slowed the footage down until the light from the laser inched slowly across the concourse wall, leaving trails behind it.

He sat up. "I got it, Edison!"

The dog cocked his head and raised his ears.

"Tik-Tok isn't pointing to anything at all. He's *writing*."

A few minutes later he had transcribed Tik-Tok's gestures. They were numbers and letters, each separated by a short pause:

40 45 10 73 59 38 južni podrum 3

He'd start with the numbers. A dozen colors flashed through his head in a long ribbon. Over four billion (green with a long stretch of black). A huge number. But they weren't one number. The pauses made them six (orange) numbers, plus the one at the end.

Joe wound the ribbons of colors around in his head, combining and recombining them. But he didn't find any patterns. He tried entering them into a couple of pattern finders online and came up empty there, too.

Then he sequenced the numbers in order:

10 38 40 45 59 73

He tried everything again, but came up with nothing again.

The numbers weren't in any mathematical sequence that he could readily find. That didn't mean that there wasn't a method to them that Nikola Tesla had known, but it did mean he should broaden his search parameters.

If they weren't mathematical, maybe they were something physical. They might be the combination of a safe. That was a discouraging thought, because he had no idea where he might find Nikola Tesla's safe. He'd read up on him recently and knew that he had kept a safe in his hotel room, but it had been emptied after his death. Surely his father wouldn't have given him a completely impossible task. He pursed his lips. His father was capable of that—he'd given Joe plenty of impossible tasks when he was a kid.

Maybe he was wrong about the numbers. He wound up the automaton and pointed his light at a piece of paper hanging on the wall. He traced each ray of light. The numbers were the same, but, in addition to the pause after every second digit, he noticed a longer pause after the sixth digit and the twelfth one. Maybe it was two separate numbers:

40 45 10
73 59 38

No patterns there, but 40 45 10 looked familiar (green, black; green, brown; cyan, black). Where had he seen those colors before? Somewhere in Grand Central Terminal, he was certain of it. He ran through combinations of tracks, of train schedules, and addresses. Again, nothing.

He closed his eyes and let the ribbon of color float free in his head, figuring out where the numbers needed to attach. A feeling of elation came over him. He knew: 40 degrees, 45 minutes 10 seconds. If you put north on the end, that was the latitude for Grand Central.

A quick check of the GPS app on his phone told him that the latitude for Grand Central was 40°45'10.08" N, and its longitude was 73°58'35.48" W. So, whatever he was looking at was close, but not in the terminal.

He entered the numbers that Tik-Tok had drawn and immediately hit a match. New Yorker Hotel, at 481 Eighth Avenue, New York, New York. A quick online search told him that Nikola Tesla had spent the last few years of his life there. He had died, alone, in Room 3327 (red, red, blue, slate) on January 7, 1943. The hotel had changed ownership several times since then and been completely refurbished, but the building still stood.

His heart raced. The automaton had a message for him. It was leading him exactly where Nikola Tesla wanted—his old hotel. His father must have figured that out and been able to find those numbers before the days of the Internet and portable GPS. It had been a much harder task in Nikola Tesla's time, and in his father's. Joe almost felt like he was cheating.

But, after that work, had his father really used the device to knock down a bridge, then hidden the device away again? Why hadn't he destroyed it himself? If it was really so deadly, why would he leave this burden for Joe?

Because he left Joe all his burdens—taking care of his mother, putting himself through school, making a name for the next generation of Teslas, and vowing to never beat on those he loved. So far, so good, but this new task frightened him. He had to push ahead, because he felt responsible for carrying out his father's last wish, and for keeping this device out of the hands of the man who had tried to steal the suitcase and then followed him onto the train. If the man knew that he had clues to lead him there, who knew what else he might know?

He had a location, but he still needed to figure out what the two words meant.

He typed them into an online translation program, taking a minute to find the z with a hat over it, which was, he found out, called a caron.

južni podrum 3
The language was Croatian, and the words meant *southern basement.*

He couldn't stop grinning. He had no idea what the final three (red) meant. But this was enough to go on.

Nikola Tesla had left the plans for the automaton with his pigeon keeper and the man's scientifically inclined young son. He must have expected them to put together the automaton and discover his message. If the newspaper clipping was right, and not the result of his father's paranoia, his father had discovered the message years ago and had taken something from the hotel's basement.

But he must have put it back or else he would never have left that yellow note: *Show the wisdom I did not and have the courage to destroy it.*

His father might have doubted his wisdom, but it had never occurred to his father that Joe wouldn't have the courage go outside and walk a mile to the New Yorker Hotel.

He'd have to find a way around that problem.

Somehow.

26

Ash opened the thick glass window. A white feather blew into the room. He watched it dance across the room before settling on his desk. Up here, almost nothing came in from the outside. Pigeons must be nesting above his floor.

He picked up the feather and studied it. Life would always find a way, no matter how much man tried to insulate himself from it.

He found the thought encouraging, and today he needed encouragement. He'd had a useless lunch with the mayor. While he agreed that solar road technology would save the city energy and money—the lots wouldn't need snow removal, the road tiles could funnel energy into the buildings they surrounded, the energy generated could recharge electric cars—it wasn't enough. The mayor needed broader political support to even consider such a radical move. The union for road builders was strong, the contracts with asphalt providers were long running, and all the other parties vested in the current system would resist. It would cost Ash a great deal of money, more than he had budgeted, but not more than he could afford.

He would win in the long run, but it might be a very long run indeed. The past was constantly reaching into the future and dragging it down. It would be easier to build a solar-powered road on Mars than in New York City.

His administrative assistant brought him a cappuccino and a printout listing his afternoon schedule. His next meeting was in half an hour with an Arizona mall owner who promised to be a strong beta test site for the solar road technology. Good numbers there would translate into sales, but good numbers in a place as far north as New York would translate into even more.

He browsed his email. Joe Tesla had not responded to his invitation. Ash didn't like being ignored, so he pulled up his tracking app. The dot that was Edison was moving at a good walking clip, then stopping for over a minute at a time—long enough for a train to pass. So, Mr. Tesla and his faithful hound were in a subway tunnel heading north and west. Probably the 7 Line.

They stopped for a long moment at Times Square, then started moving slowly north toward Central Park. Maybe Joe was meeting his dog walker at a station close to the park. If so, Ash would lose track of Joe's movements.

But from what he'd heard about Joe, he didn't go anywhere without the dog, so if he was up to something interesting, Ash would wait him out. He took a long sip of cappuccino. His assistant got it from this fantastic coffee shop on the corner. The place had insane lines, but he'd never had to wait in them. Perks of being the boss.

Edison cut left, west, which meant they were in the E subway tunnel.

Ash called his assistant in and asked her to take the meeting with the mall guy. She was ambitious and smart, and her eyes gleamed at the thought. If she landed this, he'd let her manage the project and hire someone else to fetch his coffee, and she knew it. He waved her off and went back to watching Joe. His gut told him Joe was going somewhere significant, and that was more important than handling the Arizona deal himself.

When the green dot turned south again, he looked for Quantum online. He didn't have anyone else whom he could tap at short notice for something like this, but he still hesitated. He was fairly confident that Quantum would do his best to come through for him, now that he knew the stakes. But would he be able to manage it? He had failed to retrieve the suitcase, had tipped off Joe to his presence, and missed his chance to steal the automaton.

Joe was now in the tunnel for the A, C, and E subway lines and walking ahead at a pretty brisk pace. A man on a mission. He was a couple of stops away from 34th Street and Penn Station. Ash knew what was there—the hotel where Nikola Tesla died.

He didn't have time for a different decision. He found Quantum and sent him to a dark chat room they liked to use.

ash: new yorker hotel asap
quantum: why?
ash: tesla heading there. device related? find him, take it, and go
quantum: on it

Ash grinned. It was good that he had Quantum on the case after all, and that the GPS was proving so useful. The device would be out of Joe's hands and in Ash's by the end of the day.

Then he could play with it.

27

Joe pulled Edison to the side of the tunnel and covered the dog's ears. A subway train rattled by. Stripes of light from its silver cars passed over their faces. Then the train was gone, its red taillights fading into the tunnel's darkness.

"That's the last train for a while, buddy," Joe said.

Edison wagged his tail. He didn't worry about the trains. He was used to them.

Joe directed his flashlight at the rough stone ceiling. He was right under the diner next to the New Yorker Hotel, a restaurant called, as whimsy would have it, the Tick Tock Diner. He'd seen pictures online, and it was housed in a silver train car. He would feel at home there, but he could never visit.

Before they left the house, he'd pulled up the original blueprints for the New Yorker Hotel. It had been built in 1930 with coal-fired steam boilers and generators. Ironically, it ran on direct current—Edison's invention instead of Tesla's—and it had once boasted the largest private power plant in the United States. The building hadn't been modernized to use alternating current until the late 1960s.

In Nikola Tesla's time, the basement had been divided into four (green) large rooms—the east and west basements held the boilers and power plant that kept the hotel running. The north basement had stored coal. The south basement, by far the smallest, had held food and restaurant supplies. It wouldn't have been easy for the inventor to come down and hide something without being observed, but he might have done it. Nikola Tesla had certainly managed far more impossible feats than that.

Joe'd found blueprints for renovations, too. The hotel had changed hands several times over the years and been renovated again and again, but he was hoping the basements and the steam tunnels that once brought heat into the building had been left untouched. If he was unlucky, the steam tunnels had been walled off. If he was lucky, they were still in use or had been closed off with airtight metal doors installed and certified by the city. Due to a Byzantine system of rules and regulations put in place to ensure fires were properly contained, those doors were everywhere in the tunnels.

He moved his headlamp around to find the entrance to the steam tunnel he'd seen on his maps. He had official modern maps, but much more useful was his growing collection of old ones. He had found or bought maps from the many different companies that had run subways, sewage lines, steam tunnels, electrical access, and all the other business the city kept buried beneath its feet. He'd been working off and on for months to consolidate his maps into a single real-time map that would tell him exactly where he could and couldn't go in the hundred-plus miles of subterranean New York, but he felt as if he had scarcely begun.

According to his map, the tunnel in front of him ran only a couple of yards. Branching off the side was a door labeled *Steam Operations*. Bingo.

He lifted the heavy key ring attached to his belt. Golden light from his headlamp shone on dozens of keys. The original Mr. Gallo had been very clever when he wrote the contract guaranteeing him perpetual free access to everything under Manhattan, and he and his descendants had accumulated a lot of keys in the last century. Those keys were now in Joe's hands.

He had long since organized them alphabetically by the kind of doors they opened. His fingers brushed through them until he got to the ones that opened steam tunnels. He pulled out a skeleton key with a square head and a long shank, a Con Edison master key for the branch of its company called Steam Operations. Con Edison had delivered steam to Manhattan since the tunnels were built. Its system had over one hundred miles of mains and service pipes and three thousand manholes, and the company still serviced some of New York's most famous addresses, from the United Nations buildings to the Empire State Building and the Metropolitan Museum of Art. With his keys, Joe had access to all of them—part of the reason he'd had to undergo such an extensive security screening before he moved into his underground house. He could break into a lot of basements.

He tapped the key thoughtfully. This particular Con Edison key had to be at least fifty years old. He suspected this was one of the last existing keys that would fit this lock. Not the very last key, of course. Even though it had been expressly forbidden, he'd had all the keys copied. He'd given the spare keys to Mr. Rossi to deposit in a safety deposit box. He believed in making backups.

He took a can of WD-40 (green, black) out of his backpack. He carried his most essential exploring gear—WD-40 (green, black), duct tape, dog treats, protein bars, a glow-in-the-dark tennis ball for games of fetch, water, maps, spare batteries for his headlamp, a Con Edison vest he'd stolen from the basement of the morgue, a change of clothes in case he fell in sewage, and a flashlight stun gun. He'd had to use every one of those items, although he didn't like to think about it.

Zipped into the front pocket of his backpack was a new passenger—Nikola Tesla's automaton. He felt the little guy ought to see where he'd led Joe. He'd waited long enough.

A couple of squirts on the hinges, in the keyhole, and on the key itself did the trick. The old tumblers turned over quietly, and he opened the heavy door. Back when this was made, things were built to last. Planned obsolescence had yet to become a watchword.

His headlamp revealed another tunnel, smaller than the last, so narrow he could reach his hands out and touch both sides, and so low the top nearly brushed the top of his head. The sides were painted white, but the bases of the walls had a gray patina of mold that he could smell from where he was standing.

The pipes that ran down the side of the tunnel were cold. Rust lay in drifts underneath them. They probably hadn't been used in years, and they'd probably never been used in July. According to his map, they led straight toward the New Yorker Hotel.

Edison stayed right against Joe's leg. He didn't blame him. Not so long ago, the dog had been shot in a steam tunnel that looked much like this one.

He ran his hand down Edison's back slowly, again and again, until he felt the dog relax. "It's OK, boy. We're safe in here. Nobody around."

Edison cocked his head. He closed his eyes, as if listening hard. Apparently he was satisfied with what he heard, because he opened his eyes and wagged his tail.

Joe was pretty sure they were safe, too. During their long trek through the tunnels, he had neither seen nor heard anyone. He'd waited in alcoves and peeked out, looking for the telltale glow of a flashlight. He'd doubled back a few times, once going through a long, dark tunnel by feel, to make sure they weren't being followed. Whoever had staked out the clock wasn't behind them. He hoped.

He took off his headlamp and used the stun gun flashlight to light his way, in case he needed to use it as a weapon. He swept the light from side to side, illuminating nothing but peeling paint, rusty pipes, and mold. There weren't even any rat droppings.

After another look around, he motioned for Edison to go first, then entered the tunnel after him. He carefully locked the door behind him. If anyone was following him, they wouldn't get through that door.

Hopefully.

28

Vivian dodged a pack of Swedish tourists taking pictures at the Washington Square Arch—the Arc de Triomphe of New York. She could have gone around, but she liked walking through the giant, marble monument. It always helped put her problems in perspective. Right now, her biggest problem was the Teslas.

Neither Tatiana Tesla nor her son had given her any hints as to why would try to steal Tesla's suitcase, or why she had to set up a team to protect Mrs. Tesla. It seemed like Tesla himself had been the one attacked, not his mother, and he ought to be the one that she was protecting. But he'd categorically refused to let her guard him. Maybe it was a macho thing.

Speaking of macho, the man she'd been following last night hadn't wanted to back down. He hadn't acted like someone who was easily frightened or dissuaded. If his goal was to track Tesla, he'd be back. Hell, he might be back already, and she wasn't there to protect Tesla. The best thing she could do was investigate, see if this professor had more of an idea of what was going on.

She stopped next to the fountain. The haze of water droplets scattered by the wind made the air cooler here, and she took a deep breath. The air smelled of chlorine and mildew, which was better than the exhaust fumes and hot pavement of a few moments before.

She wasn't just enjoying the view as she dug a penny out of her pocket and tossed it in. She used the motion to take a good long look behind her. The tourists she'd passed were posing next to the arch, one after the other, their white-blond hair gleaming in the sun. Nobody else had come through the arch yet.

On her journey here, she'd doubled back, cut through alleys, even hopped on and off the subway, to make sure that she wasn't being followed. A long shot, but she was still careful, especially after last night. So far, she hadn't seen anyone suspicious.

A couple paused next to her to take a selfie with the arch in the background, chattering away in Spanish. One wore a red T-shirt, the other a white one, and both wore jeans and espadrilles. Sunlight glinted off their sunglasses as they bounced their heads back and forth, trying to find the right angle for their shot. Some people's problems were easy.

She hurried toward the southeast corner of the park. Her destination was a few blocks outside the park: a tall, brick and glass building known as Warren Weaver Hall. It was part of the Courant Institute, and she had an appointment with Professor Patel. She hadn't been able to reach the other one yet.

The closer she got to the building, the older she felt. Even though it was summer, kids who seemed like they should still be in high school wandered around. She passed a group of girls who looked younger than Lucy, standing in a circle, all stabbing away at their cell phones with their thumbs and not talking.

She stopped in front of the building and texted Professor Patel. He was supposed to be in the library, working, while he waited to hear from her. She sensed that he was used to students coming late for meetings.

But he appeared immediately, walking quickly toward her across the grass.

"Professor Patel?" she asked. "I'm Vivian Torres, we met at Mr. Tesla's funeral and spoke on the phone."

"Of course you are." He led her into the building, down a hall, and into an empty classroom. Rows of desks faced a chalkboard and table at the front of the room. It reminded Vivian of high school.

He pulled one desk to face another and gestured to it. "We can talk here."

She sat across from him, although she preferred standing. "Professor Patel, I know this is an unusual circumstance."

His dark eyes narrowed. "It most certainly is. Two colleagues dead within such a short time. Nothing suspicious, of course, but still unexpected."

"Two?"

"Professor Egger, of course. You met him at the funeral. Bald man, with a beard."

And a yellow bow tie. That explained why she hadn't been able to reach him, and it made things a lot more worrisome. "Professor Egger is dead?"

"Overdose, rumor has it. Last night. Found this morning by his cleaning woman."

"Why do they think it was an overdose?"

"He had a heavy load to carry since his wife died. He never got over it, you see." Patel's voice quivered slightly.

"Do *you* think he overdosed?"

"That is a matter for the police." Professor Patel tilted his head to the side. "I thought that might be why you wanted to meet this morning, but it's not."

"Was he the type of person who would overdose?"

"The type of person who was taking sleeping pills? Yes. The type of person who also drank more than he should sometimes? Yes. The type of person who was also depressed and at risk? Yes." He patted the top of his desk with one finger. "That does not mean that he intended to die."

Vivian made a mental note to ask Dirk to look into it. "Were Professor Egger and Professor Tesla close?"

"Professor Egger had once been the graduate student of Professor Tesla. They often played chess even after Professor Tesla was…confined."

A polite term for locked up in an institution. "Did Professor Tesla have other friends?"

Patel looked past her shoulder and out the window for a second before replying. "His ex-wife. They spoke on the phone often."

So, maybe Tesla Senior had given something to Tatiana, and his good friend Egger had known about it. Maybe that something was in the suitcase that was almost stolen from Tesla.

"Were you close with Professor Tesla?"

Patel flinched ever so slightly. "What is close for mathematicians? We taught some of the same students, we played chess, we had lunch."

"Yet you went to his funeral." There was more to their relationship than he was suggesting.

"Close for mathematicians is not the same as close for others, but that does not mean we do not mark it when one of our friends dies."

"Will you go to Professor Egger's funeral, then?" She shifted in the hard desk.

"I do not believe that he will have one. He donated his body to science, so there is nothing to bury, and he hated ritual. With his wife gone, he will not want his passing to be formally acknowledged."

She thought she might have liked this Egger. They had the same idea about funerals, anyway. "If you hear of a funeral—"

"You would attend? Yet you do not like funerals. You were jumpy and angry at George Tesla's. You came to that out of a sense of duty, not sentiment. But why would you have a duty to Professor Egger?"

This guy saw more than he let on. "Did Professor Tesla have any enemies?"

"Enemies? Friends? He was not beset by either." Patel tapped his finger on the desk again. "Demons of his own, he had those."

"Do you know if he was in possession of any important papers?"

"He would have said that all his papers were important."

"He left his son a box that someone tried to steal yesterday."

"What was in it?"

"What do you think?"

He shrugged. "Professor Tesla was a mathematician, not a spy. I doubt that he had anything worth worrying about. He was a very paranoid man, but I never saw any indication that he needed to be."

"How was he paranoid?"

Patel smiled wryly. "He once said space aliens were sending him messages through his teeth because he was special. I did not give his paranoia much credence."

Had Tesla Senior been like that Joe's entire life? Joe had never told her anything about his father. But just because his father was crazy didn't change the fact that someone had tried to steal that suitcase. She questioned Patel for a few more minutes without gleaning any new information, extracted a promise that he would notify her if Egger did have a funeral, and then left him alone in the classroom, staring across the empty desks.

She called Dirk from the elevator, telling him to be on high alert. If Egger's death wasn't an accident, the threat level had kicked up a notch, and something didn't feel right about it.

After she hung up, she tried Tesla again. He didn't answer, so she left a message summarizing the results of the interview, stressing Egger's mysterious death, and telling Tesla to stay put in his house. She had no idea where he was, but she did know where Tatiana Tesla was, so that was her next stop.

Both Teslas might be in more danger than she'd thought.

29

Joe stopped in front of another door at the end of the tunnel. This door was more modern, painted blue, and also bore the Con Edison logo, a letter C surrounding the letter E. He had the master key for this one, too. He remembered to oil the hinges and the lock before unlocking the door. No point in making unnecessary noise and tipping off anyone who might be on the other side.

Slowly, he opened the door and peered inside at a room full of dusty beds piled nearly to the ceiling, chairs stacked atop each other and covered with sheets. The room smelled so strongly of mothballs his eyes watered. It must be even worse for Edison's finely tuned nose.

He put on his Con Edison vest. If he were stopped, he would say he worked for the company's still-active Steam Operations division, and Edison was specially trained to be able to smell leaky steam pipes. It might work. He knew from his time in the circus that people cut you a lot of slack if you had a convincing costume and story.

His heart raced as he stepped into the basement of the New Yorker Hotel. He was somewhere new to him, something that didn't happen often. He wanted to walk upstairs to the main lobby, take an elevator to the thirty-third (red, red) floor, and check out the room where his non-ancestor had died. He could eat at one of the hotel's restaurants and have something unexpected. He could look out the windows from a distance and see new sights. He could do all those things, but first he was going to scour the south basement to find the clues Nikola Tesla had left.

This room wasn't the south basement, so he hurried through it and into an empty corridor, shining his flashlight ahead. The lights were off, and he didn't dare switch them on. Based on the dust on the floor, it didn't look as if anyone had come this way in a long time, but he wasn't taking any chances of being caught.

He found the south basement undetected, but the door was locked. He didn't have the key for it—this was private property and not in any way related to the tunnel system. He had no access, no right to be here at all.

For a fleeting second, he regretted not being able to pick locks. Marty from the circus had tried to teach him, but he had never been able to get the hang of it. A shame Marty wasn't here right now. The lock didn't look complicated, and Marty would probably have opened it in a couple of minutes.

Joe peered through the dusty window set into the door. Inside the room various unidentifiable lumps looked like furniture covered with dusty sheets. A row of steel columns ran along the side. It looked as if no one had been in here in years.

What was he supposed to do now? Even if he could get inside, it didn't seem likely that anything Nikola Tesla had left could still be around. Hundreds of people had probably tramped through this room, emptying it and filling it over the seventy years (slate, black) since Nikola Tesla's death.

Joe pulled his phone out of its Faraday pouch and checked his GPS app.

40 45 10 73 59 38

He was in the right spot, and he was in front of the southernmost basement. He slipped his phone back into its pouch.

Nothing else for it—he had to get inside to look. He glanced up and down the empty hallway to be sure he and Edison were alone. He thought he saw a flash of movement behind them. He stared down the tunnel for several tense breaths, but nothing moved. It must have been a trick of the light.

"Back," he told Edison. The dog moved back a few steps. "Farther."

Edison gave him a dubious look, but he backed off. Whatever Joe was up to, he didn't approve. Well, neither did Joe, but he didn't see a way around it.

He broke the window with the butt of his flashlight. He carefully knocked the glass out of the frame, then reached his hand through the opening and unlocked the door from the inside. The bottom of the door scraped across broken glass as it opened.

"Stay," he told Edison.

He swept the larger pieces of glass off to the side with his shoe, then took a dusty sheet off a nearby wardrobe. He folded the sheet into fourths and laid it on top of the smaller glass shards. That should keep Edison from cutting his paws. He swung the light back and forth, checking for pieces of glass on the floor. Not satisfied, he reached over and flicked the light switch.

Bluish fluorescent light flooded the room. A high-pitched whining accompanied it. Not everyone could hear faulty fluorescent light bulbs, but he could. Not really a good thing.

In the bright light, it was clear that he'd covered up all the glass.

"All right, boy," he called. "But watch your step."

Edison walked gingerly, as if he had understood Joe's words. They were so attuned that he never really knew whether the dog recognized his commands or read his body language.

Joe wandered between wardrobes, desks, and tables. The furniture had been lined up in rows. The pieces had probably been expensive once, but when he looked under the covers, he saw burn marks, water stains, and missing legs. One table held a dusty wooden tool caddy. The furniture had probably been sent down here to be repaired long ago, but no one had ever gotten around to it.

Had these pieces been down here since Nikola Tesla's time? No way of knowing. Based on the style, it could have come from his era, but it was unlikely the inventor would have hidden anything in it. Furniture could be moved or sold at any time. Even if Nikola had assumed his pigeon keeper would build the little man and understand his clues, he had to have known it might take time, perhaps years.

So, that left the floors, walls, and ceiling. He traced the cobwebbed rafters, looked down at the concrete floor, and over at the dirty gray walls. A lot to search.

He also had the number three (red) to contend with. The automaton had written a three (red) after the words *south basement*. He still didn't know what the three meant.

He shimmied between furniture as he slowly paced the length of the room, shining his light on the dusty floor. Everywhere he looked was solid concrete. Nikola Tesla would have had to cut a hole in it with a saw—not easy to do undetected and hard to hide after.

Edison sneezed.

"Sorry about all the dust," Joe said.

He looked up. Nikola could have tucked something up in the steel beams that ran the length of the ceiling, but that was always risky—the ceiling might be enclosed one day, a lot of them were. If so, the object might have been found in the construction process. Still, he filed the ceiling away as a possible hiding place, but he couldn't look there now without a ladder. That left the walls.

The number three (red) flashed through his head. It wouldn't have been easy to design the automaton to write. Every stroke required gears and actuators to turn exactly so. Nikola Tesla had given him a location in New York (the New Yorker Hotel), the room in the hotel (south basement), and the number three (red). Each designation was more precise than the last. That number had to mean something, and it probably meant something specific in the context of this particular room.

Nikola Tesla had been obsessed with the number three (red). In Joe's research, he had discovered that Nikola often walked around a block three times before entering a building, that he ate his meals in a number of bites divisible by three, that he had to have eighteen (cyan, purple—an ugly color combination) napkins, and that he liked to stay in rooms divisible by three. At the New Yorker Hotel his room was on the thirty-third floor (red, red) and the room number was twenty-seven (blue, slate): both divisible by three (red).

Nikola Tesla hadn't chosen the first numbers the automaton had written—they were the location of the hotel. But the last number might have been his to choose.

Joe turned in a very slow circle, counting things. Colors flashed through his head. His eyes stopped on the metal columns near the wall. Those were load-bearing. No one would ever remove them, not while the building was standing. They were the perfect place to hide something.

He counted forward from the door to the third column, then hurried through the stacks of furniture to reach it. Excitement bubbled in him, and he laughed. The sound was loud in the empty room, and he stopped immediately. He was supposed to be in stealth mode, but he still couldn't suppress his excitement. If he found whatever might be hidden here, he would have solved a decades-old puzzle built by one of the most famous scientists and inventors in the world.

The third column didn't seem to have any secrets. Looking for something attached to it or near it, he pored over every inch of its surface, from the point where it sprouted out of the dusty floor to the point where it disappeared into the cobwebbed ceiling. Nothing.

He counted columns from the back of the room and went to the third one. If that didn't work, he was going to have to rethink his strategy. He started at the top and slowly worked his way down the steel, examining every fleck of peeling paint, every rivet. Maybe there was nothing there.

Joe had no particular reason to think that Nikola Tesla had hidden anything here at all. Except that his father had told him the automaton would lead him somewhere, and someone else seemed to think those papers held secrets that he had yet to uncover.

His gaze stopped at the base of the column. A second piece of steel had been welded to it. The steel column was an I shape, and someone had welded a box in the corner facing away from the door. The object was painted the same color as the other steel—an industrial gray—and it would have been easy to overlook. His heart beat faster as he stared at it.

He hurried back to fetch the old toolbox, then stood in front of the beam. These weren't a carpenter's tools—they were for fixing furniture. He unpacked the tools, setting each carefully on the concrete floor: a plane, a chisel, a sharpening stone, a pocket square, a file, and a small hammer. He left tiny nails, a metal container of brown stain, and a stained cloth in the box.

None of the items were that useful. Maybe he should get an acetylene torch and come back. He had one at his house.

But what if someone noticed the broken window by then and boarded it up or brought down additional security? He might never get back into this room.

With a sigh, he bent over the object. When his father had returned the device here, he hadn't welded it quite flush on one corner. Joe thought he could work the file into the edge and file off the old solder. Once he got through a few of the soldered spots, he could maybe use the file like a lever and pry the device loose. Maybe.

Good enough for him.

"Edison." He pointed to a spot a few feet away, far enough that the dog wouldn't get any metal dust in his eyes. "Lay down over there."

Edison walked over and lay down with his head on his front paws, watching.

"Good boy." He pitched the dog a treat.

He went back to the column and knelt next to it. The concrete was hard and cold under his knees, and that would get worse the longer he was here. Wishing it weren't so loud, he began to file. Black dust and the occasional spark fell to the floor. He settled into a rhythm.

Soon he would get this box free, and he would know what had scared his father.

30

Quantum stood in front of the New Yorker Hotel, a forty-story monument to Art Deco. It took up half a block. The place probably had over a thousand guest rooms, plus lobby, conference rooms, and who knew what else. Impressive.

The giant lobby was decorated with fashionable people, a lot of gold, and an Art Deco chandelier big enough to be buried in. But no Joe Tesla. Not that he'd expected to find him here. This place had probably gone through a lot of remodeling since Nikola Tesla's day. Not a good place to hide anything long term.

He plunked himself into a yellow leather chair as if he belonged at the hotel, took out his secure phone, and went to the chat room to see if Ash had more suggestions. Careful not to type in anything that might get him in trouble later, he sent a message from the burner phone he used to communicate with Ash: *@ hotel lobby. directions?*

He did the math in his head while he waited for a reply. The hotel must have about a million square feet. He researched the place on the burner phone while he waited to hear from Ash. The hotel had a strong Tesla connection—Nikola Tesla had died in this hotel seventy-one years before. Seemed like his old room would be a good place to start. Maybe he'd hidden something in the walls or the floor. But Quantum would never find it if he had to search all million square feet.

He checked the chat room before standing up to go see if Nikola had made it easy for everyone and left it in his room.

ash: start in south basement. GO!

The basement made sense, since Joe couldn't go outside, but how did Ash know he was in the south one? He must be tracking Joe's phone. Quantum was glad he was using a burner. He didn't want Ash tracking him.

ash: GO!

Quantum's temper flared at the command in those capital letters. Nobody told him what to do. Nobody. But he tamped down his irritation. He needed to get the device, get the Bitcoins, and get the hell out of Dodge. In that order.

He walked over to the elevators and pressed B. Nobody questioned his actions. It seemed too easy. The elevator stopped with a bump, and the doors opened onto the basement level.

No money was spent on the décor down here. The walls were a dingy white, and the smell of laundry hung in moist air. The faraway thump of dryers reminded him of childhood trips to the Laundromat.

"Hey!" An overweight guy in a security guard outfit waddled up. "Guests aren't allowed down here."

Guess he wasn't going to get lucky after all. He'd have to deal with—Quantum checked the man's name badge—Mr. Francis Ferguson personally, which probably wouldn't be that hard.

"I'm not a guest." Quantum plastered an irritated look on his face, the kind every IT employee perpetually wore. "My name is Mathison Turing."

Francis looked him over suspiciously.

Quantum glared back. He looked nerdy enough to pass as an IT consultant, and Mathison Turing was the best nerd name ever—having belonged to early computer genius Alan Mathison Turing, the guy who had practically invented modern computer science. "I'm here to fix the Wi-Fi. Someone in Reception called us."

The guard's eye twitched when Quantum said *Reception*. Apparently, that was a sore subject.

"The Wi-Fi is upstairs." Francis put one pudgy hand on a nightstick. He didn't rate a gun, which was a good thing.

"I know where the hub is, thank you." Quantum sped up his voice and injected some peevishness. "I've fixed it up there, for now, but this is a chronic problem. It keeps going out. Or haven't you heard?"

The guy nodded uncertainly. He knew he probably should have heard, and Wi-Fi went out everywhere all the time.

"I need to go down to the south basement and see where the fiber optics come into the building." Quantum had no idea if the hotel used fiber optics, but he was willing to bet this guy didn't either. "Can you give me directions?"

The security guard looked toward the noisy dryers as if they could tell him what to do.

"Or I can keep bumbling around on my own. I don't care. I'm paid by the hour." Quantum smiled. "I know your hotel is already mad about the size of the bill. What was your name again? I'll need to log it."

Francis sighed. "Give me your card. I'll check."

Quantum handed him a business card for Mathison Turing, IT consultant. The number on the card rang through to a complicated faux-voicemail system designed to keep the caller on hold until he gave up. He'd used it a bunch of times to mess with people.

The security guard dialed the number on the card and got the first voicemail prompt. He said his name, his telephone number, and the number seven, which was the code for *other inquiry*. He'd be at it for a while.

Quantum pointed to his wrist, where he'd have a watch if he wore a watch, then he rubbed his fingers and thumb together in the universal gesture for money. Time is money, asshole, he thought. Francis held up a hand to tell him to wait.

But he couldn't wait. Joe Tesla wasn't likely to stick around for long. Ash wouldn't tolerate another failure, he was sure of it.

The guard entered another number and brought the phone to his ear.

Quantum rolled his eyes and whispered, "What if we call Reception instead? I'm sure they can verify my status, and then you can help me on my way."

The man groaned. Quantum speaking had caused him to miss the voice mail prompt. He'd have to go back a step. Or maybe two. He pressed seven again.

"So," Quantum said in a slightly louder voice, "maybe call Reception?"

Francis clearly didn't want to do that. With another sigh, he pointed behind him, made a walking motion with his hands, and mouthed the word *stairs*.

Quantum set off in the indicated direction. He'd better hurry. Eventually the guy might give up on the voice mail system and come after him. All that time messing with the phone probably wouldn't improve his disposition.

Once he found the stairwell, he put on a pair of latex gloves before opening the door. He didn't want to leave any fingerprints.

He headed downstairs as fast as he dared in the flickering light of a fluorescent tube. The stairwell was painted battleship gray. It had dents in the walls and large slivers of dusty wood on the steps. It looked like someone had tried to ride a wooden crate down the steps—smashing walls and losing bits along the way.

At the bottom he had to throw himself at the door a couple of times to get it open. He wedged a sliver of wood in the doorframe to keep the door from closing all the way. He didn't want to get stuck down here. He might be lost until someone chanced upon his mummified corpse.

He hit the corridor and started a quick jog. He had to find Joe and take the device from him before the security guard came looking. No time for finesse on this one. Brute force would have to do the trick. That was OK. Sometimes he liked brute force.

He ran along quietly, listening. The corridor was deserted and had been for a long time. Guests weren't the only ones who didn't come down here.

A rasping sound reached his ears, and he slowed. Light spilled out from a door halfway down the corridor.

Cautiously, he approached. The dusty floor showed footprints coming from the opposite direction. A man and a dog.

The window had been broken out, most likely by Joe, and the door was ajar. Quantum twisted sideways and went through the door without touching anything. Covered pieces of furniture surrounded him like military ghosts at attention.

He crept forward. Joe was making enough noise that he could get close to him undetected.

It sounded as if the man had a hacksaw and was cutting through metal with a lot of noise and elbow grease. That had to mean he'd found the Oscillator.

The words pounded in his head as he slipped behind a wardrobe and peeked through a line of furniture toward the corner of the room. Joe was hunched around a steel column. His right arm was jerking forward and backward in time with the awful rasping noise.

Quantum considered his options. Best plan was to take out the dog first, the man second. He had bullets enough for both, but he didn't want to spook either one until the last second.

A flash of yellow legs showed under a squat wardrobe. The dog was heading toward him. That made the decision easy. He touched the hilt of his gun, but pulled out the Taser instead. If he played his cards right, he could take the dog out without Joe even noticing it over the sound of the sawing.

The dog walked around the corner. Its nose was raised as it sniffed. It didn't seem to sense any danger, and it was trained to help, not to attack. The dog wagged its tail and took a tentative step forward.

"Good dog," he said in a low voice that wouldn't be heard by Joe over the sound of his sawing.

The dog heard his words. It moved forward another step.

He tasered the dog. The dog went right down and lay on the ground, twitching and foaming at the mouth. That had been easier than he'd imagined.

Careful to stay away from its head, he scooped up the warm body and stuffed it into an empty wardrobe, then eased the doors closed. He turned the tiny key in the lock. The dog wouldn't be bothering him again. He hoped that someone would find it before it starved, but that wasn't his problem. His problem was in the back of the room, all alone, deaf to what had just happened because he was sawing away.

The rasping noise finally stopped, and a metal object clattered to the ground.

"I got it out, Edison!" Joe called, jubilant.

The dog whimpered. A quiet sound, and Quantum didn't see how it could carry across the room, but it did.

The man jumped to his feet. "You OK, boy?"

Quantum stuck the Taser in his pocket and pulled out the gun. He had to kill Tesla, then take the device. There was no other way.

He slipped behind the wardrobe next to the one that held the dog.

Rapid footsteps came closer. "Edison?"

The dog whimpered again, a faint sound of pain and despair.

Joe blundered past a desk and stood in front of Quantum's wardrobe, confused.

Quantum shouldered the wardrobe out into the aisle, tipping it forward onto the hapless man. Joe fell backward and struck his head against a desk on his way down. The crack reverberated around the room. The dog yipped.

Quantum walked to the end of the wardrobe with his gun out and ready to fire.

Joe Tesla lay flat on his back. The wardrobe had landed across his chest, pinning him. Not that it mattered. Blood poured out of a wound on the side of his skull, and Quantum could see that his eyes were closed.

He wouldn't have to shoot him after all. Joe, assuming he lived, wouldn't be able to identify him later. Best to just leave him there.

The dog seemed to have recovered and set to barking. He doubted that anyone would hear it. If the dust on the floor was any indication, nobody but he and Joe had come this way in months.

Still, he hurried across the room to where Joe had been working. There, on the floor next to the column, was a metal object that looked like a metal platform with a candlestick stuck to the top. He recognized it from pictures online: Tesla's Oscillator.

He scooped it up and left the man and dog to die.

To make sure that they wouldn't be found any time soon, he turned off the light and closed the door behind him.

31

Francis gave up on the damn voice mail system. He was going to have to track the guy down and drag him upstairs even if it made him look like a fool and cost the company money. Plus, he'd have to deal with the guy's snotty attitude. Mathison? What a name!

He hurried down the gray stairs to the sub-basement. The sooner he got this over, the sooner he could go on break. He wanted to call the bakery about the cake he'd ordered to celebrate his first six months on the job. He was officially out of the probationary period and was starting to save money for his own place. Things were looking up.

He flicked on the overhead fluorescents as soon as he stepped into the hall. This level gave him the creeps, and he was glad that he didn't have to come down here often. Nothing worth guarding.

A yellow dog slammed out of a door at the end of the corridor, and Francis jumped. The dog streaked toward him, barking. He turned toward the door, but the dog passed him and pushed him back a step.

Francis put his hand on the butt of his nightstick, but he didn't want to hurt the dog. What the hell was it doing down here anyway?

"Easy, boy!" he called out, wondering if it was a boy. "Good dog!"

The dog stopped barking and stared up at him. It bumped him with its nose and looked back the way it had come. It whined and took a few steps down the hall.

The IT guy hadn't had a dog with him, so where had this pooch come from, and what did it want?

The dog whined again and bumped his hand, leaving a sticky trail. Francis pulled his hand away, prepared to wipe off dog spit, then stopped. The dog hadn't drooled on him. Its muzzle was stained with blood.

He knelt next to the dog. Only now did he realize how upset the animal was. It was shaking like a leaf, and its eyes were practically popping out of its head. Gently, he felt the dog's head, body, and legs. The dog didn't shy away or yelp. It wasn't wounded.

Which meant that the blood was from someone else.

He pulled out his nightstick. He wished he'd been issued a gun, but he wasn't allowed to carry one. The hotel felt that armed security guards spooked the guests. Well, the guests weren't half as spooked as he was right now.

The dog licked his hand, then grabbed the end of his sleeve between its teeth and tugged, dragging him a step down the hall.

"Easy now," he said softly. "I'll come with you."

First, he called it in, reporting his location and a dog covered in blood that wasn't his own. Anderson, the prick, treated it as a joke, but said he'd be right down. With Anderson, that meant any time in the next hour or so.

He wanted to wait right here for Anderson, even if it took an hour, but he looked again at the blood on the dog's fur. It was still wet. Someone or something was hurt down here, and they might be dying. Maybe it was the IT guy.

Maybe he cut himself. Even a snot like Mathison deserved to have someone look for him.

He took a deep breath and followed the dog. Nobody was dying on his watch. He strained his ears, but couldn't hear a single sound. Not good.

The dog led him down a hall to another one, then stopped in front of a closed door with a broken window. He looked into the dark room. Various sheet-draped shapes stood in straight lines. He didn't see anyone inside, but someone had to have broken out the window. The IT guy wouldn't have done that. The dog probably couldn't have, not without cutting itself. Sweat trickled down his back. He thought about calling Anderson again, but didn't want to be mocked if it turned out to be nothing.

As if it knew that he wasn't going to open the door on his own, the dog took the doorknob in his mouth and turned it, which was a pretty neat trick. It must have special training. The dog pushed the door open and held it. It whined deep in its throat. It clearly wanted him to go into the room.

He wasn't sure whether he should do what the dog wanted, but he'd come this far. He stepped through the door, searching for movement and holding on to his nightstick. Broken glass crunched under his feet, although someone had put down a sheet to cover it up.

As soon as he was in the room, the dog let go of the doorknob. It made a beeline straight for the center of the room, barking.

Francis flicked on the lights. He kept his weapon up and cautiously followed, ready to dive behind the long rows of furniture if he saw any sign of danger. Not that there could be any danger in this basement. The only one who'd come past him to go down here was the IT guy, and he was a skinny little runt. The dog, he reminded himself. How did the dog get down here?

The dog had reached the center of the room and was putting up quite a racket, barking and whining. Anyone in here had to know something was up. But nothing else moved.

When he reached the dog, he saw why. A man lay on the floor, pinned under a heavy wooden wardrobe. His eyes were closed, and his head rested in a pool of blood. The wardrobe had fallen on him, and he must have cracked his head on the bloody edge of the desk when he went down. None of which explained what he was doing here in the first place.

Francis took a panicked look around the room. Empty. If someone else had been here, like that IT guy, they were gone now.

He knelt next to the man, careful not to touch the blood. The dog had stepped in it and left bloody paw prints all around, and he stayed away from those, too.

A wardrobe next to the one that had fallen gaped open. One of the doors had been knocked off its hinges. Long scratches in the wood told him that the dog had done it. Had someone stuffed the dog in the wardrobe, then dropped a second wardrobe on its master?

The dog whined and looked at the man on the floor. It clearly expected Francis to do something.

He touched the man's neck, searching for a pulse. A thready and irregular beat pushed against his fingertips. It felt as if it could stop at any time. But at least the guy was alive.

"Can you hear me?" Francis said. He didn't expect an answer, and he didn't get one.

He put both hands under the wardrobe and lifted with his legs. He got it up off the guy and back onto its four legs. That should at least make it easier for the man to breathe.

He pulled out his phone and called 911. He gave specific directions to the hotel, the basement, and the victim. He even had the operator repeat it all back.

Then he called Anderson and told him to get down here right away, and see if he could bring a doctor with him.

He looked at the man on the floor in front of him. Francis was no doctor, but he could tell this guy was badly hurt, maybe dying. The dog knew it, too. It had lain down next to its master's body as if to keep him warm, and it kept licking his cheek and whining.

He tried to remember what the teacher had said in first-aid class. For a head injury, keep the victim still. Not a problem. This guy wasn't moving. Don't move them because they might have a broken neck. OK, he wasn't going to move him either. Apply pressure to stop bleeding unless you think they might have a skull fracture. He couldn't tell, but the guy might. Best not to touch him. So he settled for taking off his shirt and spreading it over the guy to keep him warm. He thought about using one of the sheets, but they looked filthy. He felt stupid standing around in his T-shirt, and he wished he could remember more treatment options for a head injury, but that was all he could come up with.

"Sorry, doggie," he said. "There's nothing else I can do."

The dog looked over at him. Its brown eyes were wide with panic. He petted its head a couple of times. "Help is coming, doggie. Your buddy will be fine."

Francis didn't believe it.

32

Vivian waited outside the entrance to the emergency room at Lenox Hospital. Dirk had recognized Joe Tesla's name on the radio and had called her. She'd made it to the hospital before the ambulance, a tribute to the vagaries of Manhattan traffic.

She had brought Tatiana Tesla with her, of course. The woman stood right beside her, looking pale but composed. Hollingberry was next to her, holding her hand. Dirk was there, too, since he'd been on bodyguard duty when she'd called. He and Vivian were both scanning the area, looking for threats.

It would have been a lot easier if they could have persuaded Mrs. Tesla to go inside, but she wanted to see Tesla when the ambulance brought him in. Vivian couldn't blame her for that. It might be the last time she saw her son alive.

"My doing," Mrs. Tesla said. Red lipstick stood out against her pale face, making the usually sophisticated woman look like a clown.

"You couldn't have known." Hollingberry moved as if to take her into his arms, but she sidestepped the gesture, her eyes fixed on the busy street, searching for the ambulance.

"I might as well have given him a bomb." She pressed her lips together. Vivian made a mental note to follow up on that comment later.

Hollingberry murmured something that sounded reassuring, but Vivian couldn't quite make it out. Whatever it was, it didn't have any effect on Mrs. Tesla. Simple words weren't going to reassure her. Her son had been cracked on the head hard enough to have been knocked unconscious, and that was all they knew.

Vivian felt she should have kept better track of him. Her warning hadn't been enough. He'd gone wandering off alone in the tunnels. Apparently, his worry about his mother's well-being didn't extend to himself.

An ambulance braked in front of them and switched off the siren. It was the second one they'd seen since they arrived. The first had had no siren and carried an old man who'd looked dead.

Mrs. Tesla moved forward a step.

The ambulance doors slammed open. Someone lay flat on a stretcher, but she couldn't tell if it was Tesla. At the head of the stretcher was Edison. So, the man inside must be Tesla.

It was a good sign that they'd come in with the siren on. Didn't they turn the siren off if the patient died?

A man and a woman in EMT uniforms slid the stretcher out, unfolded its wheels, and pushed it toward the door.

Tesla's eyes were closed, and he was completely unconscious, which was probably a good thing. Otherwise, he'd have panicked about being outside. A blood-soaked bandage covered his head, he was strapped to a backboard, and an IV ran into his arm. He looked dead.

Mrs. Tesla was already moving toward the gurney. "My son."

"You'll have to move to the waiting area, ma'am." The EMTs didn't even look at her as they rushed forward.

"Is he alive?" Mrs. Tesla's words boomed out toward them. She had the practiced rich voice of someone used to working onstage.

"He came to in the ambulance, answered some questions." The man by Tesla's feet gave her a quick smile. "They'll do the best they can with him inside."

The dog jumped out of the back of the ambulance and started after them. He held something metal in his mouth that jangled when he walked.

"Edison!" Vivian called, and he stopped.

The two EMTs whooshed through the doors and disappeared inside. She gestured to Dirk, and he followed them. His police badge would let him stay closer to Tesla in the hospital than she could. He couldn't go into the operating room, but he could stand outside in the hall.

The dog looked between her and the disappearing gurney, a question in his eyes.

"You can't go in there," she told him. "Heel."

The dog trotted over and put his head against her leg. Dried blood was caked on his muzzle, his paws, and his chest. His master's blood. She positioned herself between the animal and Mrs. Tesla. Tesla's mother didn't need to see that.

She leaned down and took the object from his mouth. It was a giant key ring full of dozens of keys. She'd seen it before and knew that Tesla considered it irreplaceable. He used it to get through various locked doors underground. He'd probably used one of the keys to get into the basement of the hotel where he'd been attacked. She clipped it to her belt. "Good boy."

Mrs. Tesla hadn't moved from her station by the door, although she had sagged against Hollingberry. She looked as if she'd aged years in the minute since she'd seen her son go by.

The two EMTs came out the door and jumped into their ambulance before Vivian could corner them with her questions.

She called Andres Peterson, Tesla's dog walker, and arranged for him to come get the dog and keep him until further notice, then walked over to Mrs. Tesla. Edison stayed close.

"Would you like to go inside, ma'am?"

Mrs. Tesla's dark eyes met hers, and for an instant Vivian saw the fear there, but the woman blinked, and the expression was gone.

"Can we bring the dog in?" Hollingberry asked.

"He's wearing a service vest. They can't keep him out," Vivian answered.

"Why didn't he save my son?" she asked. "There's not a mark on the dog."

Vivian swallowed and told her all that Dirk had been able to find out. "My understanding is that the dog was shut inside of a wardrobe, knocked the door off the hinges, and went for help. He probably saved Mr. Tesla's life."

Mrs. Tesla crumpled to her knees and wrapped her hands around Edison. The dog was usually standoffish when he was in his vest, but right now he seemed to need Mrs. Tesla as much as she did him. He leaned into her embrace, then licked the tears off her cheeks.

Vivian looked away, not wanting to intrude on a private moment.

33

Ash ground his teeth in frustration. After sending his last enigmatic text, Quantum had gone offline. He'd ditched his phone, and he wasn't in any of his favorite online hangouts. Ash had sent men to his house and work, but Quantum wouldn't be as easy to find as Geezer had been. Meanwhile, Joe Tesla had been badly wounded, and Ash still didn't know where or what the device was. Quantum had said it was the Oscillator and that he had it in hand, but who knew how trustworthy he was?

So, here he was in the back of his limo on his way to the hospital to pretend he cared about Joe Tesla. If the wounded man was still alive, he might be able to give clues about what he'd found. Ash fiddled with his secure phone, hoping to find traces of Quantum, but the clever man stayed hidden. Instead, he verified that news of Joe's accident had been posted on the Internet, so he could say that's where he'd found it out. He found an article on the *New York Post's* website: *Multimillionaire Brained in Hotel Where Ancestor Died*. If Joe ever read it, he'd be angry at being mentioned next to Nikola Tesla, and he wouldn't like the use of the word *brained* either. Delightful.

"Shall I circle the block, sir?" His limo driver had parked and opened the door before Ash even noticed.

"I'll text you when I need you." He was out of the car and halfway across the sidewalk before he heard the door close.

It didn't take long to find Joe's room in a long corridor. Two people stood guard outside—a man and a woman, both around six feet tall. No chairs for them. They stood practically at attention. Retired military.

He approached them casually, like a man who didn't expect trouble.

"I'm sorry, sir, but you can't go beyond this point." The Amazon had a gun visible under her jacket, and she stood like someone who knew how to use it.

"It's OK," Ash said. "I'm a close friend of Mr. Tesla."

"You have my sympathy, sir, but you're not going through that door." She took his arm, and he tried to shake her off, but she wouldn't let go.

The man who'd been stationed on the other side of the door looked over at them as if ready to intervene to help her out, maybe tear Ash's head off if necessary. He wouldn't be bullying his way into the room. New tactics were called for.

"Let's start over." Ash held out his hand. "Mr. Alan Wright. You may have heard of me."

The woman did not shake his hand. "Vivian Torres. If you're lucky, you haven't heard of me either."

Ash was irritated. He was well known in New York and one of the richest men in the world. "I've known Mr. Tesla for many years, and I'd like to see how he's doing."

"I understand that, sir." She planted herself between him and the door and forced him back a step. "But only family is allowed in at this time."

He thought of making a scene, but his efforts might be better spent looking into this Vivian Torres, seeing what leverage over her he could find online. Fighting a long game instead of a skirmish here. "Is he going to be OK? Is he conscious?"

"I'm afraid I can't answer those questions, Mr. Wright."

"Is Edison all right?"

Her expression thawed by half a degree. Nobody could resist a man who cared about dogs. "The dog is fine. And I'll inform Mr. Tesla of your visit when he wakes up."

So, Joe hadn't regained consciousness yet. A good sign.

He tried to imagine Joe Tesla without the use of his magnificent brain and felt no pity. He'd had his chance, and he'd squandered it. He could have done great things.

Maybe he still could, but given the worry on Ms. Torres's face, that was no longer a certainty.

34

Vivian looked through the glass at Tesla in his bed. He'd been tested, admitted, and brought to this private room hours before. His mother sat in the room's only chair. Hollingberry had pulled it up next to the bed and fussed over her for a while, but had recently left to get everyone coffee. Mrs. Tesla held Joe's hand, her eyes never leaving his face.

He looked terrible. He was always pale, but now his skin looked as translucent as a vampire's. Even his lips were pale. A bandage on the back of his head covered where they'd stitched up his scalp. After running him through a CT scan, they'd announced that he had no skull fracture, but he did have traumatic brain injury. He would recover, but it would take time and rest.

He'd woken up a few times, asking about Edison and talking about Nikola Tesla. Vivian had looked the name up on her phone and found out that the guy had been dead since before the end of World War II. That couldn't be a good sign.

She wondered how he'd react to being out of his familiar surroundings when he woke up all the way. She'd seen him have a panic attack before, in the middle of the day in a familiar situation. In a place he'd never been and with a head injury, well, she didn't like to think about what might happen.

Tesla's eyes opened again, and his mother spoke to him. He answered, and she pressed the button behind his head to summon a nurse.

"I'm going in," Vivian told Dirk. She handed him the piece of paper that listed the doctors and nurses who were authorized to go into Tesla's room. "He's awake again. Maybe this time he'll be conscious enough to tell us who hit him."

"It's not so bad," Dirk said. "You can stop kicking your own ass, Viv."

She hadn't said a single word to indicate how guilty she felt, but Dirk knew her well. Tesla had been injured on her watch.

"I might just kick *his* ass," she said. "For getting himself into trouble."

Dirk gave her a smile, flashing his trademark dimple, and she had to smile back before going into the hospital room.

Mrs. Tesla looked at Vivian. "He wants to know about Edison again."

"Edison is with Andres Peterson, and he's completely fine, Mr. Tesla. Not a mark on him." She'd told him that three times already.

Tesla looked toward the curtained window. Vivian had drawn the curtains as soon as the doctors had left, not wanting him to see the sky outside when he woke up and panic. He had enough to worry about without that.

His gaze drifted around as he took in the room. "Where am I?"

"Hospital." His mother patted his arm. "You're safe."

Tesla's eyes met Vivian's. "How can I get home?"

Before she could say anything, a quick rap on the door announced a visitor. She tensed.

"I cleared him," called Dirk from the door.

That meant that his name was on the list, and he'd been patted down for weapons, but she didn't relax.

"Dr. Nigel Winterbottom." A pudgy white guy in a lab coat stepped into the room. "I've been assigned Mr. Tesla's case."

"What's your specialty?" Vivian had memorized the names and specialties of all of Tesla's doctors and nurses.

Winterbottom glared at her in the condescending way of every doctor she'd met. "Neurologist. I'm here to examine my patient."

She stepped away from him. She knew Winterbottom was the neurologist's name, and he was definitely behaving like a doctor.

The doctor strode across the room toward the bed, but at the last second he pivoted and pulled open the curtains.

Tesla leaped out of the bed as if the light scalded him. He listed to the side and fell to his knees behind the bed. He yanked out his IV. Blood spattered across the back of his hand.

He lunged toward the door. His blue eyes were huge and panicked—nobody home. The smartest man she'd ever met, and there was no trace of intelligence in those eyes. Just terror.

35

Quantum studied the elevated train tracks. He was at Tenth Avenue and Thirtieth Street. The tracks above him hadn't been used for years, and they were due to be opened as another part of the elevated High Line park next year, but for now they were empty.

Behind him trains rattled along the tracks at the West Side Yard, and in front of him the traffic on Thirtieth Street roared by. He'd picked this busy location because nobody would notice him standing around with his hand in his pocket. He'd scouted the area, and he'd seen no surveillance cameras that spied on this particular spot. He was invisible, a rare thing in the city these days.

He'd sell the device to Ash soon, but first he wanted to know what price to set. If the device worked, and he could prove it, then the $100K on offer was too low. If it didn't, he could collect his Bitcoins and leave Ash holding a hundred-year-old hoax. He smiled. It couldn't happen to a nicer guy than Ash.

For a test subject, he wanted something that was big and dramatic enough to show to Ash later, but not something that would cause a huge loss of life. That would attract too much attention. This unopened part of the High Line park was a perfect testing ground.

Steel support columns soared up from ground level to the tracks above. They'd been built in the 1930s and abandoned in the 1980s. After their closure, people had tried to get the tracks torn down. That hadn't worked. A grassroots movement had worked to have the elevated tracks converted into a park. A lot of money had been spent, the park was named High Line, and now people wandered around up there enjoying nature. This particular set of tracks hadn't been opened to the public yet. Nobody was up there. They were waiting for the grass to grow or something.

He patted the riveted steel affectionately. It had stood for a long time, and the time had come to see if he could bring it down. From his backpack he took wooden clamps and attached the base of the device to the steel beam. He'd chosen wood since it would resonate at a different frequency than the steel.

Before he turned the device on, he paused. If the statements that Tesla gave when he was an old man were true, then when the Oscillator hit the right frequency for long enough the steel column would shatter like a wine glass next to an opera singer. Others had tried to build the device from the description in Tesla's early patent, but it had never worked. Maybe he'd sabotaged the patent on purpose, and this device would work.

With a shrug, he turned the device on and started to tune it. He'd looked up the resonant frequency of steel, and he dialed it in now. A few minutes later, the steel shivered the tiniest bit, as if cold.

A quick glance around assured him that no one cared what he was up to. He loved the self-absorption of New Yorkers, and he was going to miss them when he left. Maybe he could come back in a couple of years.

He sat with his back against the beam and went online. He'd bought a new burner phone after he'd ditched the last one. He logged into the darknet and cycled through the chat rooms Spooky used. Geezer, who usually visited often, hadn't been around since yesterday. Did he suspect that Ash or Quantum might have recovered the device? It seemed to mean a lot to him, although Quantum wasn't sure why. Geezer wasn't the type to knock things down—he liked to lecture people on the error of their ways like some fusty professor.

Geezer hadn't been around, but Ash had. He'd left coded messages for Quantum. He wanted him to turn over the device as per their agreement. He didn't seem upset by Joe's injuries. The guy hadn't died, yet, although he was "in serious condition" according to various online news sources. Quantum hoped he pulled through. There'd be less fuss.

A train pulled into the train yard next door, but he didn't pay it any mind. Best way to remain invisible in New York was to mind your own business, especially by staring at the screen of a phone. Everyone was a phone zombie these days.

The steel behind him quivered. He pressed his back harder against it. He felt a quick pulse through his T-shirt. The steel had come alive.

This was as far as *MythBusters* had gotten. When they built their own Oscillator and hooked it up to a bridge, the steel vibrated, but nothing else happened. Or at least that's what they said on the show. If it had started to affect the bridge's structure, he bet they would have covered that up. Not a good idea to broadcast how to knock down bridges.

He had to figure out a way to get the Bitcoins before he dropped off the device. He didn't trust Ash. He'd wanted to believe in him as a crusader for the environment and freedom, but after Ash had threatened to expose his identity, he had no choice but to view him as a crook on a power trip. Or maybe a powerful guy on a power trip. Dangerous either way.

The steel behind him shivered more violently now. That hadn't happened on *MythBusters*.

He stood and stared up at the structure above. The tracks themselves seemed to shiver, as if they, too, were affected by the oscillation in this one beam. He touched the device, trying to decide whether to turn it off, and it burned his fingers.

He sucked on his fingers, trying to decide what to do. If he turned it off now, all he'd know was that the device caused low-level vibrations in steel. That wasn't particularly valuable or interesting.

An ominous crack sounded from above. He jerked his head up. Rust and dirt rained down on him. The column creaked.

His jaw dropped open. He hadn't really expected the device to work. Another crack sounded from the elevated tracks, and the pieces of rust and dirt were larger than before.

Good enough. He tried to turn the device off. The damn dial wouldn't turn. Hard to believe that the famous Nikola Tesla had built something with such an obvious flaw. He unscrewed the clamps and caught the Oscillator in his shirt before it hit the pavement. The creaking slowed as he dumped the hot device in his bag.

A siren sounded down the street, heading right toward him. He cut across the street and walked until he found a good working-class bar that smelled of beer and wood.

He ordered a shot of whiskey and drank it in one gulp. The bartender, a slight man wearing a denim shirt straight out of the seventies, held up the bottle to ask if he wanted another. He nodded, but let the second shot sit on the bar.

Sirens converged on the elevated tracks. It sounded as if they were going to exactly the spot where he had attached the device.

He swallowed the second shot of whiskey. The device in his bag was the most powerful thing he'd ever held. Nikola Tesla had been right. It could bring down the Empire State Building, or anything else.

Did he really want to give someone like Ash that power?

36

Joe had to get away from the window. Light reached across the carpet with flaming claws. They would rip him open and kill him.

Blinding pain flashed down from his head. It didn't matter. He would feel it later. Now he had to escape. He had to escape, or he would die.

He lurched across the carpet away from the light, but something caught him. A heavy bar rested against his throat. His legs collapsed under him as he fought to get away. The bar pressed in relentlessly, choking off his air. He grabbed at it. The bar felt warm under his fingers, like skin. He tore at it, but it did not move.

Darkness replaced the pain in his head. He liked darkness better than light, but he fought it anyway. He had to get away.

A screech behind him. The sunlight's claws withdrew. Safer, but not safe.

A man pinioned his arms to his sides. He tried to lunge toward him, but the bar against his neck wouldn't let him move.

He recognized a face now. The man. He'd seen him before.

"It's OK, Mr. Tesla," said a voice in his ear. "It's OK."

The voice was familiar. Even the words were familiar. A woman. He knew her.

"I don't want to choke you out, but I will." She sounded so calm and matter-of-fact.

Vivian. Vivian Torres.

"Joseph Tesla, you calm down this instant." His mother spoke behind him.

Vivian swung him around to face the voice.

His mother stood against a wall. She held the edge of a closed curtain in her hand. She looked pale and frightened, which was odd because his mother never looked frightened.

"It's Vivian Torres, Mr. Tesla," said the woman holding his throat. "I've got you, and everything is gonna be OK."

Joe relaxed. The light was gone. He trusted her.

She had him in a choke hold, but she loosened it a notch when he relaxed. He could breathe again. The black around the edges of his vision went away.

His head pounded, red and insistent, and he felt sick and faint. He'd been hurt. He was in a hospital room. It was dark now, but it hadn't been a moment ago.

A man in a white coat stood next to his mother. His mouth hung open, and his eyes were wide with surprise.

Something warm and sticky dripped down Joe's neck. Blood. He'd hurt his head, and he'd been brought to a hospital, and he was bleeding.

He tensed again. Outside. He must have gone outside to reach this place.

"Home." He tried to face the woman who was holding on to his neck, but she didn't let go. They both almost fell, but the man next to her pushed them against the wall.

"Soon," Vivian said. "I promise."

She let go of his neck and moved her hands to his shoulders as if she expected him to fall. He might. His heart galloped in panic. He had to slow it down. He had to breathe and count.

But he couldn't. His head hurt too much, and he was afraid of the window. He looked toward the window at the closed curtain.

Vivian turned him so that he faced her. Her brown eyes looked into his. She didn't look frightened. She smiled at him. She had a safe smile. "It's all going to be fine."

"Take me home." The words came out loud and fast, but that didn't scare her.

"As soon as I can." Her hands were warm against his shoulders.

"Now." He had to make her understand. "Please."

Sickness rose up inside him.

A flash of white in his peripheral vision. Someone was coming at him. Joe turned his head fast and was overwhelmed by dizziness. A man in a white coat had pulled something from his coat pocket. He broke it in two, and a piece fell onto the carpet. The cap. He'd uncapped something.

Joe stumbled toward the door again. He had to get away. His head hurt so much, he thought it might explode. The man in white kept coming. A sting in his arm. He reached a hand to his arm to feel it. But his hand wouldn't listen. His legs wouldn't listen. He threw up on the man in the white coat, pitched forward, and the world went black.

37

Vivian felt the doctor had it coming when Tesla vomited on him. The guy had opened the curtain without thinking. He clearly hadn't known about Tesla's agoraphobia, but he should have.

She couldn't blame him for the shot, though—Tesla had looked ready to bolt again. The stuff worked. Tesla went limp as a corpse, but she and Dirk caught him before he hit the ground.

Dirk took his feet, she kept his head and shoulders, and they lifted him onto the bed. She smoothed the blue blanket over him. His head lolled to the side, and she carefully straightened it. She bit back the angry words she wanted to say to the neurologist. Instead, she looked at Tesla lying there, having had to face his greatest fear in front of them.

She took Tesla's pulse. Slow and steady. He was out.

Dr. Winterbottom took off his puke-covered coat, folded it twice, then rang for a nurse.

Mrs. Tesla rounded on him. "What did you give my son?"

And where can I get some, wondered Vivian. That would come in handy in a lot of situations.

"You OK?" she asked Dirk.

"Better than that guy." He pointed to Dr. Winterbottom, who was scraping at the vomit that had gotten onto his shirt. Mrs. Tesla fired questions at him. "You?"

"I'm fine." Vivian wiped blood off the back of Tesla's hand with a tissue. The blood oozed from where he'd pulled out his IV. His head wound wasn't bleeding much. Hopefully, this whole fiasco hadn't done him any permanent damage.

Dirk went back on the door to check in the newly arrived nurse. She said something about getting another kit and left without coming into the room. Vivian supposed she was getting the needles and tubes to get Tesla hooked back up again.

Opening the curtains had been a chump move. Vivian could make sure that didn't happen again, but that wouldn't be enough to help Tesla. The neurologist was already talking about involuntary psychiatric observation, even though he looked as if he expected Mrs. Tesla to bite his head off at the suggestion. She obliged. That ought to keep him busy for a while.

Good, because Vivian didn't know how long and difficult it might be to get Tesla out of here once the headshrinkers got started on him. Tesla was a little nuts, and he'd clearly been a danger to himself when he woke up. Still, she thought he'd be better off at home.

She left them to their argument and called Mr. Rossi, Tesla's lawyer and her sometime boss. She'd called him when she first heard that Tesla was wounded and again when he was brought into this room for the night. Again, she was transferred to him right away, reminding her of how powerful the unconscious man on the bed really was.

She quietly gave him a sketch of recent events, including Tesla's desire to go home and the neurologist's suggestion of psychiatric observation. Mr. Rossi said he'd be right there, and she told him to bring a limo—not a taxi. He didn't ask why.

"How long will he be out?" Vivian asked Winterbottom, breaking into the lecture he was giving Mrs. Tesla on the dangers of mental illness and the difficult road back from agoraphobia. Clearly, he'd learned a little about Tesla's history in the past few minutes.

"A few hours, tops," Winterbottom said. "His system can metabolize—"

"Thank you, sir," she interrupted and went out to talk to Dirk. She didn't have a lot of time to follow Mr. Tesla's last order.

"I'm going to need a gurney," she told Dirk. "I'll cover the door here while you get it."

Dirk's eyebrows rose. "Last time you had that look, you got drummed out of the service."

"I'm right this time, too." She looked at her watch. "Make sure the gurney has a flat sheet on it, not just a fitted sheet on the bottom."

"Damn," he said. "Just damn."

"Mrs. Tesla," Vivian called. "Can I see you over here for a second?"

Mrs. Tesla broke off in the middle of a sentence and stalked away from Winterbottom.

"Miss Torres," she said. "Thank you for your prompt action in restraining my son."

"I didn't want him to injure himself."

"I had no idea that his agoraphobia…" She looked over her shoulder at Winterbottom and lowered her voice. "That it was so extreme."

Extreme? He hadn't gone outside in months, he'd quit his job, and he'd moved from a penthouse apartment in California to the tunnels of New York City. Those were some pretty damn extreme signs.

"He's already tried what the doctor in there was suggesting—drugs, talk therapy, hypnosis. The only thing that seems to help him is the dog and being in his house underground."

Mrs. Tesla lifted her chin. "Can we bring the dog to the hospital, for when he wakes up?"

"I'd rather not have to, ma'am."

"I beg your pardon?"

"I'd like you to take Dr. Winterbottom out of this room in a few minutes and keep him occupied for as long as you can. Can you do that?"

The nurse was back, carrying a yellow tub full of plastic-wrapped tubes. More stuff to jam into an unconscious Tesla.

Mrs. Tesla looked at her son. "Why?"

"Your son gave me an order, ma'am," Vivian said.

Mrs. Tesla cocked her head, and a small smile flashed across her face. She'd remembered what Tesla had demanded. To go home.

A few minutes later, the room was empty. The nurse had hooked Tesla back up to everything and strapped him to the bed for good measure. As tall as he was, he still looked small on the bed. Vivian hated the sight of him like that.

Winterbottom had left with Mrs. Tesla, who was leaning on his arm and asking him heartfelt questions about agoraphobia and neurology and who knew what else. Whatever she was saying, he was eating it up with a spoon. Hollingberry had come back and trailed along behind them. The coast was clear.

Dirk rapped on the doorframe and pushed an empty gurney into the room. On top of the mattress rested a flat sheet and a set of green scrubs. She hadn't asked for those, but they would come in handy.

Mr. Rossi appeared behind him. He hesitated at the sight of Tesla trussed up on the bed, then turned to Dirk and Vivian. "Good evening, Mr. Norbye, Miss Torres."

"They have surveillance cameras all over the hospital." Vivian put the folded sheet and scrubs onto Mrs. Tesla's chair. "I want to take him out. Legally, is that OK?"

"It won't be a problem," Mr. Rossi said. "I can assure you. Mr. Tesla has the full right to leave this hospital at any time should he so desire, particularly since they haven't completed the paperwork to have him admitted against his will for psychiatric evaluation. There's no legal hazard here."

"Do you think they'll let us take him out unconscious?" Vivian asked.

"He can't consent while unconscious."

"If he wakes up, we'll never get him outside and into a car, and I'm worried he'll panic and hurt himself."

"I concur," said Mr. Rossi.

"So," she said. "How about we sneak him out the back now, and you can deal with the paperwork later."

Mr. Rossi nodded.

Dirk worked at the leather straps that restrained Tesla while she eased out the IV. "We'll need a neurologist who makes house calls."

"I have one in the car," Mr. Rossi said.

"On three," Dirk said.

They counted and lifted Tesla onto the gurney. She snapped the flat sheet out and tucked it in all around him, pulling it up over his head.

Vivian jammed pillows under Tesla's recently vacated bed, tucked them under his sheet, and ran the end of the IV line underneath. The lump in the bed wouldn't fool anyone for long, but hopefully it wouldn't have to.

She slipped the green scrubs over her clothes. "How do I look?"

Dirk pointed to her black boots. "Like a badass doctor."

She took a deep breath and started pushing the gurney toward the door. The sooner she got Joe Tesla out of the hospital, the better.

She walked as quickly as she dared along the polished linoleum corridors, her face a mask of boredom while her heart thumped hard in her chest. Mr. Rossi led the way, and Dirk brought up the rear.

Tesla shifted under the sheet, and her stomach clenched. Don't wake up, she ordered him silently. Don't wake up.

It took forever to get to the loading dock. Mr. Rossi and Dirk held the double doors open for her, and she pushed the gurney outside. The heat hit her like a wave, reminding her that she had on another set of clothes under her scrubs.

She looked around the empty loading dock. Nobody here. She hoped the neurologist was right about how long Tesla would be out. This would be the worst possible time for him to wake up.

Mr. Rossi led them to a dark corner of the lot. He, Dirk, and a red-haired man she'd never met helped her to collapse the wheels on the gurney and load it into the limo. The guy didn't introduce himself, and she didn't ask, but she guessed he was the doctor.

She stripped off her scrubs and handed them to Dirk. "Keep on Mrs. Tesla. Tesla seemed to think she was in more danger than he was, so be careful."

He tossed her a mock salute and jogged back to the hospital.

She climbed into the limo and sat in one of the two seats facing the bench. Mr. Rossi came in after, and the limo driver closed the door. The red-haired guy hunched over Tesla's unconscious form, checking his pulse and bandages.

She leaned up to the panel that separated them from the driver, then glanced at Mr. Rossi for approval. After he nodded, she rapped on the glass and it slid down an inch.

"Grand Central Terminal," she said. "But take it slow."

"Yes, ma'am," said a deep voice, and the partition rolled up.

She touched the lump of keys in her pocket. Edison was a very good dog. She could use those keys to get them into the elevator. Tesla had shown her which key to use months ago, after they'd both nearly been killed not far from where the elevator let out. She was pretty sure she'd be able to figure out which key opened the front door of his house too, but that wasn't the biggest problem.

The biggest problem was Tesla's security system. There was a console at the base of the elevator. She'd walked past it many times, and she had seen Tesla enter an eight-digit code to disarm it, but she didn't know any of the numbers.

She had no idea what would happen once they got to the bottom of the elevator and set off his alarm. Would his system call the police? Release poisonous gas? Set off a loud noise? Do nothing? With Tesla, you never knew. But whatever happened, he'd be safer down there when it went off than he would be in that hospital.

"Is he OK?" she asked the doctor.

"He's resting comfortably," he said. "But he needs to be in bed, under medical supervision."

"We're on our way," she said, then leaned back in her seat to think. Worst case, they'd have to all wait by the elevator until Tesla woke up and gave them the code.

The driver had followed her directions and was moving them along smooth and easy. The sun had started to set, and the buildings and sky glowed orange. People were walking a little more quickly now, so it must have cooled down outside.

The limo drove by a beautiful blonde in a black miniskirt and a paint-spattered black T-shirt. She looked like any other terminally cool artist. The sight of her gave Vivian the answer she needed.

Celeste.

If Tesla had told anyone his alarm code, it would be Celeste. Tesla had given her Celeste's number for emergencies, and this definitely qualified.

But Celeste was sick, and Vivian didn't want to call to tell her that Tesla had been cracked on the head, and that they'd broken him out of the hospital. She dialed anyway the number and waited.

"Hello?" said a breathy voice.

"Vivian Torres here, ma'am. You don't know me, but—"

"Is Joe OK?"

"There was an incident—"

"At the New Yorker Hotel. I know. Has he regained consciousness? Can he cope in the hospital?"

"We've had to remove him from there, and we're headed to Grand Central now."

"Bring him here," Celeste snapped, as if Vivian were her servant.

"He told us to take him home."

"Let me speak to him."

Vivian didn't know how to put this delicately. "He's…sleeping right now."

"Of course. You had to knock him out to get him out of the hospital. If he's asleep, it doesn't matter where he goes. Bring him to me."

Vivian hesitated. Tesla had told her to take him home, but he hadn't really been able to think things through. What if she did take him to Celeste's house? Then he and Celeste could be trapped in her penthouse together. Who was to say that Tesla wouldn't prefer that?

But he'd told her to take him home. She kept coming back to that.

"I'll give you my address," Celeste said. "And I'll hire a doctor to come here to care for him. I already have a doctor of my own."

Vivian looked over at Mr. Rossi. He was staring at her intently.

"Just a moment, ma'am." She covered the phone's mouthpiece. "I called Celeste to get Tesla's security code."

"Does she have it?" he asked.

"I don't know. She says we should bring Tesla to her house."

Mr. Rossi shook his head, one quick, decisive movement. His decision was clearly made. "You said he told you to take him home."

"He wasn't completely lucid at the time."

"Home. If he wants to be put under anesthesia later and taken to Miss Gallo, he can make that choice himself."

She looked at the phone in her hand.

"I'll tell her. I've known her for years." Mr. Rossi held out his hand, and she gratefully handed him the phone. After a few minutes of quiet argument, he pulled a gold pen out of his suit pocket and wrote down a long number.

She texted Andres Peterson. By the time Tesla woke up, he'd have his dog by his side.

And then she'd figure out who the hell had done this to him.

38

Ash stopped pacing the length of his long living room and dropped onto a ridiculous modern sofa. Rosa had bought it when they were married, and he somehow couldn't get rid of it even though it was not now, and had never been, comfortable.

He cycled through his email and his chat rooms. Quantum was back. He'd worried that the enterprising young hustler might try to sell the Oscillator to a higher bidder, or use it himself, but he was in the chat room, waiting like a good boy. He let him stew for a few minutes before answering.

> *ash: hello*
> *quantum: thought it best to stay offline for a bit*
> *ash: can the subject id u?*
> *quantum: no*

Ash wondered if this could be true. Not that it mattered. Quantum would not be a problem for long. He'd be richly paid, and then he'd go where all the richly paid went, where everyone went, eventually.

> *ash: do u have it?*
> *quantum: yes*
> *ash: xchange?*

Quantum entered details for a Bitcoin account. He would probably pick the payoff up at a Bitcoin ATM, making it more difficult to find him. Clever, but not clever enough.

> *ash: how do i get device?*
> *quantum: the price has tripled*
> *ash: has it?*

Quantum posted a link to a video feed. When Ash clicked on the link, he saw a large metal box with a glass door. It looked like a gun safe, which meant that the door was probably not glass, but ballistic glass. He could hire someone to break into it, of course, but that would take time.

The camera zoomed in on one of two objects inside. He recognized the flat bottom and distinctive cylinder. It was the Oscillator, just as Nikola Tesla had drawn it many years ago. As if on cue, the camera panned to the left to display a bomb. Thirty minutes left on the counter, and it began to count down.

> *quantum: can detonate or stop the detonation remotely*
> *ash: intrigued*
> *quantum: triple. we both know it's worth more*
> *ash: ??*
> *quantum: hello segment*

He stared at the words, not sure what they meant. Then he realized that they were synonyms. Synonyms for two words that might be high on the NSA's radar today. Hello meant hi or high. And a segment was part of a line. High line. Ash gulped. Quantum was saying that the Oscillator was responsible for the collapse of the High Line park extension. Ash needed to make it clear that he understood the reference with some synonyms of his own for park.

> *ash: green space*
> *quantum: y*

If Quantum hadn't knocked the tracks down, it would be one hell of a coincidence that a freak earthquake had happened in Manhattan on the day that he stole the Oscillator. Ash's heart raced. It worked! And he had to have it. The clock ticked down on the video feed. Would Quantum really blow it up?

ash: triple is fine. where is it?
quantum: safe

He posted a street address on Park Avenue and the Realtor code for the lockbox. Quantum must have hidden the safe in an empty apartment for sale. Again, a clever boy.

Ash picked up his secure phone and sent a man to that address. The man said he'd be inside in twenty-five minutes. That didn't leave much margin for error.

ash: will get eyes on the device
quantum: once u verify, send me the bitcoins. when i have them in my acct, i will stop remote countdown and open safe

He admired the young hacker's audacity. Ash began the transaction, but waited for final confirmation. He'd get the money back later, regardless.

ash: waiting for verification

His secure phone beeped and displayed a picture of the safe and the device, the man he'd sent to retrieve it reflected in the glass door and the timer at four minutes. He pressed the Transfer button on Bitcoin.

ash: on its way, but bitcoin transactions can take up to 17 minutes

The number on the timer changed to seventeen, so Quantum was still there. After a few tense minutes of staring at the video feed, the countdown stopped, the clock went dark, and the door swung open.

quantum: use it in good health!

ash: thx

Not that Quantum was guaranteed good health. Not when Ash found him. Quantum must know that, so he would run.

But Ash knew a few things about the hacker beyond his real name. Quantum had exchanged emails on a temporary account with a hacker in Berlin, whom Ash suspected of pretending to be a woman. He'd learned from those emails that Quantum had never left the country, and the most logical assumption would be that he wouldn't leave it now. But a clever boy like Quantum would challenge that assumption.

Ash was willing to bet the cost of a few operatives at the international terminals of JFK, LaGuardia, and Newark's Liberty Airport that he was right.

39

Joe woke up, but he didn't open his eyes. His head, neck, and back ached so much he had trouble thinking between the electric pulses of agony that he eventually recognized as his own heartbeat. He flowed with that pain until he could relegate it to background noise. That accomplished, he used the tiny bit of his brain that didn't hurt to figure out what the hell was going on.

He was in a quiet room, and he heard breathing that wasn't his own, so he wasn't alone. He drew in a slow breath and sifted through the smells. Lilac. Dog. Disinfectant. Home.

But he couldn't be home. Last time he woke up, he'd been in a hospital. His heart raced at the memory, and he kept his eyes closed out of shame. He'd completely lost it in front of his mother and Vivian, and he might have even thrown up on a doctor. He was lucky they hadn't carted him off to the psych ward. Maybe they had.

He cracked open one eye, grateful for the subdued lighting. His mother sat next to him in a comfortable wingback chair with a crocheted doily on the back. Someone had taken that chair from his parlor and put it next to the bed.

In her hand was a leather-bound book from the Gallo collection, but she wasn't reading. She was watching him.

He was home.

A black nose slid over the side of the bed, and a warm tongue licked his cheek.

Joe croaked out, "Hey."

Joe heard the thump of Edison's tail against the rug. One (cyan), two (blue), and three (red). His head throbbed with each color. No more counting.

With a worried smile, his mother leaned forward and held a glass of water under his chin. She angled the straw between his lips. Pain knifed through his head with each swallow, but he couldn't stop drinking. He'd never felt so thirsty.

He thought he might throw up again, and his mother moved a bowl toward his head as if she thought so, too. The bowl was thick white china from his own kitchen, more proof that he was home. His stomach quieted, but the pain did not lessen.

"Sleep," his mother told him, and he did.

He slept and woke, over and over. A red-haired man in a white lab coat made him swallow pills, checked his eyes, and asked him questions. Once the man even helped him to the bathroom, although the details of that stayed mercifully murky.

Finally, he woke with the thought that he might be up for a while. His headache was still there, but his head felt clear. He heard Edison's rough breaths, and the softer sounds of someone turning a page. He opened his eyes again.

His mother marked a place in the book she was reading. "You look better."

He turned his head and groaned, then stopped because groaning only made the pain worse. "Don't feel better."

His mother patted his hand. "I'll get Dr. Stauss."

Dr. Stauss was a tall man with flaming-red hair and a calm manner. He came into the room alone. He looked into Joe's eyes with a tiny flashlight, then checked his field of vision, the sensations he could feel on his face, and a battery of other tests.

"You're doing great," he said. "Recovering well."

"Is there any long-term damage to my brain?"

His sympathetic brown eyes flicked ever so slightly to the side. "Not from your head injury. If you rest and follow instructions, you'll recover completely."

Then he made a list of restrictions: no computer, no television, no reading, no mental activity at all. Just sitting in a darkened room, maybe listening to soft music. Joe figured he'd be able to follow those instructions for a day, maybe two tops, before the boredom drove him insane.

"Over time you can do more," Dr. Stauss said. "But you don't want to push yourself. Doing too much, too soon can lengthen the recovery process and maybe even cause brain damage. And you are very likely to experience some amnesia, so don't be alarmed."

Not something Joe wanted to hear. The doctor clearly knew his business, but early on in the conversation he'd lied, and Joe went back to that. "When I asked you about long-term brain damage, you said not from my accident, but I got the feeling you were holding something back."

Dr. Stauss smiled. "No problems with your observational skills, I'll give you that."

"And?"

He closed the bedroom door. Bad sign. "The hospital did a CT scan when you were admitted, and your mother mentioned that you had one done a few years ago because of migraines, so we have something to compare it to."

"Yes." He wanted to tell Stauss to stop talking. He didn't want to know what he was about to say.

"The impact to your head gave you a concussion, and that's what we've been dealing with here."

Joe's head throbbed, almost a warning. "And?"

"And we discovered that your amygdala has become greatly enlarged between the two scans. This phenomenon has been encountered in soldiers with PTSD, but not to the degree that we see in your case, and particularly not in such a short space of time. As you probably know, the amygdala regulates memory, decision-making, and emotional responses."

"What changed it?" He wanted to ask more complicated questions, but his head ached, and he was still afraid of the answers.

"We don't know. A traumatic event maybe, or a chemical intervention."

"What kind of intervention?"

"I've spent most of my time down here in your lovely home researching that. I've been in touch with various colleagues, without using your name of course, and so far I haven't found anything conclusive."

"Can it be fixed?"

The doctor's eyes flicked to the side again. Another lie coming. "The brain is a very plastic organ. Reducing stress, meditation, adopting a positive attitude. Those could all go a long way toward sensitizing your amygdala to positive emotions instead of negative ones."

"But?"

"But you may always have difficulty processing fear."

So, his agoraphobia might never go away. No surprises there.

"You might be able to work through it. People work through traumas all the time." Dr. Stauss took his arm. "Let's get you out of bed for a bit."

A half hour later, Joe had used the bathroom, washed himself off with a warm washcloth, put on clean pajamas, and was tucked in bed between fresh sheets. Everything hurt and took longer than he would have imagined possible, but it felt good to be clean and awake.

Before he left, Dr. Stauss gave him a happy drug. His head still hurt like hell, but he didn't seem to care about it quite so much. It also didn't bother him that his head was half-shaved, or that he had a row of stitches in the back. The drug was that good.

"I brought you some broth." His mother set the bowl on his nightstand, then adjusted the pillows against the headboard so he could sit up.

The most delicious smell in the world wafted to his nostrils. Beef, vinegar, and spices—sour meatball soup, or at least the broth. His stomach growled, and his mother laughed and handed him the bowl. A few tiny pieces of meat floated in the broth, along with grains of rice and a few shreds of onion.

"You made this?" He hoped so.

"From scratch. Like you used to drink when you were a sick little boy."

He held the bowl to his lips and drank every drop. It tasted salty and rich and heavenly. It reminded him of the colds of his childhood, when his mother would bundle him up in blankets and set him propped against the trapeze net with a thermos of soup, so she could keep an eye on him while she practiced.

Edison licked his lips when Joe finished. "This is all mine, buddy. It's too good to share."

His mother smiled.

The dog rested his head next to Joe's hip. He looked as content as if he'd been given the bowl himself.

"He worried about you," his mother said. "We have to tear him away from your side for his daily walks with Mr. Peterson."

Joe rested his hand on Edison's head. "Was he hurt?"

His mother shook her head. "The police say that your attacker used a Taser on him and locked him inside a wardrobe. Edison broke the door and fetched a security guard to help you."

Edison must have been in agony when he was tased and terrified inside the dark wardrobe. Joe remembered hearing him whimper before the wardrobe had fallen on him. The sound still haunted him.

Rage welled up in Joe, and with it more pain. Apparently, there weren't enough happy pills in the world to temper his fury that someone had hurt his dog.

"Don't anger yourself," his mother said. "Dr. Stauss says that getting upset will make your head worse."

He took a few calming breaths. Self-soothing had become his new way of life. He should be able to manage. "Did they find a device in the corner of the basement?"

Someone tapped on his bedroom door.

"Come in," his mother called. "He's awake and talking sensibly."

That indicated he'd been awake and not talking sensibly before. Great.

With silent steps, Vivian entered his bedroom. She wore jeans and a gray T-shirt and her gun in a shoulder holster. She looked ready to take on a room of armed assassins, and it reminded him again how weak he currently was. "You're looking better, Mr. Tesla."

"Miss Torres has been guarding us both round the clock," his mother said. "After she took you from the hospital."

"Did they find the Oscillator in the basement?" he asked. "Was it by the wall?"

Vivian shook her head. She explained what the police had been able to piece together about his attack, and that footprints showed that someone had gone to the back of the room and retrieved something, but they didn't know what it was.

So, his attacker had taken Nikola Tesla's famous earthquake machine. He'd recognized it the instant he pulled it away from the column, before he'd heard Edison's sad whimper.

His father had warned him to tread carefully, but he'd been heedless. He'd blundered into one of the most powerful devices ever invented, and he'd let someone take it from him. If it worked, and his attacker used it, all those deaths would be on Joe, and on his father for putting him in the position to begin with. Not that shared guilt made things any easier.

"You need more sleep," his mother said. "We tire you."

"I'd like to rest," he lied.

He couldn't rest, not until he got the Oscillator back.

40

Quantum liked the anonymity of Newark Liberty International Airport. Nothing ever happened in Newark. No one knew who he was, and no one cared.

Security trusted that he belonged to the forged passport he'd used to check in. He was Matt Chang, an Asian guy on a business trip. Nobody looked twice at him.

The generic atmosphere of McGinley's Irish Pub wrapped around him like a warm blanket of anonymity. He took a long pull of dark Guinness and set his glass on the black granite bar. McGinley's clearly wasn't splashing out on authenticity. The bar was the same kind of stone used in a lot of upscale kitchens in the nineties, not a wooden bar like he'd seen in the movies, so the whole place felt more like someone's kitchen than an Irish pub.

But he didn't care. In forty-five minutes he'd be on a plane to Dublin. Then he'd see what was real, and what was leprechaun clichés. He'd mingle with the Irish lasses and keep his head down until Ash gave up on him. They had enough high tech in Dublin that an Asian geek from America wouldn't stick out too much. Plus, he had no links to Ireland. He'd taken a list of likely international destinations that he had no connection to, given each a number, and let a random number generator choose where he should go. If it were up to him, he'd have picked Berlin, which is why he hadn't let himself pick.

A heavyset man in a nondescript gray business suit sat on a nearby stool. The bar's overhead lights reflected off his shiny bald spot. He was glued to the soccer match on the bar's television. Quantum supposed he'd have to learn to like soccer in Ireland.

A commotion in the terminal drew his attention away from the game. A wiry blonde pulling a hot-pink suitcase was screaming at the man standing next to her. He had a hot-pink suitcase, too, obviously a domesticated man, and he'd apparently run over her expensive shoe. She was giving him colorful hell for it.

Quantum reached for his beer without looking and took another sip of the bitter brew. He was facing the terminal now, enjoying the show. No amount of apologizing on the man's part would make such a transgression right again, that was clear.

The woman took off her shoe and waved it under the man's nose, so that he could really understand the depth of his crime. Quantum would miss the New Jersey accent and attitude. But he supposed Dublin would have its own charms.

Nausea passed through him, and he swallowed. He hadn't had Guinness in a while, but he didn't remember this reaction. Grogginess drove his head toward his chest. He set his beer down so hard that the glass broke, and dark liquid splashed onto his shirt. The businessman was gone. He'd left a crumpled ten-dollar bill on the bar, and he'd taken Quantum's laptop.

Quantum staggered to his feet, one hand on the bar to steady himself. He'd been poisoned. Ash had found him, and he'd been poisoned, and he was going to die at a cheap chain bar in Newark.

"Are you OK?" The bartender caught hold of his elbow and was trying to get him to sit down again. His blue eyes looked concerned.

Quantum stumbled away from the stool. Plenty of time to sit when he was dead. That was coming soon.

His life didn't flash before his eyes, and he didn't think of some girl he'd missed his chance with. All he felt was a desire for revenge.

Ash probably thought he was going to die in the bar, probably had made it look like a heart attack. His death probably wouldn't even make the nightly news.

Not good enough. He was going to make damn sure that the police investigated his death, did a thorough autopsy, and that his last moments would be splashed all over the Internet for all the world to talk about.

He summoned up the last of his strength and shouted the only words that would do that.

"There's a bomb in the terminal. I put it here myself."

41

Joe closed his bedroom door. He'd promised to rest to persuade his mother and Vivian to leave him in peace. They'd agreed to go topside to shop.

Dr. Stauss was downstairs, probably in the parlor. His mother had installed him in one of the spare bedrooms and herself in one of the others. The doctor seemed to have taken a leave of absence from his regular job to look after Joe round the clock, but at least Dr. Stauss left him some breathing room.

Joe had snagged his laptop from the parlor and hidden it in his closet. Now he dug behind his clothes and shoes and an old fedora Celeste had talked him into buying years ago, and pulled out the laptop. The doctor had expressly forbidden him computers, TV, or reading. He was supposed to rest his brain, and it was slowly driving Joe insane.

His brain didn't like to rest. It liked to think and do things. A week of lying around in a darkened room trying not to think was too much.

Besides, according to Vivian, the police had only a rough sketch of Joe's attacker from the security guard who had found. Joe would be able to establish the man's identity in a matter of minutes. That would barely tax his brain at all.

With a sigh of relief, he settled down in his bed. Edison gave him a suspicious glance from his blanket on the floor. Apparently, even the dog had been briefed on the rules.

"Shh!" Joe told him. "Don't snitch on me."

Edison lowered his head to his paws and closed his eyes. Maybe he thought that if he couldn't see Joe cheating, it didn't count.

Joe logged in, connected to the darknet, and hacked into the surveillance cameras for the New Yorker Hotel. He'd hacked into those for Grand Central a thousand times before, so it wasn't really going to require much cognitive energy to do this. Not enough to count.

It took him a few tries to get through, as he kept forgetting obvious steps. Dr. Stauss had assured him that gaps in his knowledge at this stage were perfectly normal and that he would get better soon, so long as he rested. He had to hope that the doctor was right. As soon as he was done with this, he would rest.

He fast-forwarded through footage until he got a good angle on his attacker's face. It was much clearer than the old images from Grand Central. The police hadn't been able to do much with the New Yorker Hotel images, but they didn't have the same tools he did. Pellucid was founded on his ability to clean up images and match faces to surveillance videos. He'd get further.

Making educated guesses, he ran the image through a few enhancement tools. When it was as clear as it was going to get, he checked it against a backup of the criminal database that his team used for testing purposes. It was an old snapshot of the database, so crimes committed in the past six months wouldn't be listed, but he hoped that his attacker had been caught for something before that.

He closed his eyes and let his mind wander. It helped with the pain. Dr. Stauss was probably right about resting.

His computer dinged, and he looked at the match. That was the man who attacked him in Grand Central, followed him onto the train, tased Edison and locked him up, and dropped a wardrobe on his head. Michael Pham.

He took a few cleansing breaths to calm himself. If he passed out in bed with his laptop and his mother came in, she'd probably throw it against the wall. He had to be careful.

When the pain subsided, he tried again. Reading took longer than usual, too, but he was able to glean the big picture. Michael Pham had first been arrested for hacking into his school's computer network and changing his grades—an offense that should have been sealed as part of his juvenile record, but wasn't. After that he'd done time for more serious crimes—stealing credit card information from Target and an assault charge that had been pleaded down to self-defense. Not a lot of hackers with assault charges. He was also listed as a person of interest in a homicide, but the police hadn't been able to link it to him decisively. A tough geek.

Joe closed his eyes again and thought about the Target hack. It had been a sophisticated scheme using a dancing-baby video as click bait to install a virus that uploaded files while the baby kept dancing. A similar attack had been perpetrated by the hacker collective Spooky against a chemical company, except that they'd used a dancing otter. He couldn't remember the name of the company, which was odd, but he remembered Dr. Stauss's words and hoped the loss was temporary.

Meanwhile, the info gave him another lead on Michael Pham.

Before he forgot, he forwarded the Pham's name and picture to Detective Bailey. She'd have to run his name through the system to get the same match that he had, but the police would be able to do that. He hoped she wouldn't ask where he got the image from, but it was too late to worry about that.

Could Spooky be behind the Oscillator's disappearance? He shook his head, and pain knifed through it. Nausea rose right behind it, and he closed his eyes and waited it out. Once the pain subsided to a roar, he tried to think again.

No. Spooky had never been violent in the past. They were ruthless in exposing the actions and foibles of those they didn't agree with, but they had never taken direct physical action to harm someone, so far as he knew. Whoever had taken the Oscillator was willing to kill him, and might have killed his father's friend Professor Egger. That didn't sound like Spooky.

Professor Egger. What was going on with the investigation into his death? Vivian had said it was being treated as an overdose, but maybe there was more to it than that. It couldn't be a coincidence that he had died mysteriously so soon after Joe's father. Well, maybe it could, but maybe not. He sent another email off to Vivian, telling her to contact the police about Egger, and maybe check back with Patel. Maybe he'd remembered something else.

So this Michael Pham had a powerful weapon. One that could knock down bridges or buildings or, in the words of Nikola Tesla, *split the earth in two.*

42

Vivian stood at the corner of Broadway and East Twelfth. Heat radiated up from the sidewalk. As a kid she'd sometimes pretended that the sidewalks were lava and jumped from crack to crack to keep from being incinerated. Right now, that didn't seem like such a bad plan.

She envied the people around her in their shorts and T-shirts while she wore a business suit to conceal her gun. Dirk was at the house with the Teslas, because she'd had to come out here—she was still on duty, and she wasn't letting her guard down.

That was why she spotted Professor Patel long before he saw her. Tossing glances over his shoulder every block, he was an easy man to pick out of the crowd. The confident man she'd spoken to a few days ago was gone. She watched his approach and those around him. If he was being followed, his followers were very good, because she didn't spot anyone.

When he noticed her, his expression grew even more wary. She turned as if she hadn't seen him. She'd called him, and he'd said that he would call her back and hung up almost immediately. When he did, she suspected from the background noise that he was using a pay phone. Since he probably had phones in his house, his office, and his pocket, that wasn't a good sign. Patel was spooked. He'd told her to meet him here, but he hadn't said why.

She went into Strand, the giant bookstore where he'd suggested they meet. A wave of air conditioning engulfed her, and she ran her hand through her sweaty hair to bring cold air to her scalp. Shelves towered overhead, crammed with books of every shape and color. Rows and rows of shelves. Strand Book Store advertised that it had eighteen miles of books, and she believed it.

A red sign on a white pillar told her that she could browse in the Strand Underground, and it made her think of Tesla. She was sure that he would love this place with its quirky titles, the smell of books, and plain metal ladders stationed everywhere. He'd love it, and he'd likely never see it.

She moved deeper into the store and stopped at a table marked with a sign bearing the silhouette of Venus de Milo and the title *Art on the Edge*. A clear sightline of the door meant that she'd be able to see Patel and he'd be able to see her as soon as he came in. Given his paranoia level, she didn't want to approach him. Best to let him approach her.

Patel entered the store. He saw her right away, but he didn't come to her. Instead, he walked up to a table of new mysteries. Vivian picked up a brightly colored art book, but didn't even look at the pages as she slowly flipped through them. All her attention was on Patel in her peripheral vision.

He picked up a book with an orange stripe across the middle of the cover, paged slowly through it, and slipped a tiny piece of paper between its pages. Then he put the book down and walked out the front door. So much for having a conversation.

She wanted to run across the room and yank the book off the table immediately, but she strolled toward it slowly, stopping to look at other books, all the while making sure that no one else was interested in the one Patel had handled. Finally, she reached it.

The cover of his book had a woman in a hat at the top, a streetcar at the bottom, and an orange stripe in the middle that displayed the title and author's name: *City of Ghosts* by Kelli Stanley. The book looked pretty interesting, but Vivian flipped to the center and took out the paper. Patel had written:

Behind Farm City by Novella Carpenter

She slipped the note into her pants pocket and looked around. *Farm City* must be a book title, but how was she going to find it in here? Eighteen miles of books were a lot to search, especially since she didn't know what the book was about and didn't want to draw attention to it by asking. And why was Patel sending her to a book anyway? He could have written a little more on the damn note.

She pulled out her phone, brought up thestrandbookstore.com and searched for the title. Apparently, *Farm City* was about farming and raising chickens. She remembered that egg yolk-yellow bow tie that Egger had worn to the funeral. Behind an egg-farming book was the perfect place for Egger to hide a clue. Maybe Patel was sending her to something that Egger had hidden.

After a bit of wandering, she found Agriculture & Farming in the used section. She scanned through titles, eventually ending up standing atop a ladder. According to the Internet, the store had two copies of *Farm City*, and she found them in the dingiest corner on the highest shelf. She bet that no one ever came here.

As she pulled the books out, she noticed something behind them. After a quick glance to make sure no one was watching, she removed the other books around *Farm City*. Standing up behind them was a laptop.

Tesla would have a field day. A secret hidden laptop, and he wasn't allowed to use the computer. She brought down the laptop and stuck it in her purse, then bought both copies of *Farm City*, just in case. When she left the store and stepped into the solid heat outside, she felt as paranoid as Patel and had to remind herself not to give herself away by looking up and down the street.

43

Ash was in his panic room. He'd installed it so he'd have a place where he could be truly alone. None of the servants could penetrate here without the eight-digit access code, and he'd given the numbers to no one. If he died in here, they would be able to retrieve his body only by taking apart the room itself.

He had furnished the room as a gentleman's library. Unlike the simple, ecologically sound designs that he used to make a statement in the rest of his homes and offices, this one secret place could reflect his heart's desire.

An antique Persian rug covered golden oak planks. He had rescued them both from a nineteenth century house that was being demolished upstate. That house had also given him a red leather wingback chair that Jules Verne himself could have sat in. He'd had to look for the oversized mahogany desk, but it was worth the effort. Pigeonholes held notes and plans and curious objects he'd gathered over the course of his life.

Right now, the desktop was covered by a giant leather blotter with one item sitting in the center: the Oscillator. The device had rested there for a week. Every night he came in to check on it.

After he'd found Quantum and dealt with him, he'd been forced to wait again because Quantum's stunt at the airport had prompted scrutiny of the man's accounts, and

Ash wanted to be sure that Quantum's connections to Spooky, and to Ash, were not revealed. So far, there was no hint that they had been. Quantum hadn't left any little time bombs for him after all.

That meant that Ash could act now, but first he was going to take the device apart so that he would know how it was made. He picked up his camera and filmed the outside casing, then put the camera down to concentrate on the device.

A few choice curse words and banged knuckles later, he had removed the metal plate that covered the bottom of the device. When he looked inside, he saw gears and pistons and wires meshed together in inexplicable complexity. He was a software guy, not an electrical engineer. Joe Tesla had always tinkered with gadgets, but Ash never had. He regretted that now.

This left him with a dilemma. He could hire someone to disassemble the device and draw up plans for making another one—and be discreet while doing so. Then, after that person built the new device, Ash could have him eliminated so nothing could be traced back to Ash. It would all take time. The alternative was to view this as a one-time event—this Oscillator would destroy one building and that would be the end of it.

He didn't like either of those options.

Not sure what to do, he picked up the steel plate he'd removed. The outside was painted gray, probably to blend in with its surroundings in the basement, but the inside was bare metal with designs on its surface.

He brought the plate closer to the light to reveal figures etched into the metal's surface. They were too tiny to read, so he photographed them and zoomed in on the photographs. At a larger magnification, their purpose was clear—the metal was covered with plans that showed how to build the entire device. Nikola Tesla's secrets were laid bare in front of Ash.

He could hire someone to build ten or a hundred at some remote facility with no Internet connectivity. A plane crash on the way home would solve the traceability problem. It was all possible.

For now, he needed another metal plate to replace this one. He'd keep the original plate in the safe embedded in the floor of the panic room so that he would always be sure to have the plans that it carried on its surface. The photographs were useful, but he wanted the original, too.

He might not be a tinkerer, but he could definitely screw a new plate onto the bottom of the device. Then, he would use it on the Empire State Building, even though it housed his own office. No one would expect that.

He could take out the Breakers, cash in on his insurance, and be completely in the clear after the Empire State Building collapsed.

On Sunday, so that there would be minimal loss of life.

So thoughtful.

44

Joe glanced once at his closed door, then cocked his head. No noises from upstairs. He felt like a naughty ten-year-old as he leaned over and peeked under his own bed. No monsters, just two laptops and two copies of that chicken-farming book. One laptop was his, but that wasn't what interested him right now. He reached for the other one, Egger's, and pulled it out.

When he sat up, he felt light-headed. But he was improving quickly. The headaches came less often, and although he still sometimes forgot how to do the simplest things, his mind felt clearer. His mother and Dr. Stauss apparently agreed, because they'd left him alone, instead of sitting by his bed and nagging him about resting.

A faint smell of lilac drifted up when he leaned back. He adjusted the pillows behind him, then flipped open the laptop. As expected: password protected. Given enough time, he could crack it, but he hoped that he might not need to. Egger had gone to all the trouble of hiding the laptop and telling Patel. He must have known that his life was in danger and wanted someone to find it. So he would have made his password something easy to guess.

A couple of minutes later, he began to doubt that theory. He'd tried Egger's name, birthdate, wife's name and birthdate, and a handful of passwords from a list of the most common passwords, but had come up empty. If he didn't guess it soon, he'd have to run some hacking programs that would brute force it by using combinations of dictionary words and symbols, but that would feel like defeat and might take days. He should be able to think this through.

Patel hadn't given Vivian the section and shelf name to find the laptop. He'd given her a specific book title. Maybe the books had been more than a marker for the location of the laptop. He fetched them from under the bed, glancing toward Edison's empty blanket. The dog was out for a walk with Andres Peterson, cavorting in the sun and grass as he deserved, but Joe missed him.

Back to work. The book's cover featured a rooster standing on a brick wall with a blue sky behind him. Urban farming. Maybe he ought to try it. Not raising chickens, of course, but he could try to grow things out in the tunnel in front of his house. He had unlimited electricity and water, so why not hook up some grow lights and put in vegetables? If they could theoretically grow plants on the moon or Mars, he ought to be able to put some in down here.

He blinked. He'd let his mind wander again, and he reminded himself he wasn't looking at this book to find out how to grow vegetables, he was trying to get into Egger's laptop. First, he tried the author's name and book title in varying permutations. Nothing.

A fresh round of pain pounded through his head with each failure. Pity pain, he decided to call it. He turned the book over, checked the back and the spine for clues, then opened it up. A lightly written dedication was penciled on the inside of the front cover: *To my darling Ada*. He checked the second book. Same inscription.

According to the Internet, Mrs. Egger had been named Patsy, and she'd never had children. No Adas. Ada was an uncommon name, quaint to modern ears. Maybe it wasn't the name—it was the entire inscription.

He grinned. This was it. Knowing that it would work, he typed in the phrase. He held his breath and pressed the button to log in. The laptop complied. A standard desktop with a picture of a fried egg, sunny-side up, appeared on the screen. He was in.

It didn't take much searching to find the transcript from a chat room where Quantum, Ash, and Geezer had talked about Nikola Tesla and his earthquake device. Geezer, he realized from the transcript, was Egger. Joe's father must have let something slip about the device to his colleague, and Egger had decided to search for it. But Egger wasn't the one who had attacked him. Maybe that was Ash or Quantum.

Joe didn't recognize the name Quantum, but he knew who Ash was. Everyone did. Ash was one of the top hackers in a hacktivist network called Spooky. He was famous, although no one knew his real name. Was Ash Michael Pham? Or was Quantum Michael Pham? Or was Michael Pham neither of them?

Joe admired some of the hacktivists' goals, but not their methods. If they got their hands on the Oscillator, there was no telling what they might do with it. Some of them were pretty radical, maybe even violent. Maybe they'd even killed Egger.

A tap on the door made him stifle a groan. "What is it?"

"Leandro here. I have my sister on the phone, and she wants to talk to you."

He closed up the laptop and crammed it under his bed with the books. "All right."

Leandro pushed open the door with his foot. His blond hair glowed in the light behind him. From this angle he looked like a lion. He waggled a phone in his hand.

"I didn't know you were here," Joe said.

Leandro had dropped by off and on during his confinement and had even gone for a few walks in the tunnel with him, probably under instructions from Celeste. Leandro's knowledge of the tunnels suggested he had spent more time exploring them than he let on. Joe was starting to wonder how much he knew about his old friend after all.

"Just stopped by to make sure you hadn't died in Great-Grandpa's bed," Leandro said.

"I've put orders in my will to have the mattress cleaned if I do."

"Decent of you." Leandro handed him his cell phone. "Here's Celeste. Talk to her before she nags me to death."

"I heard that," Celeste called.

"Meant you to," Leandro shouted.

Joe winced at the sound. Leandro smiled at him and left.

"How are you?" Celeste asked. "And really, no sugarcoating things for me because I'm sick. I know people who can beat it out of you. I'll send them over."

"Someone got there ahead of them." His head still throbbed from Leandro's yelling.

"Tell me everything, omit nothing," her breathless voice commanded.

He gave her a quick rundown of events and ended by sending her an email with Michael Pham's photo and identity, because she insisted.

"Got your email. Are you sure this is him?" she asked. "Really sure?"

"Why?"

"This guy is dead," she said. "It's all over the news. He poisoned himself at the airport and then stumbled out into the middle of the terminal yelling that he'd set a bomb. It shut down Newark Airport for an entire day. But when they retraced his steps on the surveillance video, they found out that he never set a bomb."

So, the man who had recovered the Oscillator was dead, just like Egger and Joe's father. Joe himself should be dead, too. Tears of grief welled up, and he knuckled them off his face. He cried easily since his injury. Or maybe grief over his father's death was finally catching up to him. He pulled the blanket higher.

"What would a guy like that want with you?" Celeste asked.

He told her about the Oscillator, and also that he thought that Michael Pham might be Quantum. He was convinced he wasn't Ash. Ash wouldn't have gotten killed in the airport, and even if he had, he would have tried to retain his anonymity instead of drawing attention to himself with the bomb threat.

She coughed for a few minutes and fell silent.

"Are you OK?" he asked.

"Do you ever watch the news?"

"I'm not allowed to watch TV or use the computer or read," he said. "They'd probably tell me I can't listen to the radio if I had one."

"I bet you turn on the computer the second your keepers leave the room."

He laughed. "Maybe sometimes."

"Maybe every chance you get. But you used to use it for fun things, like flipping me off, or the time you hacked the billboards in Times Square to show me seagulls."

"Actually, I hacked the cell phones of the people wandering around Times Square and used those to hack the billboards. That's different," he said. "Tell me more about the news."

"They had a segment about the High Line. You've heard of it? It's a set of old elevated train tracks that have been converted into a park."

One more New York landmark he'd never be able to visit. "Yep."

"They have one section that's not open yet. The plants are still growing on it or something. Anyway, it was due to open soon, but it collapsed. The news called it a freak earthquake combined with metal fatigue."

His head throbbed once, as if trying to tell him to pay attention. His father's newspaper clipping flashed across his mind. Metal fatigue. "That could be the Oscillator!"

"Now, don't take that information and go off on some cockamamie quest to save the world. Call in the men with guns and helmets."

"I'm feeling weak. I need to go rest."

"Rest, as in immediately go online and start researching, quite against doctor's orders and my advice?" she asked.

"Something like that."

He disconnected a few minutes later. Leandro took his phone back, made small talk, and left.

As soon as he was alone, Joe wrote up another email, this time to Mr. Rossi. He explained about the laptop, Egger's identity and suspicious death, and his potential connection to Spooky and Quantum. Then he detailed everything he knew about Michael Pham, included his picture, and added that he thought that he was Quantum. He asked Mr. Rossi to send someone to pick up the laptop and forward it anonymously to the authorities. Then he made a copy of the hard drive because he suspected he'd never see the laptop again once it left his house.

Due diligence done, he started digging around online. It took longer than he expected to find the records for the seismographs that monitored Manhattan. In California, a state with a lot of earthquake awareness, he could have pulled them off the USGS website in seconds. Here he had to trawl through the USGS site, and Google like crazy, before he ended up at the Lamont-Doherty Cooperative Seismographic Network. Clearly, earthquakes weren't viewed as high-priority on the East Coast.

Eventually, he found the raw seismographic data. Now he had to pinpoint the time that the train tracks had collapsed and work backward from there looking for a pattern. And finding patterns was what he did.

His headache disappeared while he studied the colored seismograph readings. Numbers and colors had never disappointed him in the past, and they didn't now. An unusual wave pattern had appeared on the seismograph for about an hour before the earthquake, increasing in intensity, but always at a very low level. After about an hour, it abruptly slowed down and then stopped, as if someone had flipped a switch. After that, the wave had dissipated, and the readings went back to normal.

He had a strong sense that the Oscillator had caused those readings. That meant that it generated a clear and recognizable seismic fingerprint. He also had a strong hunch that the High Line was a test, and whoever had the Oscillator intended to use it again. If someone were to put the device into action, how could he track it?

New York didn't have a lot of seismographic stations. He wouldn't be able to pinpoint the event with enough accuracy to be useful in time. He might be able to tell if the Oscillator was being used to knock something down, but the search area was so big that he'd never be able to find it and stop it in time.

His eyes chanced upon his cell phone, plugged in next to his bed. It was outside of its Faraday pouch, like it usually was when he was home, so it was transmitting its location. Cell phones always do that, because they are constantly connected to the network. He tapped the phone with his finger. Cell phones always know where they are, and they also know their orientation relative to their surroundings—upside down or right-side up or sideways—because of their accelerometers. Millions of tiny sensors were being carried all around Manhattan, sensors that could read vibrations. They were so finely tuned to vibrations around them that it was possible for a mobile phone to use its accelerometer to determine exactly what was being typed on a nearby keyboard.

And he could hack those phones, download their accelerometer data, and monitor it.

He signed into a hacker website and pulled up a list of hackable phones in Manhattan. He'd used them before when he'd played the prank of broadcasting pictures of seagulls flying on all the billboards in Times Square. If he were going to prevent an attack, he'd need to hack all the phones, because the owners would be moving around the city, and he had no idea where the attack might come from. The more phones, the more data, and the more likely he'd be able to pinpoint the Oscillator's location before real damage was done.

He paused. Was he any better than the NSA? He was hacking innocent people's phones without their permission so he could use them as listening devices. He had no right to do that. But thousands of people might die if he didn't. That was the choice the NSA said they faced every day, too, so how could he fault them without being a hypocrite?

His head pounded, and he wanted to go to sleep, but that wasn't an option. He had to do something. He had to set up his system, and he had to take information from these phones to save lives. It wasn't private data, like pictures, emails, and phone calls, but it was still wrong.

And he was going to do it anyway.

Decision made, he returned to practical considerations. First, he would have to set up each phone so that it would broadcast its accelerometer data back to him. That was fairly straightforward. Then, he needed to convert that data to waves in order to match the anomalous seismograph output recorded from the hour before the collapse of the High Line tracks. Finally, he would have to set up an engine to compare each phone's data to the suspect wave pattern and alert him when it was detected. He could reuse his old pattern-matching code from Pellucid.

He wished that he had a group like Spooky—a place where he could outsource some of this work to get it done more quickly. But he didn't. He just had himself.

He hoped that his mother and Dr. Stauss left him alone long enough to do what he needed. And that his brain would hold up long enough for him to finish.

45

Ash stood in front of the Empire State Building, holding his briefcase. The Oscillator was tucked inside the expensive leather case. Today was Sunday, and he was ready. After he made the decision, waiting the last few days had been difficult, but he'd distracted himself with work and Mariella and fighting with Rosa.

The building's stone walls soared above him. A pair of tourists was shooting selfies from a block away to get the spire in the background, and a long line waited to buy tickets to the observation platform in spite of the fog that would keep them from seeing far. Everyone wanted to experience the building, and whatever scraps of view they could.

It was a gorgeous icon, he couldn't deny it, and it didn't just represent New York. It represented corporate greed and man's constant striving to overwhelm nature, as best exemplified by the Breakers and their shortsighted efforts. Those things deserved destruction. From the rubble of the building, great things would rise.

Things that he would build.

The spire that had once held King Kong, at least cinematically, wasn't even visible from where he stood, but he could picture it. He imagined the giant ape holding on with one hand while being strafed by fighter planes, all for the sake of love.

Ash was doing this out of love, too. Love for the entire world, not just a single building. The destruction of this building would set the Breakers back years and let him push through legislation to save the environment while they scrambled to rebuild what they had lost in the rubble.

He walked into the impressive Art Deco lobby and nodded at the pair of security guards. Both were beefy men, once athletic and now just big, probably high school athletes. They didn't look like they'd be much good in an actual emergency, but maybe they would surprise him when put to the test today.

He set his briefcase on the silver casters and watched it disappear into the black box of the metal detector. He walked through the human metal detector and waited for his briefcase to come out the other side. The Empire State Building's security would not stop him.

The security guard watching the screen, Rodney Ponder, had watery blue eyes under square glasses. Those eyes barely glanced at the contents of Ash's briefcase. Rodney wouldn't have known what to make of the Oscillator if he had noticed it. The device looked innocuous enough. "Working on a Sunday, Mr. Wright?"

"Just a few hours." Ash held out his hand for the briefcase. "Then I can get home to the family."

Like anyone would call his and Rosa's relationship a family.

Rodney handed him the briefcase, handle pointed toward him. "You have a good Sunday then, Mr. Wright."

Ash nodded without replying.

He strode across the shiny stone floor, past the Art Deco flourishes, and onto the elevator. His card key offered him access to his floor and provided a log of his presence here, as did the surveillance camera mounted in the elevator. He would have to follow his planned protocol carefully to avoid suspicion.

Keeping that in mind, he didn't glance at the Breakers' giant teak door when he got out of the elevator, unsustainably harvested as he was sure it was. Instead, he pivoted toward the green Wright logo and went through the glass doors leading into his own company. Transparent doors, nothing to hide.

The weekend receptionist, Sage, looked up when Ash stepped through the door. "Salutations, Mr. Wright."

Sage had so many piercings that he had to be wanded every time he went through security. Tattoos covered both arms. He was visual proof that Wright was a young company, vibrant and rolling with the trends. Yet he still annoyed Ash.

The young man worked weekends and evenings, trying to show his value and work his way up through the ranks, as he'd been taught. He wouldn't take the risks that Ash had taken—he would never go off to found his own world. He wasn't smart enough to recruit for Spooky, but he got things done in his own limited fashion, and he was useful.

"Sage," Ash responded, but kept walking. No one expected him to stop for conversation, and today, of all days, he would do nothing that would stand out.

Fog occluded the view from his window. A shame, because this would be the last time he'd have been able to see it, but he chose to shut down that avenue of thought. He answered emails, returned calls, did all the things that a busy executive had to do on weekends.

Until he decided that it was time.

He stood and stretched, running his fingers over the smooth grain of his bamboo desk, which was sustainably harvested. A beautiful piece of furniture, and he would miss it. Again, he glanced out the window, but fog still shrouded all but the closest buildings.

No more wishing for a final glimpse of the view. He had made his decision, and he would implement it, just as he had with thousands of decisions before. They had, by and large, helped to heal Earth, and this would, too. It was all about perspective and long-term thinking.

He gathered up his briefcase, resisting the urge to fill it with pictures and plaques that lined his walls. They mattered to him, now, in a way that they hadn't before. He had barely registered their presence, but now he knew that he would miss them.

Then he hacked into the surveillance cameras for the building. He'd done it before, just for fun, and had turned off various cameras in a random pattern often enough that he hoped the security staff would view this as a routine occurrence. He quickly knocked out the cameras that covered the front door of his company and the stairwell. He also took out those outside the Breakers' office and a few on floors nineteen, thirty-seven, and fifty-six. They'd be down for about three minutes before someone noticed and rebooted them. He'd tested that, too.

Wright was meant to be seen as an egalitarian company, and he was grateful for that as he prepared to head to the men's washroom. Most CEOs had private bathrooms, but not Ash. No one would think it unusual that he was using the regular washroom—he did it all the time.

He slipped the Oscillator out of his briefcase and dropped it into his pocket. The device bumped against his hip as he walked, but it was just a light tap. So dangerous, yet it fit in his pocket.

Sage had abandoned his post—probably to use the restroom himself. That was a stroke of luck, and Ash changed his plan accordingly. Instead of using the emergency exit behind the bathroom, he went straight for the front door and down to the stairwell. That would save him at least thirty seconds.

The stairwell was always empty. He'd never seen a soul in it. No one took the stairs to the eighty-fifth floor. Even the most ambitious health nuts recognized that as crazy. The stairs were packed surprisingly close together, so narrow that two people would barely be able to walk side by side. In modern buildings, stairwells had to be bigger.

He hurried down one flight. If he tilted his head, he could see down several floors by looking between the stairs. Vertigo gave him a thrill of panic, and he looked away.

The walls were painted gray to the height of his head, then white above that, and a utilitarian gray steel railing was on both sides. Above the railing someone had knocked a hole in the drywall and exposed a steel beam. The hole had been there for months, and no one had fixed it. Ash could have smashed through the wall anywhere, of course, but he didn't have to. This hole was the perfect place to set the device.

He took the device from his pocket and held it in his open palm. The gray paint looked shabby here, the welds attaching the cylinder to the base comically exaggerated. The Oscillator looked like a cartoon creation, not an object that could do damage in the real world.

But it had done damage. He was convinced that Quantum had tested the device on the High Line tracks as he had said. If it had worked there, it would work here.

Moving quickly, he clamped the device to the beam and turned it on. He'd already determined the correct resonance for steel, and he set the dial to match. He didn't wait to see if it worked. If it didn't, he could come back tomorrow and try again.

Instead, he hurried up the gray stairs, past Sage's empty desk, and to his office. He was sitting at his computer when the surveillance cameras came back on, and he leisurely packed up and walked to the front door on camera.

Time to go home for the day.

46

Joe's computer speakers screamed at him. He blinked at them once or twice, trying to remember what the sound was for.

The Oscillator.

His mother stood in the doorway. "What is making such a sound?"

"My computer." Joe had already pulled it into his lap. "Send in Vivian."

"You are not supposed to be—"

"Life or death. I need Vivian."

She looked at him carefully for a moment, then nodded. "I see."

She hurried down the stairs and toward the front of the house. His mother never needed extraneous explanations when things were serious. Even when he was a small boy, she had trusted him.

He pulled open the Lamont-Doherty seismograph. The wave pattern was identical to the pattern he had seen from just before the High Line park tracks went down. Something was going on in New York, but this device couldn't give him any more information. He needed something closer to the point of origin.

A few clicks brought up his network of hacked cell phones. The people carrying them moved around the city. All the phones felt the vibrations, but some more than others. He started comparing results by area. The vibrations were stronger south of Central Park. High Line was south of the park. Was it happening there again? Maybe the damage was caused by a freak localized earthquake after all.

"Sir?" Vivian was at his bedside. His mother stood behind her.

"The Oscillator has been switched on. I'll be able to give you a building name in a minute. I need to go there and shut it off."

"If we don't?" He liked that she didn't ask a lot of questions either.

"Whatever it's attached to will collapse. It's got about an hour, depending on size." Or at least that's how long it had taken to bring down the High Line tracks. He flipped through the phones as fast as he could, eyes focusing for a fraction of a second on each one as he judged the relative intensity of the vibrations.

Vivian stood quietly. That helped. No time for talking yet.

"The Oscillator?" his mother asked. "It is a true thing, then?"

"Yup." He didn't explain more, attention riveted to each passing phone until he got a match.

"Manhattan," he said. "South of the park, north of twenty-third." (blue, red)

"I see, sir."

Was it at Grand Central? His heart clenched at the thought. "Close to here."

He pulled up all the phones within a one-mile radius of Grand Central. That left him only a handful. A few in the terminal itself, others in Rockefeller Center, Bryant Park, and near the Empire State Building. The hair on the back of his neck stood up when he realized which phones were getting the strongest signals.

"It's the Empire State Building," he said.

His mother sucked in her breath audibly.

"You're sure, sir?" Vivian had pulled out her cell phone.

"As sure as I can be." That wasn't as sure as he'd like to be, but it was better to take extra precautions and look like a fool than it was to let people die.

"I'll call it in," she said. "Tell Dirk it's a kind of sonic bomb and get him to persuade the cops to evacuate the building."

"The vibration might knock down adjoining buildings, too." He wasn't really sure what it would do. But, whatever it did, it would be his fault. If he hadn't put together the automaton and gone looking for trouble, this wouldn't have happened. Egger would be enjoying his golden years. Michael Pham would be continuing his life of hacking, and thousands of people wouldn't be in danger.

He hadn't shown the wisdom that his father had hoped for. By honoring his father's wish so carelessly, he had indirectly brought death to Geezer and Quantum. Again, tears threatened to swamp him.

He climbed out of bed, ignoring the dizziness, and walked unsteadily to his closet.

Vivian was already punching numbers into her phone, but she looked over at him. "What are you doing?"

"The Empire State Building has steam heat. I'm going in through the steam access tunnels. I'm the only one who knows how to pinpoint the device's location and shut it off."

Vivian paused with her finger in midair. "Put on a hat."

He touched the back of his head. His fingers touched stubble where his head had been shaved, and spiky plastic stitches. She had a point.

While she talked on the phone, his mother helped him into a wool suit, black dress shoes, and the fedora Celeste had bought him that he'd never had the heart to throw away. Turned out, she was right. It was perfect for certain occasions—like when your head was half-shaved and you needed to go out in public without scaring anyone.

His grown-up clothes weren't what he usually wore in the subway tunnels, but with luck he'd look like any other businessman if he got caught in the Empire State Building. Instead of like Frankenstein's monster in a suit.

He tucked his phone into his suit pocket. As long as he had Internet, he could track the vibrations his phone was sensing through the online app he'd used to track everyone else's phones. Hopefully, he could use the phone to tell him exactly where to look for the device once he got to the building.

He was in the front hall before he noticed that Vivian and his mother were right behind him. "Vivian?"

"I'm coming with you. You're not getting hurt again on my watch." She gave him one of her thousand-yard stares.

He'd have to take her down to stop her from following him. Even well, he wasn't sure that he could do that, and certainly not in his current condition. "Glad to have you on the team."

Edison bounded in from the parlor and licked his fingers.

His mother looked at him.

"You can't," he said. "You have to stay here to explain. If something happens to me, no one else knows the whole story but you."

Her eyes narrowed, and he was afraid she was going to refuse, but she sighed and stepped back. "I bear the blame for starting this."

"You don't," he said. "Dad does."

"I passed his words along to you, because I thought they were not true, that they might help you understand his unreal patterns of thinking."

Joe pulled her into a hug. "All of us Teslas have unreal patterns of thinking."

She smiled at him, but her eyes shone with tears. "I will see this through to the end, but you must come back so that I don't have to. You cannot do such a thing to your mother."

"I don't intend to," he said.

He picked up two flashlights and his tool set from the parlor. He might have to take the thing apart when he found it.

Vivian had already opened the front door for him, and resettled her holster. She wasn't going to pass for a business executive working weekends.

He hurried through and led the way to the tunnel in front of his house. He quickly disabled his security alarm, and both stepped into the semidarkness of the wider tunnel system. Edison ranged a few steps ahead. Joe's head throbbed, but he ignored it.

"We'll take the tunnel for the 7 East," he said. "The steam entrance leads off from there."

He'd passed the steam tunnel for the Empire State Building many times, but had always wondered about the legality of his keys and figured that security in a building like that had to be tight, so he'd never entered. This time, with the evacuation, security would be even tighter, but he didn't have a choice.

Edison stuck close to him. The dog didn't seem nervous, just determined. They'd barely been out in the tunnels together since Joe got beaned, and he was glad to see Edison was calm. Of course, Edison was always calm. So was Vivian.

The weak link in this particular chain was Joe himself.

His head throbbed with each step, nausea came and went in waves, and he was having trouble focusing. But he didn't have the luxury of tucking himself into bed and waiting until this passed. He had to find the device.

They reached the door to the Empire State Building's steam tunnel without incident, and only one train had passed. More than that might have caused his head to actually explode, Joe had decided.

He tapped the door once, then pulled the key ring out of his pocket to search for the Con Edison steam master key. He'd need the modern one. "Thanks for saving my keys."

"Credit goes to Edison. He carried them into the ambulance and gave them to me."

"Good boy!" Joe said automatically. He wished he'd thought to bring dog treats. Edison would probably earn his weight in dog treats before this was over.

The key turned, and he pushed the metal door open.

"You can just do that?" Vivian sounded surprised.

"Came with the house." He didn't have time to explain.

Edison walked next to him as they hurried down the steam tunnel. Vivian drew her gun and went first. The pipes here were freshly painted, the ground underneath so clean it looked as if it had been swept yesterday. It was the tidiest steam tunnel he'd ever seen.

One more door, and they were in the pitch-black basement of the Empire State Building. Someone had pulled the fire alarm, and it blared so loudly that Joe swore he could feel vibrations against his skin. His headache raised a notch with each beat.

He clicked on his flashlight and shone it ahead. Clean white walls, polished linoleum, fluorescent lights overhead that were off. A gray arrow was painted on the wall next to the word *Lobby*.

"You look pale," Vivian said. "Maybe we should go back where it's quieter and rest."

He shook his head. They didn't have time for his weakness. He needed to think. Vibrations against his skin? That couldn't have come from the alarms.

Holding tight to his phone with one hand, he pressed it flat against the wall. The phone quivered under his hand with a steady heartbeat. The Oscillator was here, going full tilt. Vivian put her hand next to his and looked at him with worried eyes.

"Not much time," he said. "You can go home."

She gave him a look that left no doubt about her intentions. "Where to next?"

Following the arrow, he reached a surprisingly clean stairwell and took the stairs two at a time. The noise threatened to drive him to his knees, but he kept going. He could not let this building be brought down.

He'd take the stairs up one floor past the lobby, then he'd look like one of the evacuees, and could maybe sneak into an elevator. Up he went, until he reached the floor above the lobby. The staircase door opened onto lemon-yellow carpet and a set of closed double doors adorned with a logo that resembled a hammer. He didn't even want to know what they did in here. He made for the elevators.

Vivian touched his arm. "Stairs are safer."

"We can't climb up one hundred and three stories," he said. "We need to split up the distance. You go to forty-three, I'll go to eighty-five. When you get there, put your phone against the wall."

"Why?"

"Give me your phone." He added her number to his list of monitored phones and handed it back. "I'll know what vibrations it's registering."

Vivian pressed the up button. For a sickening moment, he feared that the elevator might be locked out by the police, or full of people fleeing, but the doors opened almost immediately onto an empty elevator. Apparently, people were following instructions and taking the stairs.

Edison went in ahead of him, Vivian after.

"I don't like being separated," she said.

"No time." He pressed the buttons for floors forty-three (green, red) and eighty-five (purple, brown).

She tried to hand him her gun, but he refused to take it.

"You'll be more use with it than I am. My vision is…impaired." A delicate way to explain that he felt light-headed and dizzy and some objects were doubling themselves whenever he looked at them.

She put the gun into her holster. "What's the plan?"

"We're going to take readings on multiple floors to pinpoint the location of the device. I'll go to the top. You start at the middle. We'll go up or down, depending on how the readings from our phones differ."

Vivian looked puzzled.

"I'm tracking the device via the sound waves it emits," he said. "The waves should get bigger the closer we are to the device."

The elevator stopped on the forty-third (green, red) floor. She held the door open with one hand. "What do I do?"

"Hold your phone against the floor by the elevator," he said. "And wait."

The doors closed on her skeptical face.

Edison nudged his hand. A question.

"I'm fine, boy," he lied. Edison knew it was a lie, but he didn't challenge him on it, just leaned against his leg, offering the support of his presence. Joe ruffled the fur on the back of the dog's neck.

The elevator shot up at remarkable speed. He couldn't hear it moving over the blaring of the fire alarm. Maybe the elevator was soundless, not like the creaky monstrosity that took him home.

He checked out the results from Vivian's phone. The waves were stronger on the forty-third (green, red) floor than in the basement. The device was up high in the building.

The elevator settled and opened its doors to the eighty-fifth (purple, brown) floor. He pressed his phone against the floor just outside the elevator, ready to compare his readings to Vivian's, but he knew already that it was stronger here. A lot stronger. The glass door vibrated visibly in front of him.

He checked the reading from her phone, then called her. "Vivian, it's stronger up here. Get to the sixtieth floor, and we can take readings there."

But his gut told him that he wouldn't need to wait for those readings. The device was close to where he was standing now.

47

Ash couldn't help himself. After he got a notification of the evacuation of the Empire State Building from Sage, Ash had a public reason to go back, so he ordered his chauffeur to turn the limousine around and head back to the building. He wanted to watch.

The car couldn't get close. Police had blocked off the street for two blocks in each direction.

"I could try to circle around," said his driver. Ash couldn't remember his name.

"I'll get out here and text you with a meeting place."

Ash climbed out and hurried down the street. Fire trucks, police cars, and people clogged the street and the sidewalk. Hard to believe so many people had been working in the building on a summer Sunday. Plus tourists.

A policeman stopped him. "You'll have to turn around, sir."

"But I have people in the Empire State Building." Ash used his worried voice. "Will they be OK?"

"We're evacuating it, and the surrounding buildings. I'm sure your friends will be fine."

He hadn't called them friends. "What's happening? Why the evacuation?"

"We received a bomb threat—a call that someone had planted a sonic bomb in the building."

Ash stopped breathing. A sonic bomb. Who could know that? "What's a sonic bomb?"

"I have no idea, sir, but I'm going to have to ask you to move away."

Ash backed away, keeping the building in sight. Who could have called in a sonic-bomb threat? Who else knew about the Oscillator? Geezer was dead. Quantum was dead. The only other person who might have an idea about the device was Joe Tesla.

Ash grimaced and moved against a nearby building to let evacuees file past. He pulled out his secure phone and called up the tracking app. The green dot that represented Edison was close. In fact, it was inside the Empire State Building.

Joe knew.

He couldn't know everything, of course, but he knew that the Oscillator was in the building, pounding away. But without any idea of where, he'd never be able to find it in time. The Empire State Building was huge—one hundred and three stories high with over two million square feet of space.

Still, doubt grew in Ash.

Even if Joe couldn't stop it, he might have told others about how the Oscillator could cause such a disaster. Had he somehow uncovered evidence that would lead him to Spooky? Ash didn't see how, but he could take no chances. He would have to distance himself from Spooky, at least for a time. He could track Joe via the device on Edison's collar for two more months, assuming Joe had the sense to get out of the building before it went down.

The building shuddered, and windows shattered. Glass fell toward the street like deadly rain.

A woman screamed, and evacuees began to run.

Ash was pushed away from the building, fighting to keep his feet in the crowd. But he chanced a glance behind him. The building shook. It was coming down soon.

And Joe Tesla was still inside.

48

Joe sprinted from the elevator to a set of giant glass doors with a green logo painted on them. Wright. It was Alan Wright's company. He'd had no idea the company had offices here. Hopefully, Alan got out. No doubt he had—taking care of himself was what Alan did best.

Edison shook his head as if the noise bothered him. Joe couldn't blame him. He was going to throw up if it didn't stop.

Before that happened, he needed to find the device. He placed his phone flat against the floor next to Wright's doors and studied the vibrations on his phone. The wave pattern was almost identical to the one he'd taken near the elevator, but the tops and bottoms of the curves looked a fraction of a millimeter smaller. Too small a difference to be sure.

The door shattered, and glass rained down. He pulled Edison against his chest, protecting the dog's sensitive eyes and ears.

After the glass stopped falling, he told Edison to stay, then crunched across the glass into the Wright office and toward the outside of the building. The floor trembled under his feet, and the giant window in front of him vibrated.

He had to get as close to it as he could, so that he would know if the Oscillator was placed near the side of the building or closer in, such as near the elevator. But the window loomed in front of him. The gray sky beyond looked as if it had climbed into the room with him. His heart started to race, and each beat brought an answering pound of pain to his skull. He hadn't thought that his panic attacks could get worse until that moment.

His hand dropped to Edison's head for reassurance, but the dog wasn't there. He'd left him near the broken door, because he hadn't wanted him to shred his feet. Good place for him. Safer than here.

Not safe for Joe. He was seconds away from a full-scale panic attack. He was going to die, right here. He recognized his fear as the truth, not a panicked response in his brain. The building wouldn't hold up long under this pounding. He would actually die.

Paradoxically, this thought calmed him enough to let him think. He took one deep, slow breath and then another. It felt like wasting time, but he had to do it. He thought of his house far below the city and Celeste's smile. Places where he was safe.

His heart still pounded, but he ignored it now. He turned his back to the giant window. Instead of the sky and the world outside, he saw Edison, sitting patiently on the other side of a mound of broken glass. Joe's legs shook, his mind screamed at him to run, but he didn't. He stared into Edison's faithful brown eyes and took one step backward, then another.

Slowly, he backed closer to the window until his shoulders bumped against its solid surface. He was right against it now. Only an inch of glass separated him from the world outside. He'd thought he couldn't panic more, but he did.

A soft sound drew his attention to the ceiling. A dirty white pigeon fluttered around near the LED lights. The bird must have flown in through an open window. Joe hoped that the open window wasn't right behind him. Wind from outside might undo him.

The pigeon swooped back and forth gracefully, as if performing a show, not flying around inside a building on the verge of collapse. Joe caught himself watching it and realized that he had relaxed. If the pigeon could stay calm, then so could he.

Still, his hands shook as much as the building as he lowered his phone to the carpeted floor. He read the waves on its tiny screen. The numbers were smaller here. The device was behind the elevators. Maybe in the stairwell. That was the best possible news. He could get away from the window.

Not even trying to steady his breathing or master the pain in his head, he sprinted across the office toward Edison, not slowing until he was out of Wright's offices, across the hall and standing in front of the door to the stairs.

"Come," he called, opening the door.

Edison bounded to him, and the pigeon followed, swooping through the open door and into the stairwell. The poor bird would be trapped in there. It should have turned tail and flown outside. Of everyone he could see, the bird had the best chance of survival.

The elevator doors opened, and Vivian strode out.

"It's up here," he said. "Close."

The whole building might collapse at any second, but she looked calm. Just an ordinary day for this retired soldier. He was glad that she was there with him.

He went into the stairwell. It was smaller than he'd expected—just wide enough for two narrow sets of stairs packed side by side with a thin stripe down the middle that presumably ran all the way down to the first floor.

He touched his phone to the gray floor, next to a white stripe that outlined the edge of the stair. The vibrations were stronger. Downstairs. He grabbed the steel railing when he stumbled. The steel quivered in his hand like a giant bell pealing out the death of the king.

The building creaked around him, and the crash of breaking glass sounded again. Hopefully, it wasn't the outside windows. They would send deadly shards of glass down onto the people below.

Edison deserted him and ran down a half flight of stairs. He was glad the dog had finally succumbed to a self-preservation instinct. Maybe the dog would make it out safely, even if the bird didn't.

But Edison stopped instead. He put his paws on the wall above the railing and barked. Joe could barely hear the bark over the alarms, but he knew what it meant.

Edison had found something.

Joe and Vivian ran after him. Edison was jumping, trying to scratch at a hole in the drywall at Joe's eye level. He clicked on his flashlight and peered into the hole.

The Oscillator, the small gray-painted device built by his father's hero, was clamped to a steel column. Joe's heart leaped. They'd found it. A needle in a huge haystack, and they'd found it.

"There!" he pointed inside for Vivian's benefit.

The device pounded relentlessly away—a million tiny taps at just the right moments to bring the building down.

Vivian's light joined his.

"We gotcha, you little bastard!" she yelled.

The flight of stairs broke free from the wall and dropped down. Edison grabbed Joe's pant leg and held on. Vivian grabbed his arm. The stairs stopped.

They'd fallen a few feet, and the stairs had canted sideways. He could still see the device, but he couldn't reach it.

He crawled up the trembling staircase until he was level with the device. The whole staircase could collapse at any second and pancake who knew how many floors.

He could see the device. He reached forward, but the device was still a foot away.

Vivian stripped off her belt and threaded it through his. He'd be able to lean farther out, and hopefully, she'd be able to hold him steady. The staircase shook underneath them.

He dangled over empty space with one foot on the staircase. His hands grazed the wall. He didn't look down. Vertigo was not one of his phobias, but he wasn't going to test that right this minute.

Heat radiated from the device. He wouldn't be able to touch it with his bare hands to turn it off. He took the handkerchief from his suit pocket and reached for the device. The dial was stuck, and the handkerchief started to smoke.

He gritted his teeth, trying to shut out the pain in his head and his hands, the noise of the alarms, the creaking of the steel, and his rising dread. The platform they were standing on quivered like a cat about to pounce.

He'd never be able to turn the dial. Instead, he focused his attention on unscrewing the clamps. His sweaty hands slipped off the clamps again and again. The device shifted, and he yanked it off. It burned through his handkerchief. He'd have a scar to match his father's.

He dropped the device into his coat pocket. It probably had evidence on it, but he wasn't going to give it to the police. That wasn't what his father would have wanted.

"Back!" he called, and Vivian pulled him back.

The shaking had already slowed. Barely perceptible, but it was a good sign.

"Steps down are clear, sir."

He looked down the broken staircase. If she'd dropped him, he'd have died.

Edison took Joe's sleeve in his mouth and gently tugged. "Right you are, boy. Time to go."

Someone had shut off the alarm. Joe's ears rang in the silence.

He dropped his hand to the top of the dog's head. "We've got a long walk home."

The device cooled as they hurried down the broken stairs. The pigeon followed, circling above their heads.

He opened the door at the next level, and a rush of warm air streamed in. Either an open window or a broken one. Either one would do.

As if it understood what he was thinking, the pigeon flew straight through the open door and out into the building like it had a plan.

Joe wished that he did, too.

49

Vivian dragged Tesla through the tunnels. He was white and trembling, but he still kept his legs moving. He'd thrown up once inside the building, and she was worried that he'd reinjured his head. She had to get him back to Dr. Stauss.

"Need break," he said.

She looked back. They'd put some distance between themselves and the Empire State Building. She lowered him to the ground.

He leaned against the stone wall and closed his eyes.

There had to be surveillance cameras in the Empire State Building. It was only a matter of time before someone traced them here. But he couldn't walk any farther, and he wasn't going to let her carry him.

She sat next to him, wishing she'd thought to bring a water bottle. The dog was crowded up against his leg, resting his head on Tesla's lap. It looked worried, too.

"How you doing, sir?" she asked.

He opened his eyes and gave her a weak grin. "Thanks for not letting go back there."

"That's my job," she said. "Rule one: Never let your client fall eighty-five stories. Bad for business."

"You have a good grip."

"I climb," she said. "Good for hand strength."

He smiled. He looked a little better now. The rest had done him good.

He took the metal device out of his pocket and set it on the ground. "My father wanted me to destroy this."

"Yes, sir." They'd seen what it could do in the wrong hands.

"It could be a force for good." He sounded like he was trying to convince himself of something. "Or evil."

"Any weapon is only as evil as the one wielding it."

"If we let this out of our hands, anyone could be the one wielding it."

"That's what 'out of our hands' means."

Tesla shut his eyes so long she wondered if he'd gone to sleep. Vivian waited. Destroying the device was Tesla's choice to make. Even if she did it, for all she knew he could build another one. She glanced back the way they had come. If they got caught here, it would be confiscated, and then there wouldn't be any decision to make.

Tesla sat back up. He picked up the device and fiddled with it. He used one of his old keys like a screwdriver and took the back off. A few minutes later, he had a pile of metal pieces in his lap.

He raised his arm and tossed a handful down the tunnel. Edison looked out at them as if deciding whether to fetch them back.

Tesla struggled to his feet, and she squelched her instinct to help him. He looked weak, but determined.

He handed her some gears. They were still warm. Back in the building the device had been practically red-hot. She flung them ahead of her. A few pinged off the metal subway tracks.

Together, they walked toward his house, scattering Nikola Tesla's invention around them as they went.

50

Joe set Tik-Tok son the tiny nightstand. The nightstand was jammed between two beds with floral bedspreads. Room 3327, the room where Nikola Tesla died, was smaller and shabbier than he had expected. Edison sat next to the door.

"I bet it didn't look like that when your creator lived here," Joe told Tik-Tok. "Back then I heard that it was over twice as big—two rooms combined into a suite."

Still, it was small, especially considering that he had lived there for ten years and had packed the rooms with pigeon cages and drawings and gadgets. Joe sat on the bed and leaned against the arched headboard. The New Yorker Hotel had been more luxurious in Nikola's time, more like the Grand Central Hyatt, where Joe himself might have had to while away his days, trapped in a hotel suite not much bigger than his non-ancestor's.

But he had escaped into the tunnels back to the Gallos' house. That was a lot to be thankful for. And his mother had scrubbed his house spotless. She'd even sent all the rugs and curtains off for dry cleaning, so the entire house was shades lighter.

Joe looked at the small window. Per his request, the curtains had been drawn closed before he arrived. He hoped that once it got dark outside, he could open them again.

He took a picture of his father out of his bag and set it next to the automaton. The photo was taken when he graduated from college, before he met Tatiana, but she'd somehow acquired it and passed it on to Joe. His father's gown billowed in front of him, and he sported a narrow 1950s-era tie and thick-framed black glasses. He looked young and happy.

Joe wished he'd met him before his father had clamped the Oscillator to the bridge. The deaths he had caused had hung heavy on him for Joe's entire life, but the picture showed that he had been carefree once.

Joe touched the top of the picture frame and then Tik-Tok's round head. He and the automaton had fulfilled his father's final wish. He'd had the courage to destroy the device, the courage that his father had lacked. But he wasn't proud of himself—he'd destroyed something that had been capable of great destruction, yes, but it had also been capable of great good. The device had been neutral, but the people who'd used it were not.

Joe wasn't about to let them go. His attempts to link the attack to Spooky, or to find out the identity of Ash, hadn't been helped much by the contents of Egger's laptop, but he wasn't giving up. It would take time, but he intended to reconstruct the actions of Spooky and find out Ash's identity.

He'd assembled a database of all of Ash's communications and was running linguistic analyses against it to find out the patterns in those texts and emails. Given enough time, he was certain that he could identify Ash and track him down. Ash wasn't someone who could stay out of the spotlight, and somewhere, either in the past or the future, his style of writing would lead Joe right to him. Then he could turn him in for the murders of Quantum and Geezer (Michael Pham and Professor Egger).

But Ash wasn't Joe's biggest problem right now. Joe took his phone out of his pocket, and checked his email. More surveillance reports. The NSA wasn't decreasing the volume of their requests. In fact, they had greatly increased it, probably in response to the attack on the Empire State Building.

But all their data collection hadn't stopped the attack. All the innocent people who were being spied on as they went about their ordinary lives were no safer. But Joe had stepped over enough lines himself that he wasn't sure he could condemn the NSA outright for their actions.

He wasn't sure what to do. He pulled out his laptop and logged into the hotel wireless, then skipped through a couple of accounts to hide his IP address, then accessed Pellucid's network. His fingers danced across the keys as he called up the final change that he needed to implement to take their power away. His pinky hung over the Enter key. If he pressed that key, he would commit the final changes to the Pellucid code line. He would distort and disable the product that he had built. He could face criminal charges. Bad guys might go free.

But so would good guys. Government agencies would no longer be able to put a name to every face. They wouldn't be able to use Joe's creation to track the movements of millions of citizens who had done nothing wrong and would do nothing wrong.

Other software would spring up to fill the gap. It would take other developers a few years longer, but they would eventually achieve Pellucid's accuracy. His action would only buy all those innocents, none of whom had complained, most of whom wouldn't complain even if they knew, a few more years of privacy and freedom.

On the edge of his screen he'd put up his father's last words to him: *I was responsible for this. May God forgive me. Show the wisdom I did not and have the courage to destroy it.*

He did not want to have to write something like that someday. He didn't want to spend his life regretting what he was responsible for. He took a deep breath, summoning up all his courage.

Then, he pressed the key.

The phone rang, and he jumped. Celeste's picture flashed on his screen.

"Hey," she said quietly. "Are you home?"

"Nope." He felt proud saying it. "I'm in the room where Nikola Tesla died."

"Morbid."

He couldn't deny that. "How's your day?"

"Five," she said.

"Brown," he answered automatically.

"How's your head?"

"Better. I'm clear for thinking now. And computers. And government interrogations."

"The news says that Michael Pham was part of a terrorist ring that knocked down the High Line park tracks, and almost brought down the Empire State Building."

"They might be right." Edison decided that the small double beds didn't count as human beds and jumped up next to Joe. He fondled the dog's ears.

"They don't mention the Oscillator."

"Guess that's going to stay out of the papers then. I've told plenty of alphabet-soup government agencies about it."

"The truth?" she asked.

"That it was invented by Nikola Tesla, stolen from the basement of this very hotel, and that I had to destroy it to take it off the Empire State Building." So, not the whole truth, but close.

"Ah, that truth," she said.

"Nobody died," Joe answered. "So I can still sleep at night."

"I heard a rumor about the Empire State Building," she said. "I think you can see it from your room."

"Curtains are closed."

"Open them."

He hesitated, then, heart beating too fast, he leaned over and opened the curtains. The night sky of New York spread out in front of him. But the Empire State Building dominated the view. It still wasn't open, as all the steel needed to be checked and certified as safe, but the lights were still working. The building was lit up in red and white, and the spire on top was blue.

"It's July Fourth," she said. "In a minute there will be fireworks, and I thought we could watch them together."

It had been months since he'd looked out a window this long. Edison crowded over onto his lap and put his head on Joe's shoulder, his furry face against Joe's cheek. Joe hugged him with one arm and held his phone in the other hand. He was safe here. He could do this.

A giant golden firework went off above the building's tall spire. That spire had almost crashed down to Earth. But it hadn't.

"It's beautiful," said Celeste. "Isn't it?"

Joe watched the glittering strands of light fall down from the sky before he answered. "It is."

ACKNOWLEDGEMENTS

Thank you to everyone who helped Joe Tesla and Edison find their feet in this story. They received literary aid from Kathryn Wadsworth, David Deardorff, Karen Hollinger, Ben Haggard, Judy Heath, and Joshua Corin; psychological advice on agoraphobia from Peter Plantec; and marvelous tea to fuel my writing from my niece Lanessa and my sister Sari. Thanks to my wonderful cover designer, Kit Foster; copy editor, Joyce Lamb; and literary agents, Mary Alice Kier and Anna Cottle. I owe the most to my husband and son—you guys are the best writing family a person could ever have.

Plus a giant thank you to all my readers—you are what make Joe and Edison's adventures possible.

ABOUT THE AUTHOR

Thank you for reading *The Tesla Legacy*. I hope that you enjoyed the story!

I'm REBECCA CANTRELL, the award-winning and *New York Times* bestselling thriller author of this book. My other novels include the Order of Sanguines series, starting with *The Blood Gospel* and the award-winning Hannah Vogel mystery series, starting with *A Trace of Smoke*. My husband, son, and I just left Hawaii's sunny shores for adventures in Berlin, Germany.

If you'd like to find out more about my novels, visit my web site at http://www.rebeccacantrell.com/. I have them all listed there, in order, plus some extra content about researching them and the worlds in which they take place.

If you'd like to receive advance notice of my upcoming books, please sign up for my newsletter at www.rebeccacantrell.com. I put it out a few times a year, and I promise never to sell or trade your name.

Or, if you want to see what I'm up to day to day, you can find me on Facebook and Twitter.

AUTHOR'S NOTES

Joe Tesla's underground world is full of secrets. Some I made up, but others are true. Before you start reading the rest of these notes, take a second to decide which is the most unrealistic claim I make in the fictional world beneath. Now, let's go through these notes together to see if it's fact or fiction.

First off, Nikola Tesla did indeed invent a device called the Oscillator or "Tesla's Earthquake Machine." On his seventy-ninth birthday, he told reporters that he had used this device to generate an earthquake near his laboratory. When asked what would be required to destroy the Empire State Building, he replied, "Five pounds of air pressure. If I attached the proper oscillating machine on a girder, that is all the force I would need, five pounds. Vibration will do anything. It would only be necessary to step up the vibrations of the machine to fit the natural vibration of the building and the building would come crashing down." Here is the quote in the New York World-Telegram dated July 11, 1935. I've also come across the quote in Tesla biographies. *MythBuster*s tried, and failed, to create an oscillator that would knock down a bridge.

On the other hand, destructive resonance may have knocked down the Tacoma Narrows Bridge near Seattle. The bridge was known as "Galloping Gertie" because it moved so much during windstorms. Although the bridge was built to withstand wind speeds of a hundred and twenty miles per hour, on a day with a wind speed of only forty-two miles an hour, the bridge collapsed. The eerie video footage of the July 1, 1940 event is on You Tube.:

https://www.youtube.com/watch?v=j-zczJXSxnw

Tesla did have someone who helped him with his pigeons, including collecting wounded pigeons from the streets, but I don't know his name, and none of my characters is in any way related to him. I'd love to learn more about him, though, so if you find anything out, please send me an email to rebecca@rebeccacantrell.com.

Spooky doesn't exist, but there are other networks of hacktivists and activists spread around the world. The most famous is Anonymous, whose members wear Guy Fawkes masks when speaking for the group in the non-virtual world. The group was named by *Time* magazine one of the world's "100 Most Influential People" in 2012 and has performed hacks against various government agencies, religious organizations, and corporations.

All of the locations in the book, besides Joe Tesla's house, are real. Grand Central Terminal does contain the information booth, the famous clock, the gorgeous constellations, the Biltmore Room, The Campbell Apartment and the Oyster Bar. If you visit any of Joe's hangouts, do please send me a picture!

Printed in Great Britain
by Amazon